ALLEN COUNTY PUBLIC LIBRARY

FORT WAYNE, INDIANA 46802

Strange and Private War

By Anthony Lejeune

STRANGE AND PRIVATE WAR

Strange and Private War

ANTHONY LEJEUNE

PUBLISHED FOR THE CRIME CLUB BY

DOUBLEDAY & COMPANY, INC.

GARDEN CITY, NEW YORK

1987

All of the characters in this book
are fictitious, and any resemblance
to actual persons, living or dead,
is purely coincidental.

Library of Congress Cataloging-in-Publication Data

Lejeune, Anthony.
Strange and private war.

I. Title.
PR6062.E465S8   1987   823'.914   87–5306
ISBN 0-385-24294-8

7138902

Contents

Strange and Private War

I

It's Warmer Down Below

Years of dangerous experience had given Bardwell an acutely honed instinct of caution. Beneath a placid exterior, which was partly natural and partly a matter of professional discipline, he could be as wary as a nervous animal with ears cocked and nose constantly sniffing the breeze. Caution had become so habitual that he was never totally off his guard even in places and at times when there was no reason to suppose he was in any danger at all. Like now. He wasn't on a job and hadn't been on one for several weeks. After lunching with a friend, he had pottered around a few shops, enjoying the mild sunshine of a spring day in London.

Nothing had happened to alert him, although there had been a moment—indeed, more than one moment—during the past few days when he felt (and it was just a feeling, not observation exactly, nothing he could put his finger on) that he was being watched. However, he hadn't felt it today.

Nevertheless, as he stood on the platform at Oxford Circus, waiting for a train, he made a swift automatic check on the people around him.

If one were to travel perpetually on the London underground, never emerging into the upper world, one would always know the time of day from the changing detail of one's fellow-passengers. Early in the morning they would be mostly workmen, reading the *Daily Mirror* or the *Sun*. Then would come the junior office staff, and shop assistants, with the *Daily Express* and the *Daily Mail* plus a sprinkling of women's magazines and a few paperback books. These would blend with, and be followed by, more senior staff reading the *Daily Telegraph* and, later still, *The Times*. After ten o'clock the shoppers begin to arrive, not reading but gossiping to each other, having travelled in from the suburbs on cheap day return tickets. And there will be parties of school-children, being herded to art galleries and museums. And there will be tourists, all the year round nowadays but increasing in the spring like flocks of migratory birds, some middle-aged and American, others young, scruffy and European, blocking the escalators by standing on the wrong side, dithering uncertainly in the entrance to every passage, peering at the indicators, poring over maps, bulky with huge orange knapsacks.

The emergence, from briefcases, of an occasional sandwich indicates the lunch-hour. In the early afternoon the tourists predominate, until the shoppers begin to reappear, laden with bulging carrier-bags. Then come the first of the returning office workers, their evening papers turned invariably to the sports news.

This was the mixture—the four o'clock wave—which Bardwell's rapid survey took in. There were more exotic passengers too—black men in white robes, an Indian woman in a sari, a young Arab with two or three days' growth of beard. How, Bardwell wondered, do they manage always to have just that much beard, never more, never less? There were two nuns: and there was a schoolgirl with freckles and a brace on her teeth, and a pudding-basin hat and a satchel full of books.

The platform was crowded, but not packed to suffocation as it would be in another hour. The train rattled out of the tunnel mouth. People moved forward, and Bardwell cast a quick precautionary glance at the young Arab. For no real reason; just in case. He didn't want to be pushed under a train. But the Arab was a safe distance away.

Nobody saw the schoolgirl put her hand in the small of Bardwell's back and shove hard, at just the right moment. The brakes squealed. A woman screamed. Bardwell's body was pushed twenty yards along the track; he was dead before anyone reached him.

II

Bedroom Scene

Richard Clayburn half-opened his eyes. He had given no sign of being awake when he heard the girl whisper his name very softly and then climb carefully out of bed. Now he saw her shape outlined against the grey oblong of the curtained window as she moved silently across the room. She paused by the dressing table. He couldn't see what she was doing, but he guessed. His jacket was hung on the back of the chair. She took something—presumably his wallet—over to the window and examined it in the dim light. Then she went back to the dressing table and, he thought, replaced the wallet in the pocket of his coat.

She moved, her bare feet absolutely silent on the thick pile of the carpet, across to the door which led to the sitting room of the flat. For a moment he couldn't see her at all, a shadow against shadows. Then, having turned the handle slowly with no noise, she pushed the door open just wide enough for her to slip through.

Suddenly there was a very small gleam of light from the sitting room. Richard, moving as carefully as the girl, sat up, swung his legs out of the bed, reached for his dressing gown and put it on. He padded silently across to the door. Now he could see what she was doing. With the aid of a pencil torch she was searching his desk. The tiny beam of light illumined a glimpse of bare flesh and the sharp profile of her face. He stood watching her as she opened each drawer in turn, flicked swiftly through the contents and pushed it shut again.

Richard switched on the light.

For what seemed a protracted moment of suspended animation, the girl remained motionless, stooping over the desk. Then she straightened up and faced him. Naked, her body slim and firm as an athlete's, red hair falling on pale shoulders, she was undoubtedly very beautiful. Her expression gave nothing away; she didn't even look surprised.

She gave a slight shrug. "May I put some clothes on?" she asked.

"Of course," he said.

"One feels at a disadvantage."

He stood aside as she came back into the bedroom. He turned on the bedside lamp, and sat on the bed watching her dress. She fumbled with a hook and he moved to help her, but she managed it herself. He was struck, not only by her composure, but by her elegance in circumstances hardly conducive to it.

"Irena," he said, "why?"

"I am a thief," she replied. "I sleep with men and I steal things from them. It is very simple."

"I don't believe it. Not you."

"You know nothing about me," she said.

"Tell me then."

"No." She was putting on her shoes now.

"Don't you owe me an explanation?"

"I've given you one."

"And I've said I don't believe it. Why didn't you take anything from my wallet? You didn't, did you? You could hardly have concealed anything about your person."

"That's why I didn't take anything. I hoped there might be something more interesting in the desk."

"What sort of something?"

"I don't know. You'd be surprised what people keep in their desks. Girls like me make a living from whatever they can find. There might have been something you'd have paid to get back."

"So you're a blackmailer as well as a thief?"

"I am what I have to be." Calmly, she was putting on her coat. "Now, do you want to search me to make sure that I haven't taken anything which belongs to you, or may I go?"

"No, dammit, you can't go. Not just like that. I want to know—"

"Will you send for the police?"

"No, certainly not. Irena, we're friends at least, or I thought we were. I'd like to help you."

"You cannot help me. I don't need help. You've found out what I am. Is it so strange? Did your mother never tell you about girls like me? Now I should like to go, please."

He stood blocking the door. This conversation was the wrong way round, he felt. He should have been dominating it. She should have been making excuses, perhaps pleading with him. After all, it was he who had caught her red-handed, and yet somehow she had put him on the defensive.

"I could scream and say you were trying to rape me," she said. "And when I wouldn't do what you wanted, you threatened to accuse me of being a thief."

"You do have some bright ideas. All right. You'd better go."

He stood aside. She walked across the sitting room, opened the door of the flat and shut it behind her, without another word and without glancing back: and she was gone.

Richard checked the desk. As far as he could see, she hadn't taken or seriously disturbed anything: nor could he see anything likely to have interested her. There was a wall-safe behind a picture, but she hadn't known about that. In the bedroom he examined his wallet: but the money—about £60—and credit cards were untouched.

He glanced around the flat. There were no traces of her presence. She had even insisted on washing up the coffee cups and brandy glasses before they'd gone to bed.

The time now was just after three o'clock. He lay down on the bed and stared at the ceiling and, through the ceiling, at the past. It was a little over a week since he'd met her. The occasion was one of those appalling publicity parties which journalists attend for the free drink and because they've nothing better to do, and which public relations officers feel obliged to give in order to show that they're doing something. The ostensible object of this party was to launch a new series of travel books.

The hotel room was large, crowded, featureless and boring. Richard recognised one or two of the journalists, but wondered who all the others were, mostly men in ill-fitting suits harvesting little bits of food as though none of them intended to have any dinner. Perhaps they were travel agents, he thought sourly. And he never knew what to drink at these parties. There was no champagne: he didn't approve of drinking spirits before dinner, let alone the currently fashionable white wine which burns a hole in your stomach or, at best, creates a pool into which subsequent—better—wine must fall uncomfortably, and two glasses of sherry were about as much as the human frame required. Another five minutes and he'd go. Publicity parties, he decided, were the antithesis of what a party should be. The guests were not invited because anybody liked them or wanted them, and no effort was made to invite anyone they might like or want to meet. There was no sense of hospitality on the one side or gratitude on the other; which seemed curiously inept, professionally clumsy indeed, on the part of the public relations men, who were presumably trying to win friends and influence people on behalf of their clients. So why didn't they try to jolly things up? Why, having made their list of journalists, or travel agents, or whatever, whom they thought useful, did they not then inject a few chorus girls or duchesses, anyone with a bit of sparkle to enliven the dreary, overwhelmingly masculine lump? Why couldn't they—

At that moment he apologised silently to his hosts: or rather he didn't, since he felt sure the woman had been invited, not because she was pretty, but because she represented some magazine or tourist organisation. Her beauty was beyond question, though—red hair, delicate features, a neat body in a cunningly simple dress. He hadn't noticed her come into the room, but now she was standing only a few feet away, glass in hand, not talking to anyone but looking at a display of the books they were supposed to be celebrating.

Thinking about it in retrospect, Richard wondered whether he had picked her up or she had picked him up. He couldn't quite remember what had happened. Their eyes had met, she gave a sort of vague half-smile.

"Do you know all these people?" he had asked.

"I don't know any of them. Do you?" She had a slight foreign accent of some kind, overlaid with a trace of American.

"A few. None that makes the heart leap up. Let me introduce myself. My name's Richard Clayburn."

"Mine's Irena Janocki. Do you travel or do you write about travelling? I gather everybody here is supposed to do one or the other."

"Well actually it's considered quite a good idea for those of us who write about travel occasionally to move across the face of the earth ourselves. Very nasty, of course, but one feels it's one's duty."

"Where do you write?"

"In the colour supplements mainly, and I've written one or two books. But what do you do?"

"Oh, nothing so clever. I'm the London agent for a Canadian tour company. Do you hate tourists?"

"Yes. Are you Canadian yourself?"

She nodded. "My parents were Polish."

"Ah, Poland—that really is the nation on our conscience. Or should be. Do you want any more of these things?" He indicated a passing dish of small undefined edible objects.

"Not really. I could do with another drink."

"The impossible takes longer. What is it—gin and tonic? Wait here, and I'll see what can be done."

He fought his way to the bar: and, when he came back, she was still there, not talking to anyone else. Soon afterwards he suggested that they might escape, and have dinner together. She had come easily enough, like a ripe apple from the bough. He took her to a Chelsea restaurant which was an old favourite of his; excruciatingly expensive, as all London restaurants had become, but well worth it that evening. The candlelight added to the glamour of her face, and she was good to talk to as well as look at. Sometimes, alas often, maintaining conversation with a pretty girl, except at the most superficial level, proved a disappointingly uphill task. But not so with Irena. She was intelligent and quick and ready to explore Richard's interests. Afterwards he took her home, which proved to be an anonymous flat off Kensington High Street. She kissed him when they said good night, having arranged to meet again two days later.

That had been the start. Memory might have truncated the details of what had been said during that first evening, but Richard didn't think he had forgotten anything significant. From then on, the affair had proceeded very agreeably along orthodox lines—lunch, dinner, a theatre, a whole Saturday spent together, the sofa in her flat, the sofa in his flat, bed.

But she was quite right in saying that he knew nothing about her. Despite all those hours of talk, the thousands and thousands of quite intimate words, something of Irena had continued to be, not just inviolably private, but elusive. She had told him the facts of her life—who her parents were, where she had been to school, some of the previous jobs she had done, about the firm for which she now worked and that she had been in London for three months. But it was the pieced-together synopsis of a life rather than a life recalled with any feeling. How old was she, even? In her early thirties, he supposed. She must have had lovers, plenty of them probably, but she had never mentioned a man and he hadn't asked.

"I can't help regarding Canadians as Americans *manqués*," he had said to her once, "although I know how much it annoys them." "We're not," she said, and they went on to discuss the nature of Canada. She hadn't said it with great conviction, though: and the fact of her being Canadian did give her background—for him, at least—a sort of haziness. If she had been English, or had lived in London for a long time, he would have expected them to have friends, or acquaintances, in common. If she had been American, there would have been points of reference. Canada was, relatively, a blank. She didn't know anyone he knew, and there was no reason why she should. He couldn't fit her clearly into a social or cultural pattern, except that she was well educated and well read; not necessarily because there was anything very enigmatic about her, but perhaps he wasn't familiar enough with Canadian social and cultural patterns.

On the other hand, perhaps there was something enigmatic about her. In retrospect, of course, there had to be.

Ah well, he couldn't do anything more about it tonight. He took off his dressing gown, and got into bed. The pillow still bore the mark of Irena's head. A few minutes later he was asleep.

Richard woke just before nine, drew the curtains and looked out over the trees in the square. It was one of those rare mornings made by God for Englishmen; a few fluffy white clouds against an eggshell-blue sky, the trees wearing the light green of early spring, the elegant pillared doorways of Belgravia looking like a street scene from an old-fashioned musical comedy. One expected to see a whistling milkman, a comic policeman and a chorus of gentlemen in morning coats and girls in Ascot dresses.

Suddenly Richard felt distinctly cheerful. The mystery of the night before intrigued rather than depressed him. Irena's hook was in him—he had realised that several days ago—but perhaps not very deeply; he wasn't fully in love with her. Not yet, though he could be—easily.

Anyway, he wasn't going to let her walk out of his life. For all sorts of reasons he had to know what last night was about.

He opened the post, which contained nothing very much, glanced at the newspapers, which also contained nothing very much, then lit the gas under a kettle and under a pan of water. He shaved and dressed in exactly the time it took the water to boil; made a pot of tea, dropped two eggs in the pan and ate his cornflakes while they were boiling. Having breakfast with Irena would have been more fun, he thought with a brief pang, but, since she wasn't there, he followed the strict timetable of long-established routine. This was the system he adopted in all his travels. If something extraordinary happened and you had to improvise, then you improvised: if not, the wise thing to do, the most convenient thing to do, was to behave conventionally. He liked the framework of his life to be as firm as possible, leaving him free to paint inside it whatever the circumstances and his fancy might suggest.

At ten past ten he sat down on the sofa, picked up the telephone and dialled one of the few numbers he knew by heart. It was the number of a small art gallery in Cork Street. "Oh, good morning," he said, "is Miss Mackenzie in yet?"

Diana Mackenzie and her friend Charlotte Hockley owned the gallery, which specialised in bird pictures, hunting prints and other rural decorations. Neither of them had known anything about business when they started it, some five years ago, but, as Diana cheerfully observed, the providence which looks after fools and drunken men had seen them through, and the gallery was now quite a success; successful enough to let them hire two other girls, so that Diana and Charlotte no longer had to be constantly on the premises. But in fact Diana was there most mornings.

"Diana?" he said. "Richard. Come to lunch."

"I can't. We're up to our ears, sorting out a whole batch of stuff I bought at an auction yesterday. Sea battles mostly. You'd like them. There's one showing armed vessels of the East India Company blowing Chinese junks out of the water. Just your sort of thing."

"You can give it me for my birthday. But, Diana, can't you get away for an hour? I particularly want to see you."

"Well, I suppose I could. But what's so urgent? I presume it's not just the aesthetic pleasure of seeing me that you want."

"I don't know why you should assume that. But I'll explain over lunch. Shall I pick you up at the gallery about one? We can go to that new Greek place round the corner."

While he had been talking, Mrs. Murphy had let herself into the flat and was clearing away the breakfast things. A large motherly woman, she had been coming in every weekday morning for years. She was fond of gossip, and—since it's wrong to put temptation in people's way— Richard kept the key of the drinks cupboard concealed beneath Volume II of *Travels in Arabia Deserta:* but nobody's perfect, and she had a heart of Irish gold.

"Top of the morning to you, Mrs. Murphy," he said. "How are all your family? In good form, I hope."

"They're all fine, thank God. Barring himself, who's got the divil of a hangover this morning. We spent too long in the pub last night, that's the truth." She pushed open the kitchen door with her ample rear, and went on talking from a distance. "I met a man who'd read your books and said how much he enjoyed them. He wanted to know what manner of gentleman you might be."

Richard, who hadn't been paying much attention, suddenly did pay attention.

"How did he know you knew me?" he asked, strolling over to the kitchen door.

"Me and my big mouth. Everyone in the pub knows all the gentlemen I work for. Mind you, I don't gossip. If sometimes there's a second breakfast cup, with lipstick on it, I wouldn't be telling anybody about that, now would I?"

"I'm sure you wouldn't. What was he like, this man in the pub? Should I be pleased that he enjoys my books?"

"If he buys them, you'll be pleased, I suppose. He didn't look like a great reader, though. More like a boxer. And he was wearing an overcoat with big purple checks. But he bought me a drink. Tell the truth and shame the divil—more than one drink. He was a decent man after all."

"Obviously. Did the landlord or the barmaid seem to know him?"

"Now you ask, I don't think they did. I've not seen him before, and I go in that pub a lot. Just to keep an eye on himself, you understand, so he doesn't drink too much and start a fight and get into trouble. He's a terror when he's had a few drinks. But 'Paddy,' I says, 'I'll thump you, if you don't come home this minute.' And he came, quiet as a lamb."

The narrative having taken a domestic turn, Richard made noises of agreement and sympathy, and managed tactfully to withdraw. He thought for a minute about what Mrs. Murphy had said, then shrugged; opened the window, tested the fresh air and decided it was warm enough to go out without an overcoat; picked up his umbrella, called goodbye to Mrs. Murphy, and went briskly downstairs and into the outside world.

It was a day for walking. Richard walked across the park, thinking about what needed to be done. There was an ostensibly humorous article, about how to distinguish good hotels from bad, which he had to deliver by the end of the week: and his current book was languishing— he really ought to try and write a few more pages: and, of course, there were letters, endless letters, which needed answering. He might deal with a few of the more urgent after lunch, and, now that Irena was gone, the evening looked boringly free. So the work schedule didn't seem too intractable. He could devote his attention, for a while, to Irena and associated problems.

The clock on St. James's Palace told him it was still only a quarter to twelve. He wandered into his club, flicked through the newspapers he hadn't already seen, toyed for a moment with the virtuous idea of writing a couple of letters, but rejected it and went into the bar instead. The pre-luncheon crowd was just beginning to gather at the water-hole. He ordered a glass of champagne, and was quite content to join idly in a conversation about racehorses. His ignorance of the subject was profound but, at least in small doses, his fellow-members amused him. There was a picture on the wall of a heavily whiskered young cavalry officer who had been killed in the Crimea. The type continued: the line had bred true. He knew young men just like that. There were two or three of them in the bar now; very brave, cheerful, rather stupid—and you could trust them to Hell and back. And if they weren't killed in wars or in motor-car crashes, or, when they became stockbrokers after completing short-service commissions in the Household Division, didn't get drawn beyond their depth and overwhelmed in some dreadful financial calamity, they mellowed into the boyish old men, with pink faces and immaculately groomed white hair, of whom there were also some fine specimens in the bar. Not to be despised, Richard thought, while lending less than half an ear to a learned disquisition on the state of the course at Newbury. Their replacement by sophists, economists and calculators, not to mention trade union leaders and bureaucrats, was a symbol, if not a symptom, of England's decline.

He glanced at his watch, refused another drink, and went into the washroom to polish his shoes ("Very important, clean boots," he often said), straighten his tie and brush his hair. He inspected himself in the mirror—well-cut grey herring-bone tweed suit, a favourite tie and, above it, a face which was beginning to look a bit lived-in. "But not bad," he decided. "I could very well pass for thirty-five?"

There are no occasions, of course, when one should not try to look one's best, and perhaps he would have been even more zealous to do so for Irena: but Diana too was special, though in a different way. He had known her a long time, he was deeply comfortable with her, and the ashes of a dormant *affaire* had never completely cooled. Seeing her still gave him positive pleasure. How she felt about him he really didn't know.

He found her now knee-deep in packing cases. Wearing a pullover and skirt, fair hair disarrayed but not unkempt, she looked like what she was, a nice sensible English girl. Her social and educational background was as immediately clear as Irena's had seemed obscure. Diana's voice, manner and intelligence spoke of Benenden and LMH. (Richard, who was interested in such things, had once held forth on the nuances which would have been different if she had been at Cambridge. "Cause or effect, I'm not sure," he said. "Do Wykehamists become Wykehamists through going to Winchester, or do they go to Winchester because they are already potential Wykehamists?") What the outward and visible signs didn't show was a streak of unpredictable adventurousness in her character; she took risks with her eyes open, but she took them.

"Ah, the life of culture," said Richard.

"Hello," she said, dumping a pile of prints on the table. "Business culture. Price, not value."

"Is there a difference?"

"Yes, there is. I'll explain it to you some time. You just look at the pretty pictures, and I'll be with you in a minute."

He looked at them, and liked them, thinking, not for the first time, that Diana and he had marvellously compatible tastes.

She gave some instructions to the rather mousey girl who was being left in charge of the shop, and they went off to lunch. The new Greek place was reassuringly full but not excessively crowded: and, because it was new, the management was still making an effort. Richard and Diana's compatibility extended to their both liking retsina, a taste which can never be assumed, and, from a menu carefully scribbled in ethnic blue ink, they both chose what was described as "moussaka—special Greek dish".

When they had exchanged a few items of gossip, Richard broached the topic of the day. He told her about Irena.

"You'll agree," he said at the end, "it's a very rum story."

"Are you in love with her?" Diana asked.

"I'm not sure. But I can't let her just disappear into the night. Maybe I could rescue her from trouble in some gallant way. I should enjoy that."

"Oh, come on! I can't see you reforming fallen women, like Mr. Gladstone."

"I still don't believe that's what she is. Not in the sense you mean, anyway."

"Could she have been looking for anything else, other than money?"

"She didn't take the money. I don't possess any valuables—except my latest manuscript. A work of genius, no doubt, but I should be surprised if rival publishers were conspiring to purloin it. And my private life, as I'm sure you know, is an open book."

"Bound in limp leather?"

"Rich Morocco."

"All right, it's a mystery. So what are you going to do about it?"

"I was rather hoping you might help."

"Me? What can I do?"

"You could meet her, and see what you think. You might get more out of her than I could."

"And how do you propose that I should meet her? It doesn't sound as if you can just ring her up now and ask her to tea."

"I've been considering that," said Richard, "and, if you're willing to have a go, this is what I suggest. . . ."

III

Girls Together

Diana Mackenzie was not the sort of girl to be particularly worried by the prospect of a tricky social situation. She had a slight tendency, which greatly annoyed her, to go pink in the face when embarrassed or angry: but she wasn't very often embarrassed or angry, such emotions being counteracted by a mischievous curiosity about how other people were reacting. Anyway, she felt no embarrassment, but considerable curiosity, at the prospect of meeting Irena.

Not that she thought there was much mystery. Irena was probably just what she seemed, what indeed she had confessed to being. Men—Richard not least—were taken in astonishingly easily by a pretty face. Diana's curiosity was directed mainly to seeing what kind of face, accompanied no doubt by other attributes (not all physical—she gave him that much credit), had hooked Richard this time.

Her train of thought suddenly stopped with an uneasy jerk. Here she was on a fool's errand, which would almost certainly prove pointless and might involve an awkward unpleasant scene. Why had she agreed to do it? Because an old friend had asked her to. Well, yes. . . . But if her real motive was that she wanted to see the woman who had hooked Richard . . . why was she so interested?

Firmly Diana started her train of thought moving again, away from such a delicate stopping-point. She could think about that question later. At the moment she'd better pay attention to the matter in hand.

This was where Irena lived, a featureless block of flats behind Kensington High Street. There was a row of bells beside the heavy plateglass door. Number sixteen, Richard had said. Yes—"Irena Janocki," the name handwritten. What were the odds, Diana wondered, on there being no reply? After last night's episode, Irena might have considered it prudent to move on, at least temporarily—particularly if this was, as it were, her business address. She wouldn't want Richard thundering at her door. Alternatively, she might be afraid that he had told the police.

Diana pressed the bell.

"Yes?" said a woman's voice through the Entryphone.

"My name's Diana Mackenzie. I'm a friend of Richard Clayburn's. He thinks he left something in your flat. May I come up for a moment?"

There was a slight pause. Then: "All right. I'm on the first floor." The electrically operated lock clicked open.

The voice, Diana thought as she walked across the small entrance hall to the lifts, was as described—Canadian with a touch of something else.

When she stepped out into the first floor corridor, she found number sixteen almost directly opposite the lift, the door slightly ajar, showing a line of light from inside. She knocked.

"Come in." Irena was standing, as though deliberately posed, in front of the fireplace, a cigarette between her fingers. Richard hadn't exaggerated. She was strikingly beautiful.

"I'm sorry to bother you—" Diana began.

"You're not. Come and sit down. How is Richard?"

"He's all right." Diana felt thrown off balance. Whatever kind of reception she'd expected, it wasn't this. But she realised that not only were Irena's voice and appearance as described, so was her performance. This was what Richard had meant when he said that she had dominated a conversation which he had expected to control: and she dominated it, not by being forceful, but by being calm.

"Will you have a drink?"

"I mustn't stay—but, thank you, gin and tonic." If this was how Irena wanted to play it, Diana was quite willing to match her. She glanced round the room while Irena was pouring the drinks. It was as featureless inside as the block had been outside. There were no clues to the nature of the occupant; no pictures on the walls; no books, except one large volume called *Canada the Beautiful* on a glass-topped coffee-table, accompanied by two or three fashion magazines. A portable typewriter stood open on a functional dining table. Irena's coat lay across a chair. There seemed to be nothing else personal at all.

But if Irena's possessions, or lack of them, gave an impression of transience, she herself—her perfect grooming, her quietly confident manners—had an air of fastidiousness and respectability. Seeing her, Diana found it very difficult indeed to believe that she was just a girl who stole from, and blackmailed, men she'd picked up.

"Richard thought he might have left his address book here," Diana said. "One he usually carries with him. Dark blue. Quite small."

Irena looked at her quizzically—unbelievingly, Diana felt. "I haven't seen it. Did he say where? In the bedroom perhaps?"

Bitch, thought Diana. "He didn't say."

"I'll look."

While Irena was out of the room, Diana took Richard's address book from her handbag and pushed it down behind the cushions on the sofa.

"It's not there," said Irena, returning.

"Well, I wonder where it could be," said Diana. "Do you remember seeing him use it lately?" Richard had told her that he did, in fact, consult his address book while sitting on the sofa a few days earlier. After a bit more prompting, Irena searched behind the cushions of the sofa and found it.

"Ah!" she said, and gave it to Diana. "Why did he send you, instead of coming himself?"

"I live nearby. No, that isn't true. He thought it would be—less awkward."

"Did he tell you much about last night?"

"Something."

"Do you know Richard well?"

"I've known him for a long time."

"Yes, he's mentioned your name." She paused, then seemed to make up her mind. "Please, I would like us to be friends. Will you sit down for a minute and tell me about yourself, and about Richard?"

"I was rather hoping that you might tell me about yourself."

Irena smiled. "You mean that's what Richard was hoping. Let's talk anyway."

So they talked. The whole point of Diana's visit was to draw Irena out, and it was proving, in a way, easier than she had expected. Diana talked freely. She had nothing to hide, unless there were things she was hiding from herself. Irena talked easily about her home in Canada and her parents, and what she thought of England. But, for a while, they both skirted the real subject.

Finally Irena said: "About last night. It wasn't what it seemed. I would like to tell you, and I think perhaps you can help me—and Richard: but I have to get someone else's permission first. Could we possibly meet again tomorrow?"

"If you want to."

Irena, it was agreed, would come to Diana's flat around half-past six the following day. "I'd rather you didn't say anything to Richard until afterwards," she added.

"All right," said Diana, concealing her gratification, at having succeeded in her mission so well, or at least being on the verge of success. Telling Richard was precisely what she wanted to do, but perhaps in twenty-four hours she would be able to offer him a positive answer to the mystery.

Having said goodbye to Irena with a certain genuine warmth—she really rather liked her—Diana took a taxi home and immediately telephoned Richard, as she had promised him she would.

"Sherlock Holmes," she said, "or Lady Molly of Scotland Yard, or whatever I'm supposed to be, has done rather better than expected."

"You saw Irena?"

"I did indeed. We had a long cosy chat."

"And?"

"My investigations, Watson, are not yet complete. Possess yourself with patience, and very shortly I think I may have some answers for you."

"Why, what happened?"

"Listen to this station at the same time tomorrow night—"

"Don't be so irritating, Diana. What happened?"

"Nothing happened. I don't know any more than you do. Honestly, Richard, I can't tell you—not now. But I'll call you this time tomorrow, and then I really may have something for you. All right?"

"No, it's bloody well not all right—"

"Don't let me forget to give you your address book back," Diana said, and hung up, smiling. It would serve him right to be kept in suspense for a while—if, that is, he was still in love with Irena. Old faithful Diana would deliver the goods. . . . Her smile became somewhat rueful.

She went out to a dinner party that evening, and next day was too occupied in the gallery to give much thought to the mystery of Irena.

She left promptly at half-past five, though, to be sure of being home when Irena came.

Diana's flat was, in fact, a mews cottage—bedroom, sitting room, kitchen and bathroom, at the top of a precipitous staircase, over a garage. Jerry-built in the eighteenth century, it had become a period gem in the twentieth. Tourists, peering down the cobbled mews, bright with window-boxes on a spring morning, sinister with dim lamps on a winter evening, said, "How sweet!" Diana too had thought it sweet when she'd first seen it, six years before, and she occasionally stood back and looked at it and thought so still: but she'd grown used to its discomfort as well as its charm. The rooms were too small, the plumbing seemed as old as the mews. Some of the other cottages had been expensively modernised. This one hadn't. Periodically she talked about moving: but her days were busy, she was often away at the weekends, and the idea of house-hunting depressed her: so she stayed.

Irena rang the bell at precisely six-thirty. Diana went downstairs to let her in.

"What a sweet little house!" she said.

Taking her coat, Diana appraised her again, and thought again what an undeniably beautiful woman she was—but perhaps (Diana noticed the lines at the corners of her eyes) a little older than she'd guessed. Her clothes weren't expensive but were absolutely right; this was a woman who knew what suited her.

When drinks had been poured and they were seated on either side of the electric fire, Irena opened her handbag and produced a small plastic-covered folder, which she flipped open and handed to Diana.

"First of all I'd better show you this," she said.

It was an identity card, consisting of a bad coloured photograph of Irena with her signature underneath, and, beside it, under the heading "United Nations Board of Narcotics Control," the statement "Miss Irena Janocki" (the name was typed in) "is an accredited agent of this Board," followed by the Director's signature.

"I see," said Diana, giving it back. "Or rather I don't."

"That explains who I am. I couldn't tell you yesterday, because I had to get security clearance. Now I want to tell you something else, which you may think absurd. In fact, I'm hoping that you can show me it is absurd.

"I won't go into a lot of detail, but we're here in London—my colleagues and I—trying to discover the route, one of the routes, along which heroin is taken from the Middle East to the United States and Canada. It passes through Britain, we believe. Indeed, it may be refined here. So we're looking for the carriers and we're looking for the laboratory or the warehouse where the stuff is kept.

"For various reasons the name of Richard Clayburn cropped up. He fitted certain descriptions. He's been in the Middle East and America lately. . . . Well, believe me, we did have reasons to think that he might be involved. Not that he was a carrier, but that he recruited the carriers. The evidence was circumstantial but it had to be investigated. My job was to get close to him."

She paused. Diana, though astonished, said nothing.

"I got close to him. The sort of thing that happened two nights ago is—part of the job. I won't try to justify it, though of course I do in my own mind. You're a friend of Richard's, and I can imagine what you must think of me. But it's because you're a friend of Richard's—and have been for a long while—that I'm telling you this.

"You see, I don't believe he is the man. I don't want to believe it. I like him very much. But it's not just that. Now that I know him rather well—it doesn't fit the sort of man he is. Which is what my colleagues would call 'a woman's argument.' It's not enough. There's still no evidence, no conclusive evidence, one way or the other.

"After what happened, I should have been pulled out anyway. But when you came to see me, I suddenly had an idea. You might be able to clear him absolutely."

Diana shook her head in amazement. "You were quite right. I do find the whole notion absurd. Of course Richard's not a drug smuggler —though, come to think of it, he has been accused of being a spy. That's an occupational risk for foreign correspondents and travel writers. But how am I to prove he's not? I haven't been as close to him, as you put it, lately, as you have."

"Quite simply. At least, you may be able to. We know that the man we're looking for, the man Richard was perhaps mistaken for, was in certain places on certain dates—some of them quite recent. If you happened to know that he was here in London, or somewhere else, on even one of those dates, that would rule him out."

"I wouldn't necessarily know," Diana said, "but he does generally tell me when he's going abroad and we have lunch or something when he gets back."

"Exactly. Don't worry, you won't be condemning him if you're not sure he was here. It would only work one way. It would just clear him if you were sure."

"All right. Let me look in my diary." Diana fetched a pocket diary from her handbag, and then, rummaging in a drawer of the desk, produced another one. "Here's last year's too." She sat down again. "Now, what dates are we looking at?"

"I know most of them by heart," said Irena, and she proceeded to mention a string of dates going back over the past year.

Diana checked them, one by one, against her diary. "No, I didn't see him that week, or the week before. At least, I haven't written it down. . . . I know he was away during the first two weeks of March. In the Far East, I think; he brought me back that little jade tiger over there. . . . We had lunch on the twenty-second of February. He was away most of January. . . . He was certainly here at Christmas. Let's try the other book. . . ."

They'd gone back some way into the previous year, piecing together Richard's movements in general terms, when finally one of the dates coincided. "Did you say September the third?" Diana asked. "I had lunch with him on September the second, and he came to drinks here on September the fourth. I had a small party and I remember he came. Does that do it? Is that enough?"

Irena smiled. "Yes, I think it is enough. I'm most grateful—and very pleased."

"Let's have another drink to celebrate." Diana put the two diaries away, took both glasses and went over to where the bottles were. Irena stood up too.

"I presume I can tell Richard—" Diana began, when Irena hit her expertly on the neck with the edge of her hand. Diana collapsed on to the floor, with a broken glass beside her and the bottle spilling its contents on to the table.

IV

Roofscape

Diana fought her way back through blurred semi-consciousness to full
realisation of where she was, although she couldn't understand for a
while what had happened. She was lying on the floor of her own sitting
room. Her head throbbed and she had difficulty focussing her eyes. She
must have fainted. Her vision was clearing now, but she still couldn't
move. . . . Suddenly she became aware that her hands were tied behind her, and her ankles were tied together, and there was a gag in her
mouth.

Irena. Recollection flooded back.

Diana managed to roll over. Irena was still there, standing a few feet
away, with the telephone in her hand. As she finished dialling, she
glanced over at Diana. Their eyes met, but Irena's face remained quite
expressionless.

She spoke in a low voice into the telephone. Diana tried to hear what
she said, and then realised that Irena was speaking in some foreign
language: and it wasn't any language she could recognise.

The conversation was brief. Irena replaced the receiver, stooped and,
with a sharp jerk, pulled the cord of the telephone out of the wall. She
put on her coat, picked up her handbag and looked carefully round the
room, as though making sure that she hadn't left anything. Then she
walked across to Diana, and looked down at her. Diana felt a stab of
apprehension. But Irena simply knelt down and checked the stockings
with which Diana's hands and feet were tied; checked the knots and
checked that the bonds were tight.

Anger overcoming fear, Diana squirmed and tried to kick, but found
she couldn't. The stockings round her wrists and ankles were joined

together. Irena stood up and, with a slight smile, said in English: "I'm sorry."

She walked briskly from the room. Diana heard her footsteps going down the steep stairs, and the front door being shut. The house became silent, except for the distant traffic noises.

Diana began trying in earnest to free herself but, the more she struggled, the tighter the knots seemed to grow. The gag in her mouth made her retch. Frightened of being sick and choking, she stopped her efforts and lay still. She tried to clear her mind, to make sense of what had happened. But it didn't make sense. Irena surely couldn't be what she'd claimed to be. The identity card must have been a fake. Or was it just possible that she might have thought Diana was involved, with Richard, in the drug-smuggling business: and, having immobilised Diana, had gone in pursuit of Richard? Or could it be that Richard really was a drug smuggler, and that Irena belonged to some rival gang and was laying a trap for him? But that made no sense either. The whole point of Irena's questions had been to establish the impossibility of Richard's involvement on certain days throughout the past year.

Whatever the explanation, he ought to be warned. Diana renewed her struggles, but with no better success. Again she flopped back, trying to recover her breath.

Could Irena have taken anything while she was unconscious? It didn't seem likely. In the first place, there was nothing much to take: and, in the second, Diana didn't think she'd been unconscious for more than two or three minutes, just long enough for Irena to tie her up. And Irena surely wasn't a casual thief. That seemed less plausible than ever.

From such speculation Diana was pulled back by an even more disturbing thought. Suppose she really couldn't untie herself: how long would she have to lie there? No one else had a key to the house. Who would ever find her? People had been known to die in that kind of situation, their bodies found weeks or months later. . . .

Again Diana pulled and twisted at her bonds. In vain. The knots were quite unyielding. Something sharp then. . . . Perhaps she could roll to the window and break a pane of glass by butting it with her head. Somebody in the mews might notice. . . . But there was glass nearer than that. Bottles and glasses. She rolled over again, and saw that the carpet was wet. She had dropped the glass she was holding when Irena hit her. But if it had broken, there were no fragments. Irena must have cleared them up, put them in the waste-paper basket or on the tray, precisely so that Diana couldn't get hold of them too easily. Efficient Irena.

But there were other bottles and glasses. Painfully, and with several pauses for breath, Diana inched her way towards them. Irena hadn't thought of this: or perhaps she had. She didn't mind if Diana escaped in a little while, after—after what?

Time enough to think about that later. By dint of much contortion and squirming, Diana managed to raise her head to the level of the shelf where the drinks were kept. The nearest breakable object was a sherry glass. She butted it with her forehead. It fell to the carpet, where, in the cussed nature of things, it didn't break. She wriggled until she was able to crush it with her shoulder.

From then on, it was just a matter of patience. Having made sure that there was a suitably razor-like splinter of glass, she rolled over, turning her back to it, scrabbled with her fingers until she had a firm grip on the splinter, then began sawing at the only part of her bonds she could reach. After a minute or so, the stocking which joined her wrists to her ankles separated.

She rested a moment; then, by squatting back on her heels, brought the stocking about her ankles within reach. She cut through it quite easily.

She was stretching her legs to restore the circulation before attempting to stand up, when the doorbell rang.

Eagerly she pushed herself to her feet, and her legs collapsed under her. She tried to call out through the gag, but couldn't make any noise loud enough to be heard down below.

The ring of the doorbell was repeated. This time she managed to struggle upright but, before she could move any further, she heard a different—very small—sound, which made her freeze. A click and a familiar slight creak. Somebody had opened the front door.

No one had a key except herself. Irena might have taken the key from her handbag while she lay stunned, but Irena wouldn't have rung the bell.

Now someone was coming slowly up the stairs. Spurred by a sharp stab of fear, Diana's mind raced. With her hands still tied behind her, she had no chance of fighting an intruder, no chance of defending herself effectively. More by instinct than with any clear plan, she decided to disguise the fact that she was partially free. Lying down again on top of the severed stocking, she resumed her original position, with her legs drawn up behind her as though they were still tied.

The footsteps were at the top of the stairs now. They certainly were not Irena's. They were cautious. Nobody could climb those old stairs noiselessly; there were too many creaky treads. But if the house had not been silent, the footsteps would scarcely have been heard. They'd stopped outside the slightly open door of the room. Diana waited in suspense.

The door was pushed open sharply. For a moment she had the weird impression that no one was there, just an empty doorway. Somebody was standing to one side, in the shadow.

Richard stepped into the room. After a quick glance at Diana, he looked coolly around, appraising the situation; checked the kitchen, the bathroom and the bedroom; and only then came over to her. She had struggled into a sitting position, and was uttering indignant noises through the gag.

"Oh dear!" he said. Kneeling beside her, he produced a penknife and cut the gag. Her mouth was so dry that she couldn't speak while he freed her wrists.

"What happened?" he asked.

Massaging her wrists and swallowing, she said: "Irena."

He gave her a glass of soda-water to drink and helped her on to the sofa. "Now tell me," he said.

She told him. He listened without comment until she'd finished, or, rather, until she was describing her efforts to escape, at which point she broke off to ask: "But what brought you here? And how did you get in? Not that I'm not pleased to see you."

"I tried to call you, and they said the line was out of order. That worried me. I don't quite know why. So I came straight round. Your light was on, but you didn't answer the door. I'm afraid I picked the lock."

"Can you? Pick locks, I mean. That's a silly question. Of course you can. You did." The relief from tension was making her quite garrulous. "You're not really a dope smuggler, are you?"

He smiled. "No. That's one thing I'm not. But, please, tell me again what dates Irena was interested in and what you said."

"I'll try to remember." She pieced the conversation together in as much detail as she could. He prompted her occasionally by asking if Irena had mentioned some particular date, and usually she had.

Eventually he stood up, and said to himself more than to Diana: "Now that's a bit awkward."

He was different somehow, Diana thought, from the Richard she was used to. Crisper, more serious. "Why?" she asked. "Did I tell her something I shouldn't have done? I didn't tell her anything in the least secret. I don't know any secrets about you."

"It's not your fault." He walked over to the window, obviously pondering. "I think I'm going to have to tell you . . ." His voice trailed away. Diana became aware of the sound of a car in the mews and the slamming of a car door, twice.

"Switch off the light," said Richard sharply. She obeyed, then came and stood beside him. He had moved to a position at the side of the window and was looking down into the dimly lit cobbled mews.

A large black car was parked near the entrance to the mews, almost blocking the archway. Three men in dark overcoats were standing beside it; another, she could just make out, was sitting at the wheel. As she watched, one of them pointed, as it seemed, straight at her, at the window of her house. Another, much taller than the other two—tall and thin, his face in shadow—made a gesture of response or command. She knew, without knowing why, that he was in charge.

"Who are they?" she asked.

The tall man stayed by the car. The other two began walking towards the house.

"Is there any way out except through the front?" asked Richard urgently. "A back door? Or can we get up to the roof?"

"There's no back door. There is a trapdoor in the ceiling. You can get up to the roof that way. Richard, is it the police?"

"No, not the police. Come on; show me the trapdoor."

It was in the ceiling of the minute landing at the top of the stairs, its outline barely discernible by the dim glow through the windows. "You'll need a chair to stand on," Diana said.

Richard flicked on the light in the kitchen, grabbed a wooden chair and scrambled on to it. With some difficulty he forced back the two bolts and heaved. The trapdoor moved. Another heave and he was able to push it open.

"Who are you running away from?" Diana asked again.

"You're coming too," he said. "These are not people you want to meet." And as he said it, she heard someone trying the front door—which Richard had shut but left unlocked.

He seized her arm, almost dragged her on to the chair and lifted her bodily to the open trapdoor. Too bewildered to make any further protest, she allowed herself to be bundled through and on to the roof. Richard clambered up after her.

He slammed the trapdoor shut, but there was no way of fastening it from above. He looked quickly round the flat roof to see if there was anything heavy he could put on top of it. But there was nothing.

A row of irregular roofs, some slightly higher, some slightly lower, stretched away for about fifty yards in either direction, sprouting an occasional clump of oddly shaped chimney pots. At the entrance to the mews there was a drop to the street, at the other end a cliff of taller buildings.

The London sky is never really dark, and this wasn't a dark night. The roofscape stood out in clear relief, though dappled with blackness. There would be ways down—drainpipes, skylights—but they had only a minute or so, Richard thought, before the men who must now be coming up the stairs would realise where their quarry had gone. He had deliberately kicked over the chair as he hauled himself through the trapdoor, but it wouldn't take them long, when they found the house empty, to appreciate the significance of that overturned chair.

"Should I yell for help?" Diana asked. "I might get some of the neighbours out."

"No. Don't do that. Here—behind these chimneys."

Grabbing her wrist, he pulled her into the shadow. They were on the blind side of the trapdoor and about five feet away from it. Quickly he took off the light overcoat he'd been wearing.

The trapdoor moved, was lifted an inch or so. Then it crashed open and a man came out fast, looking absurdly like an old-fashioned Jack-in-the-box. Richard darted forward and threw his coat over the man's head. Without pausing, he went straight in after it. His knee came up into the man's groin, his left fist drove at the stomach, his right forearm slashed across the throat.

To Diana it looked like a single blur of action: and, horrifyingly, it was over as suddenly as it had begun. Richard's second blow knocked the man backwards, still trying to claw the coat away from his face. For an instant the man's arms flailed. There was a muffled cry. And he'd vanished over the edge of the roof.

Diana had no time to be shocked. While Richard launched himself at the man, she had slammed the trapdoor shut. She was going to try and hold it down, when with a vicious whizz something punched a hole in the wood beside her. Instinctively she jumped back as a second shot whirred past.

There was no crack. The gun had a silencer.

Richard was holding her arm and pulling her again. They were running, stumbling, over the roofs. "Down!" he said. They crouched behind another chimney stack.

The second man emerged from the trapdoor more cautiously. He had thrust the door back with his left hand: in his right he held a pistol with an elongated barrel. He looked in all directions before climbing out on to the roof. For a moment he squatted, motionless, in the moonlight. He stood up, walked to the edge of the roof, looked down into the mews.

He was thick-set, bulky, with a bald head.

He turned back to the roofs, surveying them systematically. As he did so, a third man climbed out of the trapdoor. He was holding a gun too. It wasn't the tall figure who had been giving the orders. This must be the one who had been sitting in the car, Diana thought.

The two men stood together, talking in low voices, but watching all the time for any movement. Diana pressed against the chimney stack, seeing them from the corner of her eye, holding her breath.

They moved away from each other. The newcomer, the third man, began searching the shadows and corners and crannies on the far side of the trapdoor, away from where Richard and Diana were hiding. The bulky man was walking slowly towards them, his large bald head constantly turning, alert, gun ready. He crossed from one side of the roof to the other, and back again, zigzag, making sure that he missed no possible hiding place. In a few more yards he was bound to see Richard and Diana.

"Stay there!" hissed Richard, and sprinted for another cluster of chimney pots quite close to the bulky man. The man fired. The bullet ricocheted from the brickwork with a loud whine. The other man spun towards the sound, gun extended, ready to fire.

The bulky man, who had himself taken cover behind an angle of pitched roof, called to his companion in some language Diana didn't recognise. This man began moving towards Richard on the far side, while the bulky man stepped cautiously out of cover and started working his way round, keeping well away from the cluster of chimney pots on the near side.

Diana watched them, horrified, as they closed in on Richard. The time seemed to stretch out endlessly, and she found herself thinking quite clearly what she could do. There was only one thing. She did it.

As the moment came when the bulky man saw, or was about to see, Richard, she screamed. The distraction was just enough. He fired, but missed. And Richard was on him. They fell, struggling. Diana saw Richard smash his opponent's head on the roof, and, kneeling on him, lift his arm for a finishing blow.

But the other man was standing only a few feet away, gun levelled, waiting for a clear shot. He couldn't possibly miss.

For a few seconds which again seemed an eternity, the whole scene was frozen in the moonlight: the two men locked together on the roof; the figure behind, arm extended; Diana crouched in the shadow, helpless to prevent what was going to happen.

V

Into the Land of Cockaigne

The shot, when it came, was light, hardly more than a snap. For a moment Diana was bewildered. The man who had been aiming at Richard had dropped his gun. He was clutching his shoulder. It wasn't he who had fired. She became aware that there was now someone else on the roof, climbing out of the trapdoor, holding a small gun in his hand.

The newcomer spoke. "Dear me," he said. "What a lot of bother!"

Richard was staggering to his feet. The bulky man lay gasping. "You're a welcome sight," said Richard. "Unexpected." He picked up first one and then the other of their assailants' guns.

"Do you think your friend reposing down there can walk?" asked the newcomer.

"I should think so." Richard hauled the bulky man up and shoved him towards his wounded companion.

"Then let's invite them to walk. Both of you, down through that trapdoor and scarper, vamoose, run away. This is your lucky night. Hurry, dear boys, before I change my mind."

They went. One with blood now spreading through the shoulder of his coat, the other punch-drunk, shaking his head; both looking behind them, uncertainly, as though expecting a trick, perhaps a bullet. "We're following right behind you," warned the newcomer, as they started, with difficulty, to negotiate the trapdoor, "and I do advise you to be out of the house. Oh, yes, I do advise that very strongly. And don't hang about outside. Not that I think you will." The last remark was actually addressed to Richard and Diana.

"You're letting them go?" she asked.

"Have you a better idea?"

Richard, having recovered his breath and straightened his clothes, one pistol in the waistband of his trousers, the other still in his hand, said in a tolerably even voice: "I don't think you two have met. Diana, this is Jeremy Mitchell-Pearce."

"Jeremy St. John Mitchell-Pearce, if you want the whole handle. But you could call me Jeremy Fisher for short." He chuckled, went over to the edge of the roof and peered into the mews. "No great crowds," he said. "What a nice quiet place you live in. The neighbours evidently keep themselves to themselves. Ah, there go our two friends."

"Who are you?" asked Diana.

"That's a profound philosophical question. We can discuss it later. But just now I think—don't you, Richard?—that it might be wise if we withdrew quite sharpish from the field of battle."

"Yes. Diana, I will explain, but first we must get out."

She tried to protest but found herself being helped down through the trapdoor. "Grab your handbag," said Richard, "or whatever's vital. I'm afraid we've no time for anything more."

"Honestly . . . !" But she did as she was told, and a minute later they emerged cautiously into the mews. There was no sign of movement, nobody in sight. The big black car was still there, deserted, and on the cobblestones, motionless, a black heap—the man who had fallen from the roof. "Better lock the door," said Richard. He took the key from her, and did it himself.

"The great thing about the modern world," remarked Jeremy, "is that you can scream and fire off guns to your heart's content and everyone thinks it's the television. Not that this little toy makes much noise and theirs were silenced, weren't they? Let's tiptoe away."

Leaving the mews, for Diana, was like emerging from a dream into the world. Here were people, cars, lights. Richard and Jeremy looked warily in either direction. Jeremy said: "My car's parked near your flat, Richard."

He nodded. "I suppose it's not safe for me to go home."

"Better not, old chum. It's the Land of Cockaigne for you, I think."

Diana, having recovered her nerve, was getting angry. "I don't understand a word you two are saying. I don't understand anything that's happened. Aren't we going to tell the police? Aren't we going to do anything about that man who's lying back there on the ground?"

"Not the police," said Richard, "if we can help it. I'm terribly sorry to have got you into all this. Be patient just another minute. Jeremy, I must know. How did you come to arrive so opportunely?"

Richard's flat was only a few streets away from Diana's; residential streets of large Victorian houses, most of which, in the impoverished and servantless twentieth century, had been divided into flats or, occasionally, offices; not very busy streets at night. This familiar territory, which had seemed so normal compared with the bizarre events in the mews, itself took on a dream-like quality as they walked, cautiously, and Jeremy unfolded his story.

"I hope you won't be cross about this, but I was keeping an eye on your house. Not just my idea. The boss and I, we were talking—about that curious girl friend of yours and what she might have been up to, and we remembered poor old Bardwell, and we began to feel the tiniest bit uneasy. Of course we know there's nobody better able to look after himself than you. But I thought I'd ankle around and see if any undesirable characters might be lurking in the vicinity. So there I was on the street where you live, like Freddie in *My Fair Lady*. I planned to keep 'obbo,' as the police say, for an hour or so, but I didn't have to, because out you popped. And at just the same moment along came a big black car, which you didn't notice. Full of your own thoughts, you were. It drove right past you and stopped. One of the men in it jumped out and followed you on foot.

"So I toddled along after the two of you. Quite a procession we were. I had to hang back at first, because I didn't want the other fellows in the car to spot me. After five or ten minutes we arrived at that mews. When you turned into it, Chummy hovered around the entrance, and I waited at a respectful distance. In goes Chummy, I close up. No sign of you, no sign of him. Then I spotted him in the shadows. I couldn't make out what he was doing, until he lowered his hand from his face and I realised he'd been using a walkie-talkie.

"Problem again: what should I do? Prudent answer: nothing. The old brain-box ticked over, and I guessed what was going to happen. I walked nonchalantly up the road and was going to walk nonchalantly back again, when the car arrived, summoned by Chummy: and it went into the mews. Not so good, I thought, not so good for old Richard. I sprinted back to the entrance and had a look-see. Car standing in the mews, three men round it. A very tall chap giving orders. Two of them went to the nearest door, which seemed to be unlocked, and disappeared inside. That left the tall chap and a driver, who was still in the car.

"Well, I thought, two to one. Perhaps this is hero-time. Sneak up on them unobserved, I thought, that's the thing to do. They weren't looking my way, and their attention was pretty much fixed on the house. So I sneaked, shadow by shadow, but before I reached them, something—somebody—came down from the roof of the house, plop, like a high pheasant. Gave me quite a turn, I can tell you. The driver jumps out of the car and into the house, tall chap urging him on. Then the tall chap, calm as you please, strolled away towards the entrance of the mews. He passed right by me but didn't notice. I suppose he was detaching himself from the scene.

"I didn't wait to make sure. It seemed to me the U.S. cavalry might be rather overdue. So, gun in hand, heroically, I charged up the stairs. And I really did feel, for once, that I was welcome. . . ."

"You certainly were," said Richard. "We should have taken a look at the car. That might have told us something."

"I doubt it, or they wouldn't have been so willing to abandon it. And, talking of cars, here's mine."

Jeremy's car was a vintage sports model, with a leather strap round the bonnet. Diana was reminded of her deb days; in just such light-hearted vehicles she had been conveyed to many a rainswept point-to-point. Through her confusion and the headache of which she had lately become painfully aware, she thought he suited the car. He was elegant with a fine-cut profile; a bit old, though, for a deb's delight, perhaps thirty-eight or -nine.

"Where are we going?" she asked.

"To see some friends of ours," replied Jeremy, "to a safe place where you'll be out of the wind and the rain."

Richard squeezed into the back. Diana sat beside Jeremy, who drove with the kind of confidence-inspiring skill which had impressed her once when she had been out to dinner with a professional racing driver. They slid through Belgravia, along Piccadilly, past Trafalgar Square, down the Strand, up Ludgate Hill and then through an intricate pattern of back streets.

Although she wanted to press the two men with questions, Diana found she could hardly keep awake. Stirring a spark of energy, she said:

"One of you mentioned cocaine back there. Was Irena telling the truth? Is this all about drugs?"

"Cocaine?" said Richard. "We didn't—" Then he laughed aloud. "No, no, not cocaine the drug. Cockaigne with a 'k' and a 'g.' The Land of Cockaigne. The mythical paradise of Cockneys." If he explained further, she didn't hear it. She was asleep.

"Diana, we're here," he said. They were in an unfamiliar, shabby street, bleakly illuminated by sodium lamps, around the concrete stems of which were piled black plastic rubbish-bags. There was a row of small shops—a tobacconist, a launderette, a greengrocer—all closed at this time of night; only some of the windows above, where their proprietors lived, glowed more cheerfully. The premises outside which Jeremy had parked seemed as dead as the rest. "Cockney Travel" was inscribed in curly letters above a plate-glass window which could have done with cleaning; not that cleaner glass would have revealed anything except a couple of faded posters, one announcing cheap excursion tickets on British Rail, the other depicting an improbably shaped girl in a one-piece bathing costume as, like Nausicaa, she played ball in the surf to advertise the neglected delights of a South Coast holiday resort. There was no visible light inside, no sign of life.

Jeremy got out of the car, looked carefully up and down the street and then rang the bell beside the glass door of Cockney Travel. He pressed the bell-push several times, short and long. There was a protracted pause. Eventually a light went on in the shop. The door was opened by a woman, silhouetted dimly. She and Jeremy talked for a moment: then he turned, and beckoned to the car.

Diana, shaking sleep from her, waited while Richard extracted himself from the back. He put his arm round her. "Don't worry," he said. "This is a good place."

The woman waiting for them at the door was a few years older than Diana, with a softness about her face which belied the severity of the hair, pulled back into an unfashionable bun.

"Come through," she said.

The passage was lit by a single unshaded bulb. Jeremy, clearly quite at home, led the way, through another door, down a few steps to a third door, which, unlike the others, was not a flimsy piece of carpentry but seemed anomalously new and strong. There was a peephole in it. Jeremy knocked.

The door was opened immediately, and Diana found herself being inspected, not discourteously, by shrewd old eyes in a wizened face. Their possessor was quite a small man, dressed in a brown velvet smoking-jacket and wearing a skull-cap. The fringe of hair was grizzled white. He gave an impression, irrational perhaps but undeniable, of being somebody unusual, somebody to be reckoned with. Behind him, in sharp contrast with the bleak premises through which they'd come, glowed a warm and welcoming room.

Richard said: "I've brought Diana Mackenzie. She's a very old friend. Diana, this is Dr. Gabriel."

"Come in, come in," said Gabriel. "There was trouble?"

"Just a spot," said Jeremy.

"Miss Mackenzie, you're shivering," said Gabriel. "Won't you sit by the fire?"

She realised that she did feel cold. Not that the evening was chilly; it was the delayed effect, probably, of shock and of having woken from sleep. Gratefully she sank into an armchair beside an electric fire.

"You've met Maria?" he said, indicating the woman who had let them in. "Maria Konig. Now, drinks. . . ." Whisky and sherry were dispensed. When everybody had been seated and supplied, Gabriel took the chair opposite Diana and turned to Jeremy. "Two hours ago you left here, expressing some fears for Richard's safety. I gather those fears were not unjustified. Tell me, please, exactly what has happened."

Jeremy told him, with a few interjections from Richard. Gabriel listened, head cocked slightly to one side, but made no comment. When the narrative was finished, he ran his hand—violinist's fingers, Diana thought—over his face, screwed up his eyes as though visualising what he'd heard, then said: "Try and describe the tall man. Anything you can remember."

Richard said: "I only saw him from the window. He was distinctly taller than the others, very thin, wearing an overcoat which came down to his ankles."

"I was quite close to him," said Jeremy, "but I don't know there's much I can add. I think his hair was dark. His face was thin too; I suppose cadaverous might be the word. Sunken eyes. Clean-shaven, certainly. I felt he was—how shall I put this?—a person one would just as soon not meet. But I dare say that's nonsense, pure imagination."

"Perhaps. But, you know, Antoine Rivarol, at the time of the French Revolution, observed that, if there existed a race of beings superior to men, they would think little of our powers of reason but might sometimes admire our instinct. My dear," he said to Diana, "would you please tell me, as carefully as you can, what happened between you and this woman Irena. Everything she said."

Diana reconstructed the conversation, and, prompted by Richard, remembered more than she had told him before. Again Gabriel listened very attentively. Then he threw up his hands. "Forgive me," he said, "I have been most inconsiderate. You were hurt. When somebody is hit on the head there is always a risk of concussion. How are you feeling?"

"Oh, I'm all right. But if you have an aspirin . . ."

"Of course. Maria, please. And perhaps you will allow me to have a look. I am a doctor, though a trifle rusty."

He sat on the arm of her chair, laying a gentle hand on her head. "Just a bruise as far as I can see. The skin is hardly broken." There was reassurance in his touch. "A little rest is probably all you need."

Standing up, he said to Jeremy: "I suppose you are sure nobody followed you here?"

"Pretty sure. I kept a sharp eye."

"Good. Next we arrange some reconnaissance." A telephone stood on a side-table in front of a wall of books. He dialled a number. "Samuel? Here is Kingfisher. Will you do a small job for me? I want you to go to this address—what is your address, Miss Mackenzie?" She told him, and he repeated it. "Approach with care. There may be police about, and you should not let them notice you. Alternatively, there may not be police and you will find a body still lying in the mews. Yes, a body. Look at it if you can. See if you recognise him. But do not be caught. The police are not the only ones you must look out for. Other people may be watching. If there are, we want to know about them: but we don't want them to see you. When you've done that, please go to another address quite near." Gabriel gave Richard's address, which he evidently knew by heart. "Again we want to know if there's anyone watching. Then get back to me here. Yes. Thank you." He replaced the receiver.

"Even if there is no one watching, you cannot go home tonight, either of you. It would not be safe. And you, my dear, would be questioned by the police." She started to expostulate. "Please. Richard, you trust Miss Mackenzie or you would not have brought her here?"

"Absolutely."

"I think we must all trust her. My dear, your curiosity has been so aroused that, if we told you nothing, you would never rest until you found out more. It is better that you should know and, I hope, understand. I will not insult you by demanding promises of secrecy. The need for it will be obvious, must be obvious now after what you've seen tonight."

"You and Richard are in some kind of danger?"

He smiled. "You might put it that way. I must begin with a story, from long ago. I'm German, a German Jew. I was a young man in Germany, just starting to practise as a doctor, during the rise of Hitler. You are too young to remember, but you will have read what that meant. For you it's history, for me it's yesterday. Only yesterday. I shut my eyes and I can see faces. . . .

"My father was a wise man. He realised what was coming. Most of us didn't, you know. People couldn't bring themselves quite to believe it. As someone has said, the optimists died in Auschwitz, the pessimists are smoking big cigars on Broadway. There are always more optimists than pessimists. My father got me out, sent me to relations here in Britain. He wouldn't come. He was a doctor too, and he said his duty was with his patients. My mother would not come without him. And then it was too late. No one could come. Not by any ordinary route.

"I never saw my parents again. But there were others we could help. My friend Max Konig and I—Maria is Max's daughter—managed to smuggle a whole family out of Germany. Such risks we took; it makes me sick to remember them. But we were young and passionate—and lucky. And what a sense of achievement. To have done something so worthwhile, to have snatched men, women, children from the mouth of that horror, was it not worth any risk? We wanted to do it again. And we did. We succeeded again. How could we stop then? The need was so great, limitless. The appeals for help came to us—and a lot of brave people wanted to help. Before very long we had a regular pipeline, and an organisation running it. We called ourselves The Fishers, because we were fishers of men.

"Of course in the beginning we thought only of Jews and what is now called the holocaust. But it wasn't only Jews who were being killed. There were others; we couldn't distinguish. Then came Yalta, the great betrayal. Half Europe was imprisoned, and the governments of the West, who had represented freedom, did nothing to prevent it. Worse, they were handing people over to the gaolers. We found ourselves helping all kinds of refugees, victims, defectors—Poles, Cossacks, Lithuanians, Latvians, Estonians, Hungarians, Rumanians, even Germans, a desperate endless flow. We were baling the sea with a bucket, but our organisation grew.

"The Berlin Wall—but I don't have to go through the history of the post-war world. You know what politics have done to people, how even in free nations freedom has diminished. To keep our organisation going we had always allowed those refugees who had any money to make some contribution; it was up to them, whatever they could afford. Now we added, as it were, another service to our clients. We would help them get their money out of the country, any country, with a percentage for ourselves. We did this partly for the same reason—that we needed funds to support our main work—but also because I felt strongly about the principle. No man is free who isn't allowed to get up and go, taking his possessions with him. Exchange controls are wicked, halfway to the prison state, but increasingly they've been applied almost everywhere. So we were glad to fight them.

"I mention this because, more than anything else, it made our activities worldwide. Our contacts, and I suppose our reputation, spread, and, always before us, the sea of desperation opened out still more broadly, the cries for help multiplied. Occasionally there's a newspaper story—about the Boat People from Vietnam, or mainland Chinese trying to reach Hong Kong, or about the opponents of some revolution or the victims of some mad ruler fleeing with what they can carry. After a day or so the newspapers forget, but the fear, the oppression, the need to escape continue. Do you realise that half the Boat People die, from drowning or thirst or are raped, robbed and murdered by pirates? They know the odds before they set out. Imagine how desperate they must be in order to take such a gamble.

"These terrible things are going on everywhere. So many who need help, and we can help so few. But we try, Miss Mackenzie, we try. And if, at the same time, we assist emigrants to take their own savings across a frontier or perhaps smuggle out the jewels of an Indian prince, that's not a greedy diversion from what we should be doing. It's all the same job. We are not fond of governments and governments are not fond of us."

"I can well believe it," said Diana.

"I mustn't go on lecturing you, but I wanted you to understand. I wonder if you can, though. We've had to learn this lesson over many years, in hard ways. A refugee is not welcome anywhere. Ask the Poles, ask the Boat People, ask the Chinese who have been sent back from Hong Kong. You probably know that, when Communist governments allow some trusted citizen a passport so that he can travel abroad for a few brief days, they never permit the whole family to go. He must leave pledges behind. Those without dependants are very rarely allowed passports. But did you know that, even when the system relaxes, as it did in Poland, and passports are issued, then the Western governments make difficulties? Poles applying for a British visa must complete a long form, asking about their families, their jobs, and whether they own a house or an apartment—many questions which have only one purpose, to make sure they're unlikely to defect. So the countries from which people try to escape and the freer countries for which they yearn are effectively joined in a conspiracy to prevent them. That's why we feel that not only tyrannical governments, but governments of every complexion, are our natural enemies.

"I told you that we called ourselves Fishers. When Max and I chose that name, we didn't know much English history. We'd never heard of the Free Fishers, who carried Jacobites to safety in France and returned carrying brandy for the parson and 'baccy for the clerk. But that's how I like to think of us now. Free Fishers. Traffickers in freedom."

"What a speech," said Jeremy. "Not that I disagree, mind. It's just that I've never heard you talk that way before. Usually it's an everyday story of Fisher folk. It was when you took me on."

"I'm sorry," said Gabriel. "It's a long time since I have talked that way. I'm getting foolish in my old age. Second childhood. When Max and I were young we were quite idealistic." He smiled at Diana. "It must be the company of a pretty woman. I'm not used to that any more. It loosens the tongue."

"Reverting to practical matters," said Richard, "we should warn Diana that this is a dangerous business." He turned to her. "I'm afraid you've already discovered that. My fault; I got you mixed up in it. But when Gabriel talks about 'enemies,' that's no figure of speech. Half the governments of the world would like to stop us if they could. We're only pinpricks to most of them—don't imagine that we have some vast powerful organisation behind us—but governments resent even being pricked."

"Does that include the British Government?" she asked.

"In theory. The security services do know about us, of course, though not everything: but we've done them one or two favours, and we've been reasonably careful not to foul our own nest. Those men tonight, you'll agree, whoever they were, weren't British civil servants or British police.

"We've got other enemies too, besides governments. Over the years we've come up against all kinds of individuals and groups. Quite regularly, for example, somebody interested in drug running or smuggling arms makes a proposal to us—which we turn down. We've had a spat with the Triads, who thought we were trespassing on their patch, and a clash with the IRA. Revolutionaries, blackmailers, spies—you name it, we've met them, and sometimes we may have been rough."

"Sometimes they've been rough with us," said Gabriel grimly. "We do lose people, Miss Mackenzie. I told you about Max Konig. He died long ago, when Maria was a little girl. He was in Germany, trying to get back from the East."

Jeremy said: "Do we really connect poor old Bardwell's untimely end? I know we talked about it earlier. . . . Bardwell," he explained to Diana, "was a colleague. Not very important. A courier, mainly around the Middle East. Last week he fell under a tube train. It may have been pure accident, but one does tend to look at accidents with a jaundiced eye."

"We simply don't know," said Gabriel. "Accidents happen. But I've been thinking. Peters in Singapore was killed in a car crash a few days earlier, and Miller in Athens was injured recently. And we've been trying to reach another of our contacts in the Far East—without success. That is rather a lot of accidents."

Richard nodded. "I agree. But I suppose in a way it doesn't really matter. Those gunmen tonight weren't imaginary, nor was Irena. Someone's after us. After me, anyway."

"If there is a pattern," said Jeremy, "they—whoever they may be—

seem to have changed it. Bardwell and Peters were supposed to be accidents, but these people went after Richard quite openly. Blazing away like Buffalo Bill."

"What that suggests, I'm afraid," said Gabriel, "is that they really mean business. The important thing is to break us, not to conceal what they're doing. And they knew that, in Richard's case, we wouldn't have believed an accident."

"How does Irena come into it?" Diana interjected. "What was the point of all those questions she asked me? Those dates?"

"I think I understand that," said Richard. "They know about some of our operations, where and when. What they don't know for sure is who we are. But they've got my name. I was probably seen in one, or more than one, relevant place. So Irena's job was to find out about me. She didn't learn anything useful from me when we were together—I am quite careful—or find anything in my flat, but, when she met Diana, that suggested a new idea. If she could establish that I was away from London at all the times they were interested in, or enough of those times to rule out coincidence, they'd have their proof. Then they'd hit me. At once. Which is what happened tonight."

"They'd have been better advised, surely," said Jeremy, "to keep an eye on you, and let you lead them into the network."

"After Diana had told me what Irena was asking?"

"Of course. Silly me."

"We must assume—" Gabriel began but was interrupted by the telephone. He picked it up. "Yes, Sammy." He listened. "Really? And no one visibly watching? No, you go home. We'll be in touch later. Thank you very much."

Replacing the receiver, he turned to the others. "In your mews, Miss Mackenzie, there is no car and nobody lying on the cobblestones. And there are no police, which there certainly would be if it was they who had taken the car and the man away."

"Do you think we invented it all?" asked Diana indignantly.

"Of course not. What I think is that the opposition came back and cleared up."

"Thank God we weren't still there," she said.

"Quite so. Sammy had a look all around and couldn't see anyone watching, but Richard is plainly a target. We must keep you out of the way for a bit. They're probably not interested in Miss Mackenzie any more, but I think it would be as well if she accepted our hospitality for a day or so. Will you, my dear?"

"I suppose so. I certainly shouldn't feel very safe on my own."

"Off to the Land of Cockaigne," said Jeremy.

Gabriel smiled. "That's an old joke of ours. When we first set up The Fishers, all those years ago, we acquired these premises here to be our headquarters. An inconspicuous shop in an inconspicuous street, and the most useful cover, we thought, was to make it a travel agency. I lived in these rooms, behind the shop. "What shall we call it?" Max said. "You and I are not so English, so let's give it a very English name. We'll call it Cockney Travel." And when we needed to keep someone under cover, we called it sending them to the Land of Cockaigne."

"I see."

"Rather charming, don't you think?" said Jeremy.

"We have other houses now," continued Gabriel. "But I should be honoured if you and Richard would stay in mine. Not here. In the country."

"Truly rural," said Jeremy. "All mod cons, though."

"Could I pick up a few things from my house on the way?"

"I'd rather you didn't. I'll send Sammy round tomorrow."

"I can lend you some night-clothes," said Maria.

Maria's room above the shop was little-girlish, her clothes were frilly, in a style contrasting oddly and, Diana thought, rather touchingly with her spinsterish appearance. Together they packed a small case. When they came downstairs again, the three men were already waiting in the passage.

"We're taking Gabriel's car," said Richard. "You'll find it rather more comfortable than Jeremy's rocket-propelled rattletrap."

"Ingrate," said Jeremy. "Diana, it's been a pleasure. I shall see you soon, I hope."

"I'll come down tomorrow," said Gabriel. "We have much to do."

The car was a venerable Daimler, spacious and solid. As they purred through the darkness, Diana soon became drowsy again.

"Less than forty-eight hours ago," she murmured, "you told me your life was an open book."

"I may have exaggerated."

Richard, steady old Richard, her friend for so long, wasn't the man she'd known at all. But then the world was no longer the world she'd known. She'd stepped through the looking-glass into the Land of Cock-aigne, where everything was different and dangerous. Familiar outlines shifted and changed. . . . She slept.

VI

"Just a Word, a Whisper"

"There's a man called Shaman," said Gabriel. "Or perhaps Shaman isn't a man. It could be a group or the code-name of an operation. It's really just a word, a whisper. But apparently it frightens people."

Neither Richard nor Jeremy commented. They waited for Gabriel to continue. He stood by the French windows, looking out into the garden, which sloped, fresh and green, down to the little river. He seemed tired, Richard thought, the lines in his face deeper, the eyes more melancholy. Gabriel loved this house, not very far from London but secluded among gentle woods and hills. It represented everything which he had found romantic and consoling about the England where he had come, so long ago, for refuge. The intervening years had, to some extent, disillusioned him, or, he would have been more inclined to say, England itself had changed, losing or discarding much of the rooted stability and respectability which had fascinated him. But this old house, Shadowlawn, acquired when he first had a little money and since devotedly restored, was an English dream, mellowed over centuries. Only a foreigner, Gabriel used to say, could really appreciate such a place.

Perhaps he imagined himself in the role of an eighteenth-century hunting squire, a bluff John Bull, surveying his own rich acres and complaining about modern times and manners: but, if he did play such games, there would always be a double picture in his mind. His strong sense of irony would constantly compare the role with the reality, the robust simplicity of the grand old English gentleman with the subtle plottings of the European refugee. Instead of a swallow-tailed coat and a Union Jack waistcoat, he wore a hard blue suit and a bow tie.

In this drawing room, on previous occasions, Richard had seen Gabriel as near to completely relaxed as he ever became. Today, though, he was tense: and, as he turned back from the window, the tension had dispelled the tiredness. Here was an elderly man, who had seen too much, but this was the man who created The Fishers.

"Sammy and various other friends of ours have been making enquiries. They didn't come up with very much. Just that word. Shaman. It stands for something or somebody new, at least in London. Sammy asked in particular about the man your cleaning woman said approached her in the pub, the one she described as wearing a purple-check overcoat. He's a small-time agent who'll work for anyone who pays him. He was paid to make enquiries about you. There's been money spread around. We don't know yet how far. Sammy's still digging. What we want to know, of course, is how much they know, how many of us they may have identified."

"It would also be nice," observed Jeremy, "to know who employs them, or, if they're self-employed, what their racket is."

"Their racket at the moment appears to be destroying us. It seems quite clear now that Richard wasn't a solitary target. This isn't any kind of personal feud. The only good thing is that we've discovered we are under attack before the attack reached our heart. I'm sorry, Richard; I didn't mean to imply that what happened to you doesn't matter."

"No, you're quite right. It looks as if they made a mistake. They'd have been wiser not to move until they got closer—well, to you."

"Not necessarily to me. I'm not crucial nowadays. You could carry on without me. But they should have hit as many of us as possible simultaneously."

"Which could mean," said Richard, "that they're under pressure to show results. Which, in turn, would mean that they're not self-employed."

"I don't wish to appear timid," said Jeremy, "or, indeed, looked at from another point of view, conceited, but, do you think we can rely on the assumption that, since nothing nasty has yet happened to me—or to most of us, we're not so far in their little black book?"

"Rely—no," answered Gabriel. "But it seems probable. I'd have expected a bomb in the travel agency if they knew about that."

"Or a break-in," said Richard. "If it was me, I'd be looking for records, files, names."

"You wouldn't find them," said Gabriel grimly. "Not there, and not much anywhere. That was a lesson I learned early."

"Addresses? Telephone numbers?" asked Jeremy. "I know you've always told us to have nothing on paper, but they must surely exist."

"In coded form. Different parts in different places. From the beginning we've always worked on a cell system, nobody knowing more than a little. You two know more than most. Shaman—let's use that name—perhaps gives us credit for running a network which won't be easy to roll up."

"Shaman . . ." mused Jeremy. "Interesting name. Russian connections? It rather suits the tall bloke I saw. Maybe that was Shaman."

"Maybe. The first thing, anyway, is to warn everyone. Then, if we can only discover a bit more, we might make some moves of our own."

"Like what?"

"That depends on what we discover. There are options."

"A war?"

"Maybe. Not necessarily. We might tip off the security services and let them do the job."

Richard, glancing out of the window, said: "Diana thinks that Irena was probably talking some Slav language."

"Her flat's empty," said Jeremy. "We've checked. Her clothes are gone." Following Richard's gaze, he saw that Diana was walking beside the little river which flowed past the bottom of the lawn. "Did she ever give you an office telephone number?"

"Yes, she did. It's in my book."

"Where was it supposed to be?"

"She said it was in the City. I never actually called her there. I wonder who would have answered if I had."

"Someone. Perhaps Irena. But even if we managed to trace the address, I fancy all we'd find is an empty office or another empty flat."

"What are we going to do about Diana?" asked Richard. "She's been down here three days now, and she's restive. Her partner's running the gallery, but that can't go on indefinitely. Besides, she has a life to lead. Boy friends, I expect."

"The question is," replied Gabriel, "whether, if she goes back to her normal life, she would be in danger. She is no part of The Fishers. There is no reason why Shaman should be interested in her."

"Except," observed Jeremy, "that she now knows about Cockney Travel and about this house."

"Well, she can't stay here for ever," said Richard, "any more than I can. It seems to me the fairest thing, the only fair thing, is to explain the situation to her, just as we've been discussing it, and let her make up her own mind. She could go away. Disappear for a while. She has a sister in New York; she could visit her."

"I'm not sure that would be wise," Gabriel said. "If Shaman is what we think he—or it—may be, crossing the Atlantic mightn't be enough. At least in London we can give her some protection. Is she frightened?"

"Not visibly. She's quite tough. I'll talk to her."

"Yes, do. Tell her that she is, of course, welcome to remain here as long as she wishes. It is now twelve o'clock. Let us all meet for luncheon at one, and we can make a plan."

Richard went out of the French windows. Gabriel and Jeremy watched him walk down the lawn to join Diana. She took his arm as they strolled by the river. In the fields beyond, cows were grazing. On the water a line of baby ducks were following their mother.

"When I was at Oxford," Diana said, "there used to be baby ducks like that on the Cherwell at the beginning of the summer term. And by the end of term they were quite grown up. I used to think of it as a symbol of transience. Oxford generations pass so quickly. I was always very much aware of that."

"This is a beautiful place, isn't it? What do you really think of Gabriel?"

"He's a remarkable man. I'd like to know him better. What's he been telling you?"

"Not a great deal, I'm afraid. But it does create a problem—for you." He repeated to her the scraps of information which Gabriel and Jeremy had brought and their assessment of the situation. She listened without interrupting. Then: "I see. But you're the one they're really after. What are you going to do?"

"I must go back to London with Jeremy. We—I mean The Fishers —can't just sit still. We should never be safe again."

"You're not exactly safe at the best of times, are you? Oddly enough I've rather enjoyed these past three days, and I've learned things about you that I never knew before. But I have been rather good about not asking questions, don't you think?"

"Wonderfully good. There are two reasons why I'm grateful. One is that some secrets—about The Fishers—aren't mine, the other is that I thought the less you knew, the less dangerous it would be for you. I'm not sure now that the second reason applies. That is, I'm not sure it makes much difference. Is there anything you particularly want to know?"

"About you. How did you meet Gabriel?"

"He met me, seven or eight years ago. I'd written some articles about refugees, and he saw something in them which made him think I was recruitable. The original Fishers had grown old. He needed new blood. He checked me out, of course—my politics, whether I had any family; which, as you know, I don't. . . . Then he asked me to lunch at Claridge's. All he wanted, at that stage, was my help in one, relatively easy, matter. From then on, the connection just grew."

"Eight years ago. That was just after we were seeing each other regularly. I'm glad about that. I shouldn't like to think you were keeping so much of your life from me then. And Jeremy—where did he come from?"

"Household Cavalry. SAS. Then he drifted out to the Far East on some sort of business venture which collapsed. I met him in a bar. He saved my life or at least saved me from being very badly beaten up. I recommended him to Gabriel."

"Are there a lot more of you? Or is that one of the questions I shouldn't ask?"

"Not a great many. Of course we've a lot of contacts all around the world. If you wanted to disappear for a few months, we could certainly arrange it."

"In the Land of Cockaigne?" she smiled. "I shall always think of this house as Cockaigne, a place where everything is made of sugar and marzipan. But Gabriel's right, isn't he? It would be like those KGB defectors you read about, or people who've squealed on the Mafia. They're given new names, perhaps new faces, and sent somewhere remote. But all their lives they can never be quite sure whether the postman is really a postman or who may be inside any strange car which comes down the road. Living like that can't be very pleasant. I'd rather be in London. At least I know all the runs through the briar patch."

He looked at her curiously. "You've been thinking about it? Wouldn't you prefer to stay here for a while, though? Nowhere's a hundred per cent safe, of course, but everyone here can be trusted and we do take some precautions."

"I don't think so, not by myself. What does Gabriel advise?"

"I'm not sure. He said you were welcome to stay. Ask him yourself at lunch."

"I bet I know what Jeremy would like. He'd like to use us as bait."

"You have been thinking about it. Is that how you see him?"

"As being pretty ruthless—behind that camp surface."

"I doubt if that's altogether fair. What's true—I hope this doesn't sound too pompous—is that I joined The Fishers because I believed in what they were doing. Jeremy joined for the fun of it. He's the most absolutely fearless man I've ever met."

"Do you find that admirable?" asked Diana.

"What an interesting question. Of course he isn't really. One could only be fearless if one had no imagination. And Jeremy has plenty of that."

They strolled back towards the house, with spring sunshine gleaming on grass which was still damp from an early shower. Richard thought how well Diana fitted the scene, just the sort of unmistakably English girl whom Gabriel might have imagined when, moved by a romantic vision of England, he had bought the house.

Sherry was provided in the drawing room, and afterwards, on an immaculately polished dining table, a luncheon considerably better, or at least lighter, than any traditional English squire would have commanded. There were limits to Gabriel's role-playing.

Jeremy was loquacious and entertaining. Only when the coffee had been brought did the conversation revert to serious questions. "I've loved it here," said Diana, "but I want to go back to London with you."

"You really shouldn't be on your own," said Richard. "Would you like to stay in my flat? There's a spare room."

"Which was not used by Irena," she said, a trifle tartly. "Well, that's an idea."

"But not, I'm afraid, a suitable one," interjected Gabriel. For a moment she thought, incredulously, that he was worried, in some fatherly way, about her virtue. But, as though reading her mind, he went on, with a smile: "I'm not speaking of impropriety—"

"I should think not indeed," said Jeremy, looking shocked.

"—but, for the next week or so, Richard won't be there."

"I won't?"

Gabriel turned to Richard. "I was going to tell you about this later. A job has come up which won't wait."

"It's really my job," said Jeremy, "but Gabriel thinks I need you to hold my hand."

"Nothing of the sort," said Gabriel, "but you know some of the people involved, which should be helpful, especially now when we're not sure who can be trusted."

"Where is it, this job?"

Diana realised that she was frightened. Not for herself. Gabriel said to her: "My dear, would you consider it very rude if I asked you to withdraw?" Again he immediately answered the objection which she had no time to utter, even if she had been going to do so. "It is not in the least that we do not trust you, but, for your own sake, the less you know, the safer you will be." His eyes, very liquid and melancholy in a deeply lined face, were fixed on her. Objections melted from her tongue.

As she stood up, Gabriel said: "Will you at least let us offer you the hospitality of the travel agency for a few days, while Richard is away or until you can safely return to your own house? There is quite a comfortable spare room."

"Thank you," she said. "I'd like that. Now I'll go and pack."

When she had left the room, Richard looked expectantly at Gabriel, who was lighting a cigar. Extinguishing the match, he said: "The job to be done is in southern Africa, a place which you know far better than Jeremy. He will run the field operation, but I want you to go with him for the setting up. You've had dealings before with Van der Bruin, haven't you?"

"In Johannesburg? Yes. He's a good man."

"I hope so. It's he who suggested that we take up this case and who says that the project is feasible."

"Can't it wait a little while? Isn't the situation here more urgent?"

"Apparently it can't wait. Of course the situation here is urgent, but

I shan't be completely helpless without you. We mustn't let Shaman stop all our work. That may be just what they are trying to do."

"I suppose you're right. So what's the job?"

"Three mercenaries are held in Angola. Van der Bruin knows the wife of one of them. She says that, if her husband isn't got out soon, he'll die."

"The urgency," Jeremy put in, "comes from the fact that there is now an opportunity. An unrepeatable opportunity, as the advertisements say."

"You go on, Jeremy," said Gabriel. "You've worked on the details."

Jeremy produced a small notebook from his pocket and flattened it on the table in front of him. "Code-name—Operation Moneybags," he said. "Not that I've anything against mercenaries, being a kind of one myself. These three are called Pieter Villiers—he's the South African; Ben Smith—he's American; and Charles Carter, who's English. They were fighting, not for UNITA, the main rebel force, but for a separate faction. I won't go into the politics now—they're largely tribal anyway —but it is an anti-Marxist group. The Angolan Government has always denied their existence, or at any rate their significance. They may get a bit of South African help, with weapons and money, but nothing much. The point is that nobody in the outside world cares a jot about them.

"So, when these three men were captured over a year ago by Cuban troops, there were no press reports and no diplomatic representations on their behalf. They simply disappeared. Not that diplomatic representations would have done them any good. You know my opinion of diplomats.

"Anyway, last week the wife of Pieter Villiers arrived on Van der Bruin's doorstep—if they have doorsteps in South Africa. Stoep, perhaps. I've spoken to him on the telephone: I'm telling you what he told me. He said she was very agitated and tearful. She had assumed for months that her husband was dead, but now she had received a message, through some black man who had just come across the border from Angola into Namibia or South-West Africa or whatever you like to call it, saying he was still alive but in a fairly desperate condition. The Angolans had kept moving him and the other two, who are with him, around from village to village, and they're being held at the moment in a place not too difficult to reach. But of course we don't know how long they'll stay there.

"Mrs. Villiers wanted Van der Bruin to tell her what to do. Should she appeal for government help or ask the Angolan Government for clemency or start a public campaign or what? And she wanted to get in touch with the families of the other two men. She didn't know about The Fishers or Van der Bruin's connection with us. He was merely an old friend."

"A coincidence?" asked Gabriel.

"Yes, but not an incredible one. Quite a lot of South Africans have lost relatives in Angola or Rhodesia or the Congo. Most of them are dead, but there may well be some other prisoners nobody knows about. Van der Bruin has his own contacts of course, and he found out as much as he could before telephoning us. I don't think he's talked personally yet to the man who brought the message, but he's going to. Meanwhile, he has confirmed that there have been rumours about three white captives and that there is a small unit of soldiers in the relevant village. And he says the village is accessible." Jeremy sat back in his chair. "That's about it."

Gabriel said: "Point one. If we do nothing to rescue these men, certainly no one else will and they will probably die. Point two. Jan Van der Bruin, who has helped us on several occasions in the past, makes a personal request. Point three. He assures us that rescue is practicable. I think, therefore, that we must try, or at least explore the possibility. In view of what's been happening, it is conceivable that the whole thing may be a trap. That is why I particularly want you to go, Richard. I want you to form a judgement."

"Field work for me," Jeremy said, "brain work for you. The story of my life. Everyone knows that I'm a bear of very small brain."

"That doesn't sound at all a comfortable decision to have to make," said Richard. "And isn't there a risk, now, that I might be recognised and blow the whole operation? If, for example, Shaman—he, it, they— is really the Russians, they'll have agents in South Africa."

"True," said Gabriel, "but it's the kind of risk we can't avoid until we've solved this problem. They might recognise any of our people. We don't know the extent of their knowledge. You must simply be alert and take as much care as you can."

"All fixed, then?" said Jeremy. "You'll join me on this picnic?"

"I suppose so."

"Good," said Gabriel. "I will get Maria to make the travel arrangements."

Outside, spring clouds had covered the sun. Rain spattered against
the windows.

VII

"I Think It's Go"

The sky above Jan Smuts airport was bright cloudless blue but the air had none of the heavy heat which, in tropical Africa, enfolds the arriving traveller like a blanket. It was just a warm autumn day. South African Airways stewardesses in their light-blue uniforms herded the passengers, including Richard and Jeremy, through the short journey to the arrival lounge. Jeremy's passport described him as "Farmer," which was true since he owned a few ancestral acres in Norfolk. Richard's said "Writer," which provoked a question or two at the immigration desk. If it had said "Journalist," he would have needed a special visa, since journalists are ranked by the South African authorities, along with musicians oddly enough, as a dangerous class of character.

As soon as they were through the barrier they were greeted by a slim sun-browned man in a crisply laundered safari suit. "Richard," he said, "how good to see you."

"And you, Jan. You don't know my colleague—our colleague—Jeremy Mitchell-Pearce?"

"We've spoken on the telephone." They shook hands. "Is this all your luggage?"

"Yes," said Richard. "Important principle. Never travel with more than you can carry yourself."

"I've often thought," observed Jeremy, "that the philologists of the future will be very puzzled by the derivation of the word 'porter,' since it clearly has nothing to do with carrying things."

"That's not quite true here," said Van der Bruin with a smile, as he led the way to his car, a new-model estate wagon, which was parked outside. "Have you put us in the Carlton?" Richard asked.

"No, I felt it would be better if you stayed with me." He flipped a hand towards the airport hotel which they were passing. "That's one of the few absolutely honest hotels I've ever been in. There was a notice in the bedroom which said 'Our room service is slow and expensive.' I suppose they wanted you to use the bar."

Richard laughed. "I must remember that for my next powerful piece about South Africa."

"You'll be writing one, I expect, to justify this trip?"

"Probably. How long is it since I was here last? Two years?"

"About that, I'd think. You'll find Jo'burg is becoming more and more like an American city. Everyone's moved to the suburbs, so it's dead at night. And at the weekends it's full of Africans."

"Have you been doing much Fisher business lately?"

"A bit. Mostly helping people from Rhodesia get their money out. When Mugabe took over, a lot of the young ones left, the ones who thought they could earn a living here. Durban especially is full of them. But the older people, who'd made their lives in Rhodesia, building up farms and small businesses, were trapped. They're allowed to bring out hardly anything, only a few hundred pounds. Not even a kitchen stove. Helping them struck me as proper sort of work for us."

"Strange, isn't it," said Jeremy, "that anyone should imagine the fall of empires makes people freer? Of course it makes local politicians freer, but for everybody else it simply multiplies frontiers. Mind you, I'm a simple soul. I just can't forgive British politicians for throwing away my empire."

"It wasn't my empire," said Van der Bruin rather grimly. "Plenty of English-speaking South Africans would agree with you, though. They resent the fact that they're not still in charge here. But it's a paradox. I tell them that, if Britain had remained the ruling power in South Africa, there wouldn't now be a white man south of the Limpopo. We should have gone the same way as the countries to the north. And they know it's true."

"When I first came here, fifteen years ago," said Richard, "I kept being told that the split between Afrikaners and English-speaking South Africans was growing less. But is it? I still get the impression that you hardly ever see an Afrikaner in an English-speaking house or English-speakers at an Afrikaans dinner table."

"I'm afraid that's largely so. Of course there are far more Afrikaners in business now and some English-speakers have joined the Nationalist Party. But socially there's not a great deal of mixing."

"And what about the security situation? How's that?"

"A few bombs. An occasional cache of arms. And sometimes the army catches a group of terrorists trying to come down from the border. There won't be a bush war, like the one in Rhodesia. The terrain and the population are too different. Urban terrorism's the danger, but it hasn't made much impact on ordinary life. Until recently there were fewer precautions here than I gather there are in the U.K. against IRA bombs."

"On the subject of security," Richard said, "did London tell you that The Fishers have a problem?"

"Yes, Kingfisher telephoned. He warned us to keep our eyes open."

"And have you noticed anything untoward?"

"Nothing. But we're small fry, down here at the end of the line. I don't suppose this mysterious opposition, whoever it may be, is bothered much about us."

"Maybe. I hope not."

They were driving now along roads flanked by large houses with well-tended gardens. There was a cluster of shops, mainly of the modern supermarket kind, looking new, and then another characteristically suburban road. Although the leaves were starting to turn brown, the colours were brighter than they would have been in England or America, and there were a few Africans sitting beside the road and a couple of African women walking along with bundles on their heads, but the general effect was quiet, comfortable and not at all exotic. Many of the houses had English names—Windermere, Rose Lodge, Eleventrees.

"It might be stockbroker Surrey," observed Jeremy.

"You're an exception, Jan, aren't you," said Richard, "to what we were saying about the Afrikaners and the English? You mix."

"My grandparents spoke Afrikaans at home," he replied, "but my mother was Scottish. I went to an English school. I think I was the only one there with *voortrekker* ancestors."

"Meaning that your family came up from the Cape?" asked Jeremy.

"Yes. To escape the English. Of course everybody's supposed to be bilingual now, but most of them aren't, not really. That may be changing, though. We've only one white television channel still, and the evening is divided into half Afrikaans and half English: then, the following day, it's the other way round. So if the children want to watch for more than a couple of hours—which mine certainly do—they have to sit through both languages. We get American programmes dubbed into Afrikaans. But here we are. . . ."

He turned in through an open gate. A short gravel drive led to a sprawling bungalow with big shade-trees on the right and, on the left, a wide expanse of lawn, which was being watered by two sprinklers. An elderly African was lethargically weeding the flower beds. Two large dogs bounded out to greet them. A smiling African in a white jacket came and took their bags.

Ensconced in a pleasant airy room, with prints of South African birds and flowers on the wall, Richard changed into lighter clothes, did a little unpacking and then went to find the others. They were sitting in canvas chairs outside the living room, which overlooked the lawn. There was a tray of drinks on an iron table. Jan's wife, a small plump woman with a quick smile and an eager manner, having made sure they were supplied with everything they needed, asked them to excuse her because, she said, she wanted to see to the lunch.

The company included one other person. He was a tall handsome black man, wearing a European suit with a waistcoat. His grip, when he shook Richard's hand, was strong.

"This is Luke Matiwane," said Jan. "An old associate of mine." When Mrs. Van der Bruin had left, he explained further: "Luke knows all about this business. In fact he knows more than I do. He's been to see the man who brought the news about Piet Villiers. Do you want to discuss it now or shall we wait until after lunch? You've had a long flight; you probably just want to relax for a while."

"Oh, we're quite used to long flights," said Richard.

"Like birds on the wing," said Jeremy, who was fondling the ears of the dogs, both of which were stretched at his feet.

"Since time appears to be important," said Richard, "perhaps we could at least have an outline, so we can be thinking about it."

"All right. I'd better begin, then we'll come to Luke's bit in a minute. Just over a week ago Sara Villiers—Piet's wife—came to see me. I should add that I've known Piet since he was a boy. He's always been an adventurous type, getting into more scrapes than most of us. He enjoyed his military service and, afterwards, got involved in several hair-raising schemes. He was passionately anti-Communist. Marriage didn't seem to slow him down much. So I wasn't particularly surprised when I heard, last year, that he'd disappeared into Angola. Afterwards I heard that he'd been killed.

"But it seems he wasn't. That's what Sara came to tell me. She was in a great state, almost hysterical. She'd received this message from someone who'd just come out of Angola. Piet was alive but in a bad way. She knew I knew him, and wanted advice. She doesn't know about The Fishers, but she'd probably heard that I've been able to help one or two people. The news that Piet was alive had really hit her."

"That's hardly surprising," said Richard.

"No, but not because they were a devoted couple. On the contrary, they squabbled like mad. I suspect that may have been one reason why Piet went up to Angola in the first place, as much to get away from her as for any political motive or even for the money. And believing he was dead, she'd taken up with another man. Someone she was proposing to marry. Hence the agitation. The wedding was fixed, she told me.

"She couldn't disbelieve the news; there were personal things which convinced her. The man who brought it was an Ovambo—they're the biggest tribe in South-West Africa, straddling the border with Angola. They provide the bulk of SWAPO, the South-West Africa People's Organisation, which is Communist-backed and wants to take over an independent Namibia. But this fellow was one of the rebel group which Piet Villiers had been fighting for. He made contact with the recruiter in Windhoek, who got in touch with Sara.

"I calmed her down as much as possible and said I'd see what could be done. I gave her the impression, I think, that it would be through friends of mine in the government. But, of course, that's not possible—or, at least, it's highly unlikely—as she'd have realised if she were a bit brighter. I don't know how familiar you are with the situation in Angola?"

"Not very," said Richard.

"You can safely assume that I know nothing," said Jeremy.

"Well, forgive me if I'm lecturing you on what's common knowledge, but I'd better, perhaps, just explain that the principal rebel faction in Angola is UNITA, led by Dr. Jonas Savimbi. UNITA means the National Union for the Total Independence of Angola. It's been fighting against the Marxist Government ever since the Portuguese pulled out in 1975. The Marxists, with Soviet backing, brought in 25,000

Cuban troops to crush any other claimants to power: but Savimbi's
been waging a very successful guerrilla war. He probably controls a
third of the country. And the South African Government has given
him a good deal of discreet, and sometimes not so discreet, backing.

"But though UNITA is very much the largest rebel faction, with
perhaps 40,000 men under arms, it isn't the only one. There are several
other groups or combinations, local or tribal or ideological, and it was
one of these, calling itself the Spear of Freedom, which was recruiting
mercenaries a couple of years ago. It's a relatively small faction. The
object was to form an independent breakaway state in a fairly inaccessi-
ble region, taking advantage of the general chaos caused by the civil
war. The South African Government has very good intelligence sources
in Angola, and gave a bit of assistance, or maybe just made encouraging
noises, to several of these anti-Communist groups: but most of them
have fizzled out or been absorbed by UNITA. And South Africa's
careful not to get involved. All the real backing goes to Savimbi.

"The Spear of Freedom didn't have a chance. There were a few
skirmishes and finally a bigger clash with Cuban troops. That's where
Piet Villiers was presumed to have been killed. But no one really knows
what happened. The Angolan Government has never officially admitted the existence of a breakaway faction, nor, for its own reasons, has
UNITA. So the South African Government has followed suit. There
were rumours, and some of us knew that mercenaries were being recruited, but, again, nothing's been admitted officially by anyone. Since
the Spear of Freedom wasn't supposed to exist, the Angolan Government never complained about the mercenaries or boasted about killing
them or held show-trials of any who were captured. And the South
African Government didn't want to know. The mercenaries were on
their own. They just disappeared. Until now.

"Why these three should have been kept alive, one can only guess.
Probably so that they could be produced for propaganda purposes if it
became politically desirable. And I suppose it's because they don't officially exist that they've been moved around with the army rather than
being held in prison. Now I'd better ask Luke to tell you what he
learned."

The big black man spoke English with barely a trace of accent. "Mr.
Van der Bruin asked me to go to Windhoek—" he began.

"Excuse my interrupting," said Jan, "but, in case you're worried about cover, I should explain that I'm a consultant mining engineer and Luke works for me." He grinned. "We're both quite genuine, I can assure you. In fact we're rather good at our work, aren't we? And we have legitimate business in South-West, or Namibia."

"I call it German South-West," murmured Jeremy.

"The recruiter in Windhoek arranged for me to see this Ovambo," Luke continued. "He was still quite weak from the journey. He'd had fever and not enough to eat and he'd been dodging SWAPO guerrillas and South African army patrols. And that's difficult country, first swamp, then desert. But he was all right. I questioned him for quite a long time."

"And you're satisfied that he was telling you the truth?" asked Richard.

"Yes. I saw no reason to disbelieve him. He had been a scout with the MPLA forces—"

"MPLA?" asked Jeremy.

"The Marxist Popular Movement for the Liberation of Angola. That's the Angolan Government. But secretly he'd been spying for the rebels, he said because he didn't like Communism but perhaps really for money. He was afraid that the security officer attached to his unit was becoming suspicious, so he ran away. The night before he left, he talked to one of the three white prisoners, who asked him, if he reached South Africa safely, to let his wife—Mrs. Villiers—know that he was alive. He could find her through the recruiter in Windhoek."

"You mean this man casually told a prisoner in the camp that he was a spy on the point of escaping to South Africa?" asked Richard. "That doesn't sound very probable."

"I think it does," replied Luke. "He knew no one in South Africa. He needed someone to go to. He needed money. Here was a chance of both, and the prisoner wasn't very likely to give him away. So he made a deliberate approach. It wasn't casual at all."

"Would he have had access to the prisoners?"

"That was no problem. They're scarcely guarded. There's no need. The village is surrounded by wild bush country. Anybody who didn't know it, particularly a white man, would have almost no possibility of surviving. And the prisoners were too weak, anyway, to attempt such a journey. They're living together in a hut, with one man on guard outside at night: but, during the day, they're allowed to wander more or less where they like in the village."

"That's what made me think a rescue was conceivable," said Jan.

"But what about all that wild bush country?" asked Richard. "How would the rescuers get there—and out again?"

"There's something Luke hasn't mentioned. The village is near to the sea. It's a difficult coast but not impossible. The man in Windhoek who recruited the mercenaries, he accepts some responsibility for what happened to them and wants to rescue the prisoners if he can—or rather if we can. He's arranging a boat and some men. But I told him, of course, that I couldn't move without the approval of my backers. It's up to you."

Richard turned to Luke. "What's your opinion? You've talked to the man who knows the ground. What are the chances of pulling it off? How dangerous is it?"

"I believe the chances are good," said Luke. "As I told you, there are virtually no guards. The soldiers are not a fighting unit, merely a small escort for the women and children and for the prisoners. They don't expect an attack by South African troops—they're quite a long way from the border—and there are no UNITA forces in that area. So they're not alert."

"How many soldiers are there?"

"If my friend the Ovambo can be relied on—and we must rely on him if we're going to do anything—there are just twelve, plus a few armed men belonging to the village."

"My idea," said Jan, "is that, if we create a diversion, we should be able to slip the prisoners away, in the dark, before anyone realises what's happening."

"We? Would you be coming?"

"Naturally. And Luke."

"And how many others?" asked Jeremy.

"There's the boat's crew—it's a fishing boat—and eight men to go ashore. The Ovambo has agreed to come with us to show us the way, for a price. And both of you?"

"Me," said Jeremy, "not Richard. This isn't his kind of work. It is mine."

"No," said Richard. "If I authorise this jaunt, I'm coming too. I can't stay behind while you—well, I can't stay behind."

"Rubbish. You'd only be in the way."

"I'll try not to be. I mean it; I won't let you go otherwise."

"Does that mean you're satisfied?" asked Jan. "We go ahead?"

Richard hesitated, sighed. "Before I give a final answer, I want you to go through the whole plan and then I shall need to telephone London. I can't pretend I'm very happy. Despite what Luke says, it obviously is dangerous. We'll be risking a dozen lives. But if I say no, I'll be condemning those three prisoners. And our whole purpose is to help people who have no other help. That's why we exist, why we take risks."

At that moment Jan's wife reappeared. "Lunch is ready when you are," she said.

After lunch maps were produced and there was much more talk. Eventually Richard went alone into Jan's study, dialled the code for London and then the familiar number. When Gabriel came on the line, he said: "I think it's go."

The fishing boat, which was called the *Blue Heron* and was quite large, had already put out from Walvis Bay with a bigger crew than usual and some items of equipment about which the harbour authorities were not informed. The recruiter from Windhoek knew the right strings to pull and how to induce blind eyes.

It was arranged that Richard and Jeremy, who might have attracted attention, should join the *Blue Heron* from Swakopmund. They flew, together with Jan and Luke, to Windhoek, and, from there, took a Land Rover across the desert. Their story, if they met anyone, was that the two Englishmen were Jan's guests; that he was an amateur naturalist (which was true) and wanted to show them the strange harsh landscape of the Namib desert, the creatures and plants which survive there, and that afterwards they would be looking at birds and at the salt pan. But during the five or six hours of the drive they saw no other human being. Twice they stopped and surveyed the road behind them, and the bare dunes, with binoculars. If anyone was watching them, or watching for them, they might have been spotted at Windhoek airport but they were certainly not being followed across the desert.

Late in the afternoon, their shirts sweat-dampened from the heat, they suddenly drove into a wall of fog as thick, as blinding, as the old-

fashioned London Particular of which the Clean Air Act has deprived
romantic Londoners.

"What an astonishing thing!" said Richard.

"There's a fog in Swakopmund more than two hundred days a year,"
Jan explained. "It's where cold air from the sea meets hot air from the
desert." And the fog indeed hung clammy around them. The buildings,
which they were passing now, were only dim shapes. The one beside
which Jan pulled up was tall and somehow, Richard thought, un-Afri-
can. There were three steps leading up to the door, and beside it a
wooden board on which were neatly painted the words "Gasthof Barbarossa". "Everything's German here," said Jan.

The proprietor was expecting them. He was gaunt and taciturn; the
few words he spoke were guttural. He took them into a room at the end
of the hall. It smelled musty. Heavy velvet curtains covered the windows: the table-cloth was fringed and tasselled: the chairs were upright
and unyielding. The proprietor, having brought coffee and schnapps on
a tray, withdrew. There was no sign of any other living creature in the
house, and sounds from the street were muffled by the fog.

"Cosy little seaside guest-house," observed Jeremy.

"This was an assembly point for the mercenaries," Jan replied. "A
kind of safe house." He looked at his watch. "We shan't be here long.
Rendezvous in just over an hour."

A clock on the chimney-piece ticked ponderously. Desultory at-
tempts at conversation seemed swallowed up by the gloom. Richard
tried to pour himself another cup of coffee, but the pot was empty. He
could have asked intelligent questions about the history of the town
and the political problems of Namibia, but inertia silenced him. They
waited.

Eventually the proprietor returned. "It is time," he said.

They collected their bags from the still deserted hall, and followed
him out into the fog. They walked in silence. A large object loomed up
beside them. "That's a memorial to the German marines," Jan explained, "who were killed in the First World War when the South
African column arrived."

"Is the South African army here now?" asked Richard.

"No, they're a long way to the north, in the operational area. As
you've seen, this is impossible guerrilla country. But up there on the
border the swamps are so difficult that the army can sometimes see a

guerrilla group and not be able to reach them. The navy uses Walvis Bay and wants to keep it, if and when Namibia becomes independent."

Richard could hear the sea now, gently splashing. They crossed the road, and there were wet flagstones under his feet. They were walking out on to a jetty. On the way they had passed only a couple of shadowy figures; the whole town seemed almost as empty as the Gasthof Barbarossa—or perhaps they had merely avoided the places where people were. They halted by a flight of stone steps, which ran down to a dark, gently heaving sea. The proprietor, drawing a flashlight from his pocket, blinked it three times, then twice more, out into the opaqueness. It was answered immediately by the sound of a muffled engine.

A dinghy emerged from the mist and slid in beside the steps. There were two men on board, one in the stern, steering, the other in the bows with a boathook. The proprietor pointed to the boat and muttered something to Jan. They shook hands. Then Jan led the way down the steps. Richard said thank-you to the proprietor, who simply nodded without a smile. One by one they were helped into the dinghy by the man in the bows, who was swarthy and unshaven and wore a seaman's pullover above stained jeans. The engine gave a quiet roar, and, in a moment, the jetty and the proprietor had vanished behind them. Their world became nothing but chilly sea and clammy mist.

The whole experience, by now, was so dream-like and disorienting that Richard seemed to lose track of time and space. Then, quite suddenly, they emerged from the fog. There was open sea and a bright gibbous moon, the fog bank behind them and ahead, Richard saw, the silhouette of a vessel, riding high in the water, with two masts and only a dim glow, which, as they approached, became the outline of a cabin door. The moon, drifting in and out of clouds, revealed several men on deck.

A rope ladder already hung from the side. The sea being calm, climbing it proved quite easy even for Richard, who was unused to such nautical exercises. Jeremy went up like a cat. Luke and Jan came last. Firm hands pulled them on board. A fat man in a peaked cap stood beside the rail. "Welcome," he said. "I am Captain Gomez."

A few minutes later they were in his diminutive cabin. "I'm afraid your quarters will not be very comfortable," he said. "We sling hammocks in part of the hold. Maybe it smells of fish a little. There is the deck, of course, if you prefer, but you will have to keep out of sight if a plane should come over or we should meet a patrol boat. We have more men on board already than if we were really out for fish."

"Are we likely to be stopped by a patrol boat?" asked Jan.

"I hope not. We have a special bulkhead which we can pull across to conceal that part of the hold. But if anyone really searched . . ." He shrugged and spread his hands.

They all chose to sleep on deck, but they were shown how to get below quickly. An Indian cook had brought food and wine to the captain's cabin. Gomez proved a cheerful and expansive host, full of anecdotes. Richard gathered that, though ostensibly a fisherman, he took more pleasure and certainly found more profit in smuggling. "My luck and my cunning," he said, putting a thick finger beside a greasy nose, "keep me out of trouble. Well, not too much trouble. Everyone has a little, no? Luck and cunning and maybe a bit of money to the right people." He chuckled.

Only the constant throbbing of an engine showed that they were under way. The depression which had overcome Richard in that oppressive house at Swakopmund had lifted. He looked around the cabin, at the little group with their faces illumined by the single lamp like figures in an old painting, at his friend Jeremy, at Jan and Luke, good men both, at fat Gomez, felt the stir of the boat, alive, beneath his feet, knew that they were moving inexorably towards danger, but towards a danger cheerfully undertaken for a good cause which gave his life meaning, and he was glad. This was adventure, a crusade. There was nowhere on earth he would rather have been at that moment.

When they went out on deck, the night was warm and the sky filled with African stars. "In the books one used to read," said Jeremy, "the Southern Cross always 'blazed,' but it's really rather a disappointing constellation, don't you think? One has to be pointed in the right direction even to see it."

"Like most things," answered Richard, "it depends what you expect." He was in no mood to be disappointed.

Gomez provided rough blankets, with which they made the best accommodation they could, a row of nests against the wheelhouse. In such uncomfortable circumstances, Richard expected sleep to be difficult: but his eyes closed immediately, and, when he opened them again, a spectacular dawn was already flooding the sea. There was no land in sight. Shortly afterwards a smell of coffee and frying bacon came up from the galley.

After breakfast Richard met the rest of his miniature expeditionary force. They were gathered in the hold, eight very tough-looking white men and one black. "That's the Ovambo," Luke whispered to him.

Jeremy pinned a large sheet of paper to the bulkhead, rather dramatically since, having no drawing pins, he did it with two knives. Then he addressed his troops, who sat on the deck around him or leaned against the bulkheads.

"My name is Colonel Fisher," he said. "I'm in charge of this party." There was a crispness about him, an authority, in sharp contrast with the figure he normally chose to present. ("All an act, dear boy," he had said once, on another occasion, when Richard had remarked on the difference.) "You probably know our objective. It's to rescue three men —some of you, I believe, served with them—who are being held prisoner in a village about a hundred miles north of the border. According to our intelligence, the geography is like this." He drew on the paper, in bold lines, with a fibre-tipped pen. "That's the coast. There's the estuary of a small river, and beside it—that's the village.

"The village consists of about two dozen huts and some other light wooden structures. There are trees and scrub around it. The prisoners are held in a hut, just there, close to the northern perimeter. One guard is normally watching them. He and eleven others are uniformed soldiers, armed with Kalashnikov rifles and revolvers. Some of the villagers also have guns, although probably nothing very modern.

"We shall land, after dark, there." He made a cross on the paper. "We shall use two boats, with room in each for eight people—ourselves and the three we are going to bring back. Three of us will go round to the far side of the village, and at zero hour create a diversion. The rest will approach behind the prisoners' hut"—he tapped the paper—"and fetch them out, using minimum force. With luck there should be only that one guard to deal with, perhaps not even him if he can be distracted to the other side. They'll have no reason to suppose that anyone is interested in the prisoners or that the prisoners themselves will try to escape. The prisoners are in bad physical condition but they should all be able to walk.

"Our diversionary party will try to draw the opposition off into the bush and then fade away. The main party, with the prisoners, will move back—quietly, I hope—to the boats. No shooting, if we can avoid it. Then we all get the hell out as fast as possible. The bush between the village and the shore is thick enough to provide cover but won't be difficult to traverse. As I'm sure you know, we have a guide who's familiar with the area. Before we go in, at nightfall, the day after tomorrow, there'll be another briefing. By then I'll have a map with as much detail as we can work out—paths, obstructions, that sort of thing. Now, any questions?"

A large, deeply weather-browned man spoke with a heavy Afrikaans accent. "You've got a bloody lot of optimistic assumptions. Suppose the main party's seen. We'll have the whole village after us, including those twelve soldiers."

"In that case," said Jeremy, "we stop them. We shall have the fire-power." Richard felt a chill at the implications of that reply.

"And where's the *Blue Heron* while all this is going on?" asked an older man. "If she's spotted, mayn't that already have alerted the village?"

"She'll be hove to, well out at sea," answered Jeremy. "Too far away to be noticed, I hope. But if she is spotted, at a distance, she's just a fishing boat. There's nothing unusual about that."

"The troops will surely be in radio contact with their headquarters. Won't we be chased by planes or patrol boats?"

"I'm not sure they are in radio contact. There's been no sign of it. But even if they are, we shall try to be outside territorial waters as quickly as possible and soon after that, we shall be joining—by arrangement—some other fishing vessels. These prisoners aren't of any great political importance. The Angolans won't want to create a major incident over them."

A fair-haired boy in faded blue denim asked: "What weapons do we take?"

"Four Uzi sub-machine guns," replied Jeremy. "Browning automatics, semi-automatic rifles. And commando knives. They'll be issued tomorrow morning, so that you can familiarise yourselves with them."

It went on, question and answer, for about half an hour. Then they dispersed. Luke took the Ovambo away to interrogate him again, as closely as possible, about the geography and routine of the village. Jeremy, Richard and Van der Bruin went back to the captain's cabin. Gomez was there, with a vile-smelling black cigar between his teeth.

When they were settled around the table, Jeremy asked him: "The crew. If the situation gets sticky, can they be trusted?"

Gomez removed the cigar, and grinned, showing the gleam of a gold tooth. "Absolutely. They are all first-class reliable crooks."

Jeremy produced a notebook from his pocket. "I've been working out how we should go in the boats," he said. "I'll go in the first with Luke, the Ovambo and three men. Richard and Jan, you'll go in the second with five men. That means that, on the way back, we'll bring two of the prisoners. You'll bring one. Jan, I'd like you to take two men round to the far side of the village, where you'll create the diversion. . . ."

Gomez recited the names—it was agreed that Christian names only should be used—of all the men who would be in the party, and Jeremy allocated them between the two boats. He asked about their qualifications, but Gomez didn't know, or didn't admit to knowing, much about most of them. Exhaustively they discussed various things which could go wrong and various contingencies to which they might have to respond. Eventually there seemed no more to be said.

The day wore on, the *Blue Heron* ploughing steadily through calm seas. The only ships they saw were a couple of tankers on the horizon and a fishing boat, which passed them, heading south, the crew waving cheerfully. For Richard the hours moved slowly, because he had nothing to do, but relentlessly. He had insisted on coming, romantically perhaps, out of a sense of duty, but of course Jeremy had been quite right in saying that this wasn't his kind of work. He had never been a soldier. He was out of place among those tough men with whom he would be going ashore. How would he conduct himself, he wondered, if it came to a battle? When he had decided that the attempt should be made, he hadn't envisaged, though he realised now that he should have done, the possibility of a fire-fight in which quite a lot of people might be killed. If they were, how would the ethics of his decision look then, the balance sheet of lives lost and lives saved? He tried to shake such thoughts away, like a dog shaking off water. He was committed and had committed the rest of the party: there could be no turning back now. The time for debate, for moral reflection, would be afterwards. If there was an afterwards.

Night came again. They dined in the captain's cabin. Most of the talking was done by Jeremy and Gomez, both of whom seemed in ebullient form, swapping outrageous tales. Later, wrapping himself in his blanket on the deck, Richard lay awake for a long time but then fell into a deep sleep. He awoke feeling cold. A pearl-grey sea-mist had cut the boat off from all sight or sound, except the steady throb of the engine. But soon the heat of the sun burnt the mist off, and they were again in the midst of an empty blue sea with an empty blue sky above.

A false bulkhead was lifted away and the equipment produced—camouflaged battledress, weapons well oiled and wrapped in sacking, ammunition, a box of grenades and some medical packs. Jeremy supervised the distribution. He took one of the Uzis for himself. He gave Richard a carbine, a Browning automatic in a holster and a sheath-knife.

"Satisfy yourselves," said Jeremy, "that your weapons work and that you know how to use them." He allowed several shots to be fired at tin cans which were thrown into the sea but wouldn't permit great fusillades. Richard tried two shots and missed the can with both, but not, he told himself, by very much; then it had floated beyond accurate range.

The day passed, another night, morning, and this was *the* day. After twelve—to Richard almost unbearable—hours darkness fell, quickly, like a purple curtain. The *Blue Heron* had changed course and was moving now, obliquely, towards the land, as he could tell from the curve in the wake. They were all wearing their battledress, as they sat on the deck, faces blacked, weapons beside them, in two groups while the boats were got ready. The cook and his assistant brought round mugs of steaming coffee. Gomez had taken the wheel himself.

No one, it seemed, felt like talking; just an occasional muttered remark. Sitting next to Richard was the older man who had asked a question. His name was Steve, and he had told Richard earlier that he was in the South African army when they invaded Angola. "We were right up at Luanda," he said. "We could have captured it easy, but the Americans let us down. They'd promised support, you know, and it never came. So we pulled back. Mind you, the Cubans weren't bad fighters. At least this bunch tonight won't be hitting us with Stalin Organs."

The Stalin Organ, Richard knew, was a multiple rocket-launcher. I might as well stick close to an experienced soldier, he thought, not some young tearaway. Steve was reassuringly calm now, sucking a pipe.

The night was dark; the moon wouldn't rise for another hour. The dinghies were in the water. Two rope-ladders were over the side. Jeremy walked back from the rail, glanced at his watch and signalled to Gomez. "All right, chaps," he said.

With his rifle slung across his shoulders, Richard clambered down, taking his seat beside the steersman in the number two boat. Looking towards the shore, he could see a faint white line of surf and fancied he could hear it booming. Jan was the last to clamber aboard. He took the bow seat, matching Jeremy's position in the number one boat. They bobbed very mildly up and down. Jeremy had one arm raised in the air. He lowered it sharply. The outboard motors coughed fully into life. The dark bulk of the *Blue Heron* began to recede behind them as the two laden dinghies headed for the distant shore.

VIII

Assault

Halfway to the shore, the motors were cut and paddles produced. The booming and sucking of the waves across the rocks which lay ahead was clearly audible, though still faint; it would surely have blocked off the noise of the motors so far, and of the paddles now, from anybody on the shore beyond. The night was clear and calm, and, until the moon came up, reasonably dark. Were the boats visible from the shore, Richard wondered, if anybody was watching, with night-glasses perhaps?

He could see a line of phosphorescence, the spray on the reef. No boat much larger than these dinghies could reach the shore at this point, and even for them there were only two narrow passages available between the jagged rocks. The Ovambo, sitting beside Jeremy in the number one boat, would guide them in. Richard tried to remember what the man's name was, but it had been a tongue-twister and he couldn't reconstruct it. They had talked to him at length during the first day on the *Blue Heron*, checking his story again and forming their own view of his reliability. But his English was poor and Richard felt that he had no means of assessing the man—a man on whom his life now depended. An uncomfortable doubt haunted the back of Richard's mind even at this moment: but then, he thought, how good am I at telling whether a man can be trusted when we speak the same language? Not very. Perhaps not at all. Mentally he shrugged, and concentrated on the black water and the line of foam and the dark shore.

Out of some kind of deference, or perhaps mere distrust of his skill, he was the odd man among the seven in the dinghy and had not been given a paddle. In the other boat, just a few yards ahead, he could barely make out the figure of the Ovambo, who was gesturing, indicating that they must steer to the right. Suddenly they were pitching and bobbing, turbulent water splashing over the side. Foam outlined a protruding bulk only a few feet to the left. The sea gurgled and slapped, and controlling the boats at all became an urgent struggle. The spray was dripping from Richard's face. Then, with equal suddenness, they were in calm water, the noise of the surf behind them.

Wiping the salt water from his eyes and collecting his breath, Richard looked up and saw, unexpectedly near, the shape of a beach with a low cliff and trees behind it. The final hundred yards of tranquil sea glided rapidly beneath the boats. Now men were jumping out of the number one boat, pulling it up on to the sand. Now the first man was out of Richard's boat too. . . .

It was a relief to move. He knew what to do; the briefing had been exact. Warm water splashed round his ankles, then he was stumbling up a gentle slope of sand, holding his rifle, thumb on the safety catch. Most of the others were ahead, Jeremy and the Ovambo leading, except for those who had been detailed to drag the boats above the waterline and, if possible, into whatever concealment there might be. The first objective, Jeremy had said, was to get everyone off the beach, out of sight.

To the left, Richard was vaguely aware, the beach, behind its guardian reef, stretched away indefinitely: to the right, the land bulked into a cliff with rocks at its foot. The strip of sand was no more than twenty yards across, after which the ground rose quite gently to a crest, a low cliff topped with rank grass, merging into scattered bushes and small trees.

The sand sliding beneath his feet, Richard panted behind Steve. He was afraid of hearing a cry of alarm or a shot, but there was nothing. The welcome shadows of thickening vegetation enclosed him. Jeremy had halted, crouched beneath a tree, and each of the others, as they arrived, knelt or squatted beside him. The silence felt blanket-thick, like the warmth of the tropical night. There was only the murmur of the surf, no nightbird, no cicada. When they were all present, they just waited, listening, for a minute. A silvery glow in the sky showed that the moon was almost up; it made the shadows blacker. Richard could see that they were not in the middle of serious woodland or undergrowth. This was merely a fringe of trees. Ahead shimmered grass with only a scattering of thorn bushes and, here and there, a taller wide-branched tree.

Jeremy and the Ovambo rose together. The Ovambo led the way, and the whole party followed in single file, weapons at the ready. Jan, then Steve, were immediately in front of Richard, behind him the two men who had waited to pull their boat ashore. Richard couldn't make out if they were actually following a path, but the Ovambo walked confidently, threading between bushes, and the ground was not difficult.

After some twenty minutes, the path, if it was a path, grew harder and began to climb. They were surrounded by a tumble of rocks, from which they emerged on to the crest of a wide shallow basin, spread out before them in the moonlight. They paused. Jeremy beckoned them to close around him. The far edge of the basin dropped in the middle to the silver line of a small river. The inside slopes were more thickly, though still not densely, covered in vegetation: but, in the cleared centre, was a ring of huts.

Lying prone or crouched behind the available cover, they surveyed their objective. There was not much sign of activity; a fire smouldering, beside which they could make out three seated figures; somebody crossing from one hut to another; and, in front of a large hut on the nearside of the circle, a man standing, a sentry perhaps. The Ovambo pointed and murmured something to Jeremy and Luke, who were on either side of him.

Turning to the others, Jeremy said in a low voice: "That's the hut where the prisoners are kept. Guarded by one man. There should be two other men keeping watch, probably those by the fire."

"Probably or certainly?" whispered Jan. "Could the watchmen be outside the village?"

Luke spoke to the Ovambo, who replied. "He says it's unlikely," Luke interpreted. "This is a safe area and the sentries are lazy."

Jeremy said: "There's a chance we can do this thing with no trouble at all. Jan, that's your place, in those trees beside the path leading to the river. I should think it'll take you about half an hour to get there. Let's say three-quarters of an hour." He looked at his watch. "That's five to eleven. We'll make it eleven o'clock exactly. No need to start all hell breaking loose if we don't have to. See if you can draw those watchmen away. We'll cope with the guard outside the prisoners' hut. But if we're spotted, or if the watchmen won't move, then hit them."

"There are three people by the fire," Jan said. "I think the third's a woman."

"Likely enough. Just make sure she looks your way, not ours. Afterwards, get out fast. Our friend here thinks they won't follow you into the bush. But if they do, you've got to lose them or stop them. Take your time getting back to the boats. We'll wait for you."

The plan which had appeared so simple when Jeremy first outlined it now seemed to Richard full of possible, even probably, dangers. Suppose it worked, and Jan's diversion really did draw everybody's attention to the far side. Suppose Jeremy did get the prisoners out. Surely it wouldn't be more than a few minutes before the absence of the guard, and then the absence of the prisoners, was noticed. And then what? The only hope was that the villagers and the soldiers might be reluctant to go charging out into the dark in pursuit of an unknown enemy.

Jeremy and Jan, although they had synchronised their watches before leaving the *Blue Heron*, checked them again. Jeremy touched Jan's shoulder. "Good luck," he said. "Off you go." And Jan, accompanied by the two men he'd picked earlier for the job, slipped away through the rocks.

"We'll wait for a bit," said Jeremy. So they waited. The brilliant moon climbed higher, shortening and blackening the shadows. In the village below, one of the watchmen threw a log on the fire, sending up a shower of sparks. The guard outside the prisoners' hut stretched his legs by walking up and down, then strolled over to the group by the fire, stood chatting for a while and returned more or less to his original position. There was no other movement. There were sounds—a nightbird's call, and the cicadas, accustomed now to the presence of the motionless intruders, resumed their constant rustle.

"Let's go," said Jeremy at last. With the Ovambo just ahead of him, he picked a cautious, devious way down the slope, being careful not to expose the party in patches of open moonlit ground. As they went lower the vegetation thickened again. Where the slope, the side of the basin, levelled off, perhaps three hundred yards from the clearing round the village, a large rock formation towered above bushes. The path, which was now discernible as being man-made, ran beside it. Jeremy lifted a hand to halt the party. Then he waved two men, one of them carrying an Uzi, into cover among the bushes. Jan had also taken an

Uzi: Jeremy had another and one of the older, and presumably more experienced, of the mercenaries carried the fourth.

Leaving the two men, the party moved forward again, very slowly, scrupulous not to kick a stone or crack a twig. A bird suddenly flew up ahead of them, sending Richard's heart into his mouth. They all froze. But nothing happened. Forward again.

Now they were at the very edge of the trees and scrub. Twenty feet of cleared ground separated them from the back of the prisoners' hut. Looking past it, Richard could see the shadow of the guard, though not the man himself, who was concealed by the structure. Beyond were the leaping glow of the fire and the three figures beside it, two men and a slim African girl. He heard the girl laugh.

Jeremy gestured an order to lie down. Richard felt baked mud and sharp stones beneath him. He looked at the luminous dial of his wristwatch. Ten fifty-six. His hands, grasping the rifle, were sweaty, although he suddenly felt that the night had become cold. He scrutinised the dark bulk of the prisoners' hut, remembering the discussion on the boat about whether it would be possible, and safer, to penetrate the wall or perhaps go through the roof without being seen or heard. But the walls, the Ovambo told them, were solidly constructed, and getting up on to the roof and through it, in the moonlight, had seemed riskier than the plan they settled on. Richard looked at his watch again. Ten fifty-nine.

The sentry's shadow moved, and the man himself came into view past the hut. Slung across his chest was a rifle with the characteristic curved magazine of a Kalashnikov.

The time must be eleven by now. It was. One minute past eleven. But still nothing had happened. Then there was a cry from one of the two watchmen. They and the girl were all on their feet, looking towards the other side of the village. The intervening glow of the fire made it difficult for Richard to see what had drawn their attention, but a moment later it was unmistakable—flame leaping up from the roof of one of the furthest huts, and another flame beside it, spreading. Both shouting an alarm, the watchmen ran towards the burning hut. The girl stood still. The sentry turned to see what was happening.

Now there were figures everywhere, movement, clamour. Too many figures surely. Some who weren't black. Cubans?

Even as that thought struck Richard, he saw Jeremy slip forward across the few feet of moonlit ground into the shadow of the prisoners' hut. The sentry hadn't left his post but he was facing away. Moving so quickly and fluidly that even Richard scarcely realised what was happening, Jeremy had grabbed the sentry and pulled him back into the shadow. There was no cry, and no sign that anybody else had seen. All attention was concentrated on the spreading blaze. Luke followed Jeremy, and rolled a canister out in front of the hut. It started belching smoke. Richard saw them both, Jeremy and Luke, emerge from the shadow and slip round to the entrance of the hut. He brought his own gun up, ready to give covering fire if necessary.

Jeremy had a flashlight for use inside the hut. But there was too much light, suddenly, shining out on to the smoke, and the fearful rip of automatic fire. Several guns. And a scream. Immediately shots began on the far side of the village too.

Two figures, three, four, emerged from the hut into the smoke, weirdly illumined by what seemed to be a powerful lamp. The first was Luke, half-dragging, half-supporting a white man, who wore only a pair of underpants. Then came another white man, then Jeremy, backing out, machine-gun pointed. He fired a burst into the hut.

The four of them were running across the moonlight now. Behind them, an armed man appeared out of the smoke. Steve, crouching next to Richard, shot him.

As Luke and the man he was helping staggered towards them, Richard saw that Luke was wounded too, a dark patch spreading across his chest. "Out of here. Quick," said Jeremy. And they were all up and running, back along the way they'd come, not caring about noise now, stones slipping beneath their feet, thorns catching at their clothes. Richard snatched a glance over his shoulder to see if they were being followed, but there was no one yet, just a maelstrom of shouting and shots and flame and smoke.

Then there was someone. Several men. A burst of shots which ricocheted somewhere near. A movement in the bushes ahead and a gleam of metal in the moonlight made Richard's stomach turn over, until he realised that it was their own two men who had been posted there. Waving the rest of them on, Jeremy too plunged into the shelter of the bushes.

The ground was rising now. Panting for breath, Richard stumbled, pushed himself back on to his feet, and, as he did so, heard two bursts of machine-gun fire and some rifle shots behind him. Then silence. Or, rather, only distant shouts. The gunfire from the village had stopped too.

Richard was at the rear of the fleeing party, perhaps because he was the least fit among them. Steve, helping Luke, was a few yards ahead. They were scrambling up between bushes. The rim of the hill, above them, was a sharp black edge against the stars. Richard froze. He could hear feet on the path behind, quite near. He turned, his finger on the trigger of his gun.

Loping into sight came Jeremy and the two mercenaries. Richard let out his breath with a sigh.

"Mind where you point that thing," said Jeremy.

"What happened?" asked Richard.

"Keep jogging, dear boy. We stopped the ones who came after us."

"But in the hut?"

"They were waiting. Don't know quite how many. But I'd say it was a trap. I don't mean they were expecting us tonight. If they had been, I shouldn't be here now. I'm afraid one of the prisoners bought it."

"And Luke was hit."

"Yes."

"There were far more than twelve soldiers in the village."

"Exactly."

They were close to the brow, where the rest of the party had halted, waiting for them to catch up. Luke was sitting on the ground, leaning against a rock. The man he'd supported from the hut lay beside him, whether hurt or merely exhausted Richard couldn't tell.

"Not me, boss," pleaded the Ovambo, "not me. I told you truth." Richard saw that he was terrified.

Jeremy ignored him. They all looked back down the path, which lay empty and silent, although the bushes and rocks had ominous shapes. A cautious attacker might well get close to them unobserved. Below, the fire in the huts had been brought under control. Smoke still drifted up to the sky. Figures scurried like ants whose nest has been disturbed.

"Jan started firing as soon as he heard our shots," said Jeremy. "That's what saved us. The question is, did he and his men get away? If he did, he'll head for the beach. Which is what we must do."

"How many of them do you reckon there are?" asked Steve. "Cubans, I mean. Proper soldiers."

"There were four or five in the hut," said Jeremy, "and we killed six on the path. But there must be more, the ones we heard shooting on the far side of the village."

"There were thirty-six altogether," said a new voice. "I counted them. They arrived in two trucks, five days ago." This was the other man who'd been rescued. He had on a pair of tattered denim trousers and nothing else, not even shoes. His feet must have been cut excruciatingly by the stony path. But his voice was remarkably calm, and the accent American. Of course, thought Richard, searching for the name; yes, that was it—Smith, Ben Smith.

"That leaves two dozen," said Steve, "plus the villagers. They'll be a bit cautious when they see what you did to their chums, but, from what I know of them, they won't sit tight. They'll be working out now which way we're likeliest to have gone."

"Then let's not wait for them," said Jeremy. "We'll get back to the boats."

They ran, bushes, trees, patches of moonlight flickering by. It seemed unlikely that their pursuers could be ahead of them but every turn in the path made Richard grip his gun more tightly, his eyes searching the shadows. Luke was still supporting the man he had rescued. He brushed aside an offer of help, but Richard, seeing him stagger, wondered how long he could keep going. Jeremy ran steadily in front of the party. Steve kept just behind Richard, turning constantly to see if there was any sign of pursuit.

There wasn't. The noise from the village had died away. Sooner than Richard expected they were back in the clump of trees at the top of the little cliff. Silhouetted on the horizon lay the *Blue Heron*. The line of breaking waves boomed across the reef. The silvery beach was blessedly empty, with the two dinghies concealed among the rocks on the left. Leaning against a tree, recovering his breath, Richard felt, for the first time since the whole plan had exploded in the village, that they had a real chance of escaping safely.

But time—how much time had they? Every nerve in Richard's body cried out that they had no time to spare; they must go now.

Steve asked the question which Richard had forced himself not to ask: "How long are we going to wait?"

Jeremy didn't answer directly. He said to two of the mercenaries:

"You two, down on to the beach and get the boats to the water's edge. We'll follow."

"We must wait," said Luke. "They've got to find a way through the bush. But Mr. Van der Bruin will do it. I know him."

"We'll wait as long as we can," replied Jeremy. "Steve, go back just beyond that last turn of the path. You should have quite a view from there. If you see the opposition coming, fire one shot, then get down to the beach double-quick. We'll be ahead."

"Right," said Steve and, rifle in hand, marched back down the path.

Excruciating minutes crawled by. On the beach below, the two mercenaries had hauled one dinghy to the water's lapping edge, and went back for the other. The silence was eerie. The loudest noise was the stertorous breathing of the rescued man, slumped now against a rock. Jeremy had been helping to bandage Luke's wound. "At least we can stop the bleeding," he said.

A noise in the bush brought them all to their feet—all except the man lying against the rock—weapons pointed. "It's us," called Jan's voice. "Hold your fire."

Jan and his two companions emerged from the scrub. "We threw them off, I think."

"Glad to see you," said Jeremy. "It's going-home time."

"Not for this one," said Luke, peering down at the man by the rock. "He's dead."

"Leave him," said Jeremy. "Come on. I'll fetch Steve."

But, before he could move, a shot echoed like doom from around the turn of the path, followed immediately by a burst of automatic fire. Richard, spurred by a sense that he had been useless so far, took a step back towards the firing.

"No," said Jeremy, gripping his arm.

The first of the mercenaries were already slithering down towards the beach, with Jan and the Ovambo close behind them. Richard, Luke and Jeremy followed, and were halfway down when Luke shouted and, as they turned to see what he had seen, fired. A group of figures had emerged on to the higher clifftop, on their left, about fifty yards away. Luke's burst of fire took two of them. A third was firing over the cliff edge when Jeremy cut him down. Bullets zipped somewhere very close as Richard fired, and the fourth man fell. That was all.

They plunged down the slope, and Luke, in the lead, almost fell over the body of the Ovambo. Jeremy and Richard jumped across it. No one else appeared to have been hit. The others had reached the open sand.

The flash and the clap of noise were so unexpected that Richard didn't realise what had happened. And then, appalled, saw. Jeremy, twisting round, fired another burst at the clifftop. Two men with a grenade-launcher collapsed. Again there was no one left on the clifftop. But on the sand, midway between the rocks and the water's edge, was a crater where the second dinghy had been. One of the mercenaries lay motionless beside it; the other, wounded, was trying to crawl.

Before Richard had fully grasped the magnitude of the disaster, Jeremy spoke quite steadily: "I'm going to hold them off. That dinghy should just about take the rest of you—with luck."

"You can't—" began Richard.

"Don't argue. Do it."

"I'll stay with you," said Luke.

"Do as you're told. There's room."

"Maybe. But I don't think I'd make it anyway. The wound's bleeding."

For a moment the three of them stood there in the moonlight. The remaining dinghy was already being pushed out into the water. Jan, beside it, the waves lapping around his thighs, looked back at them, beckoning. Far off lay the *Blue Heron*. On the path and the cliff were dead men. That scene, frozen into momentary stillness, was etched ever afterwards in Richard's mind.

"Go on," said Jeremy quietly to Richard. "No point in us all hanging round." And when Richard still hesitated, "It's your show now. Go on."

Jan was calling to them. With a gesture of helplessness Richard backed away for a step: then, hardly making a conscious decision, ran towards the dinghy. The water was round his legs. He heard the motor spluttering, roaring into life as Jan hauled him into the crowded boat. As he sat up and looked back, spray from the reef was already lashing his face. He caught only a glimpse of the two figures walking away across the bright sand into the shadow of the cliff.

The dinghy was perhaps four hundred yards out to sea when they heard the sound of firing. It didn't last long.

IX

Rendezvous at Dusk

"We lost Jeremy, Luke, even the man we were chiefly trying to rescue —Piet Villiers—and three others. It was my decision to go. How can I help, if not actually blaming myself, at least feeling so wretched about it that I still can't think of anything else?" Richard sank back in the chair with a sigh as much of exasperation, Diana thought, as of anguish. Before Gabriel could answer, he interrupted him: "I know, I know. Good soldiers make decisions, accept the consequences and march on. Well, I'm not a good soldier. I found that out."

They were in Gabriel's homely sitting room at the back of the travel agency. Two standard lamps shed kindly circles of light. No sound of traffic penetrated from outside. Maria, having supplied them with coffee and brandy, withdrew to a chair discreetly away from the others and got on with her sewing. Gabriel's face was almost invisible in the shadow thrown by the wings of his comfortably shabby armchair. Diana sat on a pouffe between the two men. The terrible events of just a week ago might have been as remote as Africa: but they were obviously being played over, again and again, in Richard's mind.

"There was nothing else you could have done," Diana said.

"I could have stayed with Jeremy. Or perhaps tried to get them off in the boat. Instead of which, I just went. And I wanted to go, that's the truth of it."

"You must stop this," said Gabriel sharply. "Now listen to me. Of course you feel wretched over Jeremy. We all do. I was very fond of him too. But what happened was not your fault. He was in charge of the operation. It was what he was trained for. When it went wrong— through no fault of his either—he assessed the situation, saw what must be done and, very bravely, as we would expect, did it. He ordered you to leave, and he was quite right, and you were quite right to obey. If you had stayed with him, you would have been sacrificing your own life for no reason."

"Self-respect. That's a reason."

"No. There's nothing to be ashamed of. In a battle everyone except a fool is frightened. Believe me, I know. And when a friend dies, one weeps. I lost a friend, a very close friend, on an operation which I had approved. But Max would not have wanted me to weep for very long. Or at all." He paused. Diana glanced across at Maria, whose head was bent over her sewing. "As for your decision, when you had heard all the facts, that this operation was worth trying—no, please, listen still— about decisions one has made, there is only a single question to consider. Was the decision sensible in the light of what you knew at the time? If so, there is nothing to regret. Your decision was sensible. I agreed with it, remember."

"All right. So we were both wrong," said Richard.

"No. We weren't wrong. The operation was betrayed."

Mainly to relieve the tension between the two of them, Diana interjected: "Do you think it was the Ovambo? Was he sent to lay a trap?"

Richard shook his head. "Jan believes it was probably Piet Villiers' wife. She didn't want him to come back."

"How terrible."

"When I left, he said he was going to squeeze the truth out of her. 'I'm going to sweat that bitch,' he said. He and Luke were really very close friends."

Gabriel asked: "The man you rescued, who survived—the American —what did he say?"

"Ben Smith. Well, of course he knew nothing except what had happened in the village, but he confirmed that the soldiers had arrived just a few days before we came and that some of them were always with the prisoners, even in the hut at night. Nothing of the kind had ever happened before. He thought they were expecting a rescue attempt."

"This end," said Gabriel thoughtfully, "no one except us knew. But in South Africa quite a lot of people must have known. The recruiter in Windhoek, for example, and whomever he talked to when he made the arrangements."

"Yes," agreed Richard, "and, although I'm sure both Jan and Luke kept their mouths shut in the ordinary way, one can never be certain who may have picked up a hint from something they said or did. Luke, after all, had been to Namibia, before we arrived, to meet the Ovambo. But if that's right and the leak was from the South African end, it means there's no connection with the troubles we've been having here. Which may be true, but it is rather a coincidence."

"Coincidences happen," said Gabriel. "That's another thing I've learned."

"I've not asked you yet," said Richard. "Any progress—about Shaman?"

"Yes and no. No information exactly: but Sammy's been working on the contacts used by Shaman to find out about us. He's been trying to work back up the pipeline, as it were. He's got some more names. Nothing we can act on yet."

"What sort of action—if you could?" asked Diana.

"That depends on what we learn. But a counter-attack, yes, I think we must. And now I have Richard again to help me."

"I told you," said Richard, "I don't think I'm up to it any more. Perhaps I never was. I'm a danger to other people. From now on you must count me out."

"Richard, Richard." Gabriel leaned forward, gazing intently, speaking earnestly. "You want that I should lose both my lieutenants together? My right hand and my left hand? You have been through your baptism of fire. Before you weren't a soldier, now you are. What do you think Jeremy would say? Would he like to have destroyed your courage?" He sank back into the chair. "And there's a practical point. You may withdraw, but you won't cease to be a target. Are you going to send Shaman a message, saying, 'Please don't shoot me. I'm not a Fisher any more'?"

"Oh," said Richard. No one spoke. Eventually he said: "I can't deny that. All right. I've not much choice. We carry on." Diana put her hand on his knee and squeezed, as though to give him comfort.

"Good," said Gabriel. "If you want to regard it that way, think also that you are protecting me. I need your help. Meanwhile, you are staying at Haggard's Hotel?"

"Yes."

Gabriel explained to Diana: "They are friends of ours. From the old days. We put people there sometimes. If anything suspicious happens, anybody asking questions, they would tell us."

"And it is very convenient," said Richard. "All of fifty yards from the club."

"Do you really think it's still not safe for us to go home?" asked Diana. "Richard or me?"

"For you, perhaps," replied Gabriel. "But better we don't take risks. You are comfortable here, I hope?"

"Very. And I love being with you and Maria. But I shall have to go home some time."

"We'll see what happens. But now I have work to do. Why don't you two go out to dinner?"

"Would you like to?" asked Richard.

"I could bear it. Would you believe, I've not been out at all since you left? I don't know where Charlotte thinks I am. I've only been allowed to telephone her."

"She probably thinks you're having a wild affair with some new man."

"The Land of Cockaigne," said Gabriel, "where all things are possible. I'm afraid we haven't supplied much milk and honey. But you never know. Off with you now."

"I'll get my coat."

They went, almost without discussing it, to a little restaurant in Chelsea off the King's Road, where, once upon a time, they had dined together regularly. The familiarity, they both felt, would be soothing, and they were in no mood for anywhere brash.

Before they entered, Richard glanced quickly up and down the street, making sure they hadn't been followed. Watching him, Diana felt a pang of—she didn't quite know what: pity, affection, curiosity? He had changed, aged, in the last two weeks. But perhaps I have too, she thought.

The proprietor, a central European of some indeterminate kind, greeted them as though they had never been away. The decoration of the room hadn't been altered at all; dark red wallpaper combined with red candles to create cosy pools of flickering light amid friendly shadows. The waiters, uniformed in blue smocks with scarlet sashes, were new but might just as well not have been. They were recognisably the same breed of out-of-work actor, not very efficient but eager to please, whom Richard and Diana had known when the world was younger.

The food and wine were distinctly better than respectable, much better certainly and less expensive than in the newer tourist traps of Covent Garden. Game soup for Richard, *pâté maison* for Diana. When the wine waiter had poured the claret and faded from view, she said: "Tell me honestly. Do you want to talk about Africa or not?"

"I thought I didn't, but perhaps now I do." So he did, with Diana prompting him very gently. "Jeremy leaves a sort of audible gap," he said at the end. "Losing the others was terrible, of course, but I didn't know them."

"I hardly knew Jeremy," she said, "but I could see he was rather a special person. Gabriel was right, though. He wouldn't want you to blame yourself or to feel you couldn't go on doing the job."

"I remember his saying once, when somebody we knew had been killed, that the army had the proper idea at funerals. Slow march up, quick march away. But is the job worth doing? Are we entitled to do it at such a price? That's what's been worrying me."

She put her hand on his for a moment. "It's very much worth doing. I've talked to Gabriel an awful lot during these past few days. Or, rather, I've listened to him. He's told me stories, about The Fishers, and about his own life. What he's been doing, what you've all been doing, is a wonderful thing. I haven't said so to him, but I hope you may allow me to be part of it."

He looked at her in some astonishment. "Really? It's a far cry from your normal beat."

"What's normal? If there was a war, I'd want to be in it. And there is a war. Besides, I'd like a crack at Irena. She gave *me* quite a crack, remember."

"Ah, yes, Irena. I'd almost forgotten about her. We still don't know how she fits in, do we?"

"One of Mr. Shaman's circus, I imagine. Have you really forgotten about her? Aren't you at all in love with her still? What would you say if you found her in your bed when you went back to the flat? Would you throw her out?"

Richard laughed for the first time in a long while. "Don't be so wicked. In love with her? No. Attracted by her? Yes. And intrigued by her. If I found her in my bed, I should have a number of questions for that young woman."

"All a wonder and a mild desire."

"Jokes yet!"

"A poor thing but mine own."

"You are in sparkling form." He topped up her glass. "This is quite like old times." He surveyed the room. "I used to think, when I went back to Oxford and saw a pretty girl or a cheerful crowd of young men, that I wished I knew them: and then I realised I did know them—that is, that I'd known others exactly like them. I'd had my share. A lot of these people are familiar, don't you feel, in much that way?"

"Look not for last year's birds in this year's nests. Or is it the other way round? I can never remember."

"I should like this year's birds better if so many of them didn't make the worst of themselves. Look at that girl in the corner. . . ." Richard was perceptibly relaxing, as though some pressure had been relieved, some barrier breached. Was there a line or two on his face which hadn't been there before, Diana wondered, or was that her imagination? His tenseness earlier had frightened her, but now gradually he was becoming himself again.

They talked widely and lightly. Only at the coffee stage did they touch again on the subject which, though temporarily suppressed, was still obtrusive and painful in Richard's mind. Diana had said something about vintage cars, and then stopped abruptly.

"I wonder what we should do about Jeremy's car," said Richard, "and his house indeed. I suppose he made a will."

"Had he any relations?"

"Nobody close that I ever heard of. He seemed somehow complete in himself; I can't imagine him with a family. Gabriel may know who his next-of-kin are. Funny, I never thought of that aspect before. Somebody will have to be informed."

"I'm sure Gabriel thought of it. Gabriel struck me as the kind of man who thinks about most things. Where did Jeremy live, anyway?"

"He had a little house in Notting Hill. He gave dinner parties there sometimes. He was a good cook."

The words "and as good cooks go, he went" rose, unbidden, to her lips: but, shocked by her own levity, she firmly suppressed them: and she eased the conversation back to less hurtful ground as soon as she could. Twenty minutes later they left the restaurant, with Richard happier than at any time since he returned to London. At the travel agency they found Gabriel still sitting by the fire, a block of writing paper on his knees, a drift of documents around his feet.

They drank a nightcap together. Then Diana, after seeing Richard to the door, said good night and went up to bed. Watching her, and thinking what a transformation she had achieved in Richard, Gabriel said to himself: "That's a clever woman."

Over the next few days the situation developed, if at all, invisibly. Richard, accompanied, at Gabriel's insistence, by a minder from the East End who had done occasional jobs for The Fishers, visited his own flat to collect a typewriter and some clothes, but continued to live in the hotel, wandering up St. James's Street to his club for lunch. There was no sign that he was being watched or followed. Diana stayed at the travel agency but went each morning to her gallery, travelling in a minicab whose driver Gabriel knew. Gabriel talked on the telephone to various contacts and received a number of mysterious visitors. The three of them—four, actually, including Maria—dined together or else Richard took Diana out. Neither Richard nor Diana felt inclined yet to pick up the threads of what had been their customary social life.

The Fishers were not, at the moment, operational anywhere. Gabriel had warned all his agents that they might be in danger, and told them to report anything untoward: but there was nothing. Richard asked Gabriel what they should do about Jeremy's possessions.

Gabriel said: "I've got a key to his house. He told me once that, if anything happened to him, we'd find an envelope in his desk. I'm afraid that's a duty I've been postponing. Perhaps you would go?"

"Of course. You know, it's something I never thought of. What would you have done if I hadn't come back?"

"Told your solicitor, after a discreet interval, when I had invented a nice story."

"Do you know who my solicitors are?"

"Oh yes. You probably don't remember, but I asked you a long time ago." He smiled slightly. "I try to be delicate in these matters."

"Diana was right. She said you'd have thought about it."

Richard took Diana with him to Jeremy's house, which was a gentrified artisan's cottage, built in the early years of Queen Victoria's reign. The street was lined with ornamental cherries, from which the blossom had lately fallen. One of the advantages, from Jeremy's point of view, was that the pocket handkerchief-sized garden at the back ended in a wall, through which a door opened on to the street behind. Since the

Fishers had never, until now, been under attack at home, this option had not been needed: but Jeremy was a man who always liked to keep an escape route open.

The familiar, unmistakable old sports car with the leather strap over the bonnet was parked a few yards away from the house. Diana ran her hand lightly across the mudguard as they passed.

Caution having become instinctive, they walked around the block before mounting the two tiled steps to Jeremy's red-painted brass-knockered front door. Opening it with the key Gabriel had given him, Richard led the way into a narrow hall, where there were sticks and an umbrella in a stand and a row of regimental prints on the right-hand wall. To the left a half-open door took them into a miniature drawing room or study, with two armchairs and a fireplace at one end and at the other, overlooking the garden, a leather-topped desk, flanked by book-cases.

"I'd better look in the desk," said Richard. While he opened the drawers, one after another, Diana inspected the books. Military history rubbed shoulders with P.G. Wodehouse and Evelyn Waugh. There were three volumes of *Burke's Landed Gentry, Who's Who, The Oxford Dictionary of Quotations*, a book called *Floreat Etona* . . .

"Here it is," said Richard, holding up a long envelope. "It says in large letters, 'Will' and, underneath, 'For friendly eyes only. To be read if the occasion demands.' So, we read."

Slitting the envelope with a silver paper-knife which lay on the desk, he extracted a single sheet of foolscap and ran his eye down it. He smiled. "The first paragraph says: 'My will is lodged with Worrals and Stone of Gray's Inn Square. I hereby reappoint George Worrals and my accountant, Stanley Hyam, to be my executors. This is a codicil, which I shall ask my excellent cleaning lady, Mrs. Dobbin, and the next person who comes to the door to witness. I don't see why I should pay Worrals and Stone another fifty guineas every time I want to change anything. If I get the wording wrong, no doubt they will earn far more than that in clearing up the mess. But I warn you, George and Stanley, that if you don't implement my wishes, I shall return to haunt you. My wishes are that from my residual estate the following gifts should be made.'"

"Then," Richard explained, "there's a whole succession of paragraphs, each one separately dated and several of them crossed out. The crossed out ones leave gifts to various ladies." He read on, silently, for a moment. "He leaves the books in this house to be shared between Gabriel and me. And he says, 'I leave my walking-sticks and umbrella to Richard Clayburn because, without me, he'll need support and he doesn't always know enough to come in from the rain.' "

Richard paused again, then looked up at Diana. "The final paragraph was written on the day we flew to Africa. It's very short. It just says, 'I leave my motor car to Diana Mackenzie, because she likes it.' "

Diana did something which, in all the years of their acquaintance, he had never seen her do before. She burst into tears.

After quickly touring the rest of the house, to ensure that there were no papers which ought to be removed (but Jeremy was much too careful to have left anything of the sort) and that there was no sign of intruders, they locked up and returned to the travel agency. Richard handed the envelope to Gabriel, who barely glanced at the foolscap page, nodded and put it on the table beside his chair.

"I have news," he said. "You know I've been trying to learn more about Shaman. Our friends have been, as it were, feeling in the dark. Now they've had a catch. Sammy found one of the men who were asking questions about you, Richard, the man who was handing out cash, and he leaned on him a little. Just a little. Enough to make him co-operative without frightening him too much. And he agreed to take a message."

"A message? What kind of message?"

"To Shaman. From me. I said I'd like to arrange a meeting."

"You really think he might come? Why on earth should he?"

"For the same reason that I want to see him. To get his measure. To learn, if I can, something about his organisation."

"And what's the meeting supposed to be for?"

"I didn't say. To ask for a truce maybe. To see if we can buy him off."

"Well, I suppose it could be possible. But I still doubt if he'll come."

"Apparently he will come. At least, that's the message I've got back."

"It'll be a trap."

"For him or for me? Shaman and his colleagues are probably having just the same discussion. The meeting place they have suggested is in the open. But of course you are right. They may still not know who I am, and I don't propose to make them a present of myself. But someone must keep that assignation, don't you think?"

After a moment's pause, Richard said: "Me?"

"You are the obvious person, since they already know you."

"But he's a target," protested Diana. "You said so yourself. And so soon after Africa—"

"I'm all right now," said Richard. "And we can't leave the situation as it is. We must try to flush them out. Otherwise I shall go on being a target. We all shall."

"I don't think there's much risk," said Gabriel. "The message told me to come alone, but they will assume we shall have people watching, just as I assume they will. The place they've chosen is Parliament Hill Fields. Are you familiar with it?"

"Oh, yes," replied Richard. "I once had a girl friend who lived in Highgate. We used to walk there."

"Then you will remember, there is a hill from which children fly kites."

"Not only children. There are more grown-ups, actually."

"On the top of the hill there is apparently a wooden seat. They say we are to approach from the south-east. The time is seven-thirty tomorrow night."

"When it's getting dark."

"And when there won't be many people around. You will have to walk up the hill by yourself, but we shall keep you in sight. I shall keep you in sight. I very much want to see our friend Shaman."

"I'm coming too," said Diana. She expected them to protest, and they did: but she was adamant, and eventually they yielded.

They took two cars. Gabriel and Diana went first in the Daimler, parked in a side street and walked, conversing earnestly together, into Parliament Hill Fields through the gate at the bottom. Two of Sammy's people were supposed already to be in position. There were, indeed, one or two strollers, but the children—or adults—with their kites had gone. It would be difficult to get very close without being noticeable. Gabriel and Diana stayed on the lower paths. They could make out the bench, empty, at the top of the hill. Beyond, the sky glowed with sunset.

Richard, in his own car, arrived a few minutes later. He glanced at his watch; he was exactly on schedule. Entering by the same gate, he headed straight up the hill. At first he made a point of not looking around him, in case, spotting Gabriel and Diana, he should give them away, but then realised that this was an unnatural way to behave and therefore, in itself, revealing. He surveyed the territory. There was a cluster of trees not very far from the brow of the hill, and another off on the right. But there was no undergrowth, really no cover anywhere. He thought he saw Gabriel and Diana beside the children's playground, but he wasn't sure. Darkness was falling quickly now. Sammy's people could be anyone—the jogger who panted past him, the young couple absorbed in each other. Or these could be Shaman's people. The jogger might suddenly turn. The young couple might produce guns. A shot in the back, a silenced pistol . . . He pushed such ideas out of his mind.

A solitary figure appeared at the top of the hill. Richard peered through the dusk. This man wasn't tall, as Shaman was supposed to be, and he had a dog on a lead: and he was walking on, down the hill, past Richard. The brow of the hill was deserted. Shadows filled the hollows to the north and east; here too there were still a few walkers but no one came close.

Richard sat down on the bench. In front of him stretched London, a bowl of lights. He could make out the illumined dome of St. Paul's and the curious shape of the Post Office Tower. He always had thought it a magnificent view. He remembered the days when he used to come here. That was a long time ago, but nothing seemed to have changed. Except him. How straightforward life had seemed then, how safe. How innocent he had been. . . .

Sunk in these memories and meditations, he remained aware that there was nobody approaching along the path from either direction, but failed to hear a footstep on the grass behind him.

"Hello," said Irena.

X

Blaise

He had forgotten quite how pretty she was; romantic and mysterious in the half-light. She wore a swagger coat, with the collar turned up, framing the pale and perfect oval of her face. She sat down beside him.

"Do you know," he said, "these used to be called Traitors' Fields, because it was where Guy Fawkes's fellow-conspirators gathered for the original good view of the fireworks? Eventually the local residents found it embarrassing and changed the name."

"No," she said, "I didn't know that."

"How are you? Are you well?"

"I'm well. Should I start by saying I'm sorry?"

"Not much point. I presume you are the person I'm supposed to meet here tonight?"

"We weren't expecting you particularly."

"I wasn't expecting you. Unless, of course, Shaman is one of your names."

"He sent me. What are we going to talk about?"

For the first time, he turned to her. "I should like to talk about you. We did part rather abruptly."

"Now it's my turn to say there's no point. You know why I'm here. And I should warn you that, if you make any attempt to hold me or take me away by force, you won't leave here alive. There's a rifle pointing at us now."

"With a night-sight and a telescopic lens?"

"Exactly. But you are quite safe if you do nothing foolish. We are under a flag of truce, aren't we? It was you or your friends who wanted to talk."

"Irena, what's this all about?"

"I'm not allowed to answer questions. I'm just a messenger. I have to listen to you, and report what you say."

"What I have to say is a question. What would we have to do in order to get Shaman off our backs?"

"The Fishers would have to stop."

"Stop everywhere?"

"I can't answer that. But you can guess." She smiled. "If you like to smuggle Pakistanis into Britain or Mexicans into the United States, we shan't mind." Then she turned to him, and said earnestly: "Richard, I don't expect you to believe this, but I am fond of you. It wasn't all pretence. If you carry on, you'll be killed. Go away. Take Diana and go on holiday, somewhere far off. I think I can persuade my masters that you're no danger to them, once you've left."

He looked at her curiously. "There was a time when I thought I was getting to know you quite well, but, of course, I wasn't. I do wonder what makes you tick. I suppose you're entitled to say that I wasn't frank with you either. But I hope you know me well enough not really to imagine I could accept your suggestion."

She sighed. "Yes. But you can't beat these people. They are too powerful, they have too many resources. Couldn't I at least tell them that you will avoid"—she hesitated—"politically sensitive matters for a while?"

"Our business is with what you call politically sensitive matters. I seem to remember we talked about Poland once or twice. Was that pretence?"

She didn't reply. They sat in silence. The darkness was now complete. Above the glow of London, and against the emerging pattern of stars, aircraft lights marked a procession of planes descending towards Heathrow.

"I must leave," said Irena, "and you mustn't follow me." She stood up.

"I wish—" began Richard.

"So do I. Please tell Diana I'm sorry."

Richard held out his hand as though to touch or detain her, but she was already walking away across the grass, down the slope to the north into deep shadow. Almost before he realised it, she had disappeared. For a moment he stayed there, fixed by the emotional impact of that strange meeting: but then, recalling that he was on the skyline and that a rifle might be, or had been (at least, so Irena had said), pointing at him, he turned and went back down the hill in the opposite direction.

Two figures emerged from the clump of trees. He stiffened, but recognised them.

"Diana says that was Irena," said Gabriel.

"Yes, it was. Will your men try to follow her?"

"They will try, but they've been told to be very cautious. I'm not sure they were close enough."

"And what did the darling girl have to say?" asked Diana.

"Among other things that I was to tell you she was sorry."

"Did she indeed?"

"I couldn't get anything much from her. I'm not sure what to make of it. She was frightened, I think, or anyway tense, unhappy."

"An agent, not a principal, would you say?" asked Gabriel.

"Definitely. She talked about "these people" and "my masters," and implied they were political."

Diana said: "I was afraid she might have stabbed you with a poisoned umbrella or something."

"To be honest," said Richard, "there was a tiny part of my mind which had the same idea. If she'd made any sudden move . . . But she said we were meeting under a flag of truce."

"When we get back," said Gabriel, "you must try to recall everything *verbatim*. It might give us some clue, something to follow." They emerged from the gate on to the Highgate Road. "Our car is just around that corner. We'll meet at the travel agency, shall we? Or would you prefer to go with Richard?" he said to Diana.

"No, I'll come with you. He can moon about Irena." She said it with a smile but she meant it.

They turned right, while Richard crossed the road towards his car. Something, perhaps the roar of a suddenly accelerating engine, made Diana glance over her shoulder. A big black car, sweeping down the hill, was being aimed at Richard as he was about to step on to the far pavement. Diana screamed. Richard hurled himself forward and, as the car mounted the kerb, half-vaulted half-tumbled over the low wall of a garden. He felt the wind of the car swish past him.

Unhurt except for a bruised knee and scraped hands, he got rather shakily to his feet. A middle-aged couple, who had been only a few yards away, hurried forward to help him.

"Are you all right?" asked the man.

"Whoever was driving that car must have been drunk," said the woman indignantly.

"I expect so," agreed Richard.

"I didn't get the number. Did you, Shirl?" asked the man.

"I'm afraid not," said the woman.

"One never does," said Richard.

"You should report it to the police," she said.

"Won't do any good," said the man. "Did you see what happened?" he asked Gabriel and Diana, who had run across the road.

Gabriel said that he had indeed seen what happened, and the driver must certainly have been drunk, and that there was never a policeman in sight when you wanted one. They all agreed that it was a very shocking thing: and, after mutual assurances of goodwill, the middle-aged couple resumed their walk. Diana helped Richard brush the garden mud from his clothes, while Gabriel inspected the tyre marks on the kerb.

"Did either of you see who was in the car?" he asked.

Diana shook her head. "I didn't really see the car at all," said Richard. "I just heard it."

"A pity," said Gabriel. "You might have recognised him. Not the driver, the man in the back. I got a glimpse. Thin, pale, probably tall."

Nobody spoke the name. Diana said: "Now I will go with Richard. I'll drive."

"I am a bit shaky," he agreed.

On their way back to the travel agency, Diana took a slightly circuitous route, making sure they weren't followed; a precaution which, not so long ago, would have struck her as absurdly melodramatic but now seemed merely sensible. Gabriel was already there to welcome them when they arrived. Maria made a fuss over Richard, bringing a bowl of warm water to sponge his grazed hands and seating him nearest the fire, while Gabriel poured him a very large brandy. Never had that small cluttered room seemed more comforting.

The telephone rang. It was Sammy. One of his men had followed Irena, but had been knocked down from behind as they were about to emerge from the heath on to the road. The other man, who had been positioned some distance away, found him lying on the path. He wasn't seriously hurt, just angry that he should have been taken out so easily.

"Tell him not to mind," said Gabriel. "We are dealing with experts."

Richard then reported, as accurately as possible, everything Irena had said. Maria brought chicken soup. They mulled over the events of the evening, discussing the implications but agreeing, inevitably, that they had learned very little more than had been clear before.

"We were lucky tonight," said Gabriel. "I exposed you to a risk which wasn't worth it for anything we were likely to gain. I shall not repeat that mistake."

"But what can we do now?" asked Diana.

"Starting tomorrow, we put the boot on the other foot. We go hunting."

Everything always takes longer to arrange than one might hope. All that Gabriel was, in fact, able to accomplish on the following day was a number of telephone calls, made while Richard and Diana, both of whom had spent the night at the travel agency, ventured out together on brief expeditions, more cautiously than ever. And he fixed a luncheon appointment for the day after.

Next morning Diana went to her gallery. Richard agreed to hold the fort at the travel agency, where they were hoping to receive a further report from Sammy and perhaps from Jan in South Africa. Gabriel took a taxi to St. James's Street. His engagement was at a club on the other side of the road from Richard's. When he arrived, just before one o'clock, his host was already there, sitting in a leather chair beside the fire in the elegant marble-floored hall.

Sir Arthur Blaise was a slightly built, dapper man, with grey hair immaculately trimmed and shrewd blue eyes. Of course eyes cannot really be shrewd (or, for that matter, blank), but it was the impression they gave because they were part of the man and his alertness was like a crackle of electricity. Only very foolish people underrated him, which had been a disadvantage when he was an agent in the field; he could never be unobtrusive. In the deadlier battles of Whitehall he had provoked jealousy and made enemies, over all of whom he had eventually triumphed. He had now held the top job for longer than any of his predecessors since the war. He knew where a great many bodies were buried; which made him more formidable than ever.

He and Gabriel had occasionally been opponents but never enemies. Sometimes, in practice, they had been allies, when The Fishers had been of help to the service over which Blaise presided: and he, in return, had given them a degree of unofficial protection. Favours are coin of the realm in that shadowy world where their interests met, but the genuine regard in which those two strange men held each other drew more on personal affection than on a lively sense of favours given, received or due.

Although, or perhaps because, he was a servant of government, Blaise shared Gabriel's contempt for governments. "Order is better than anarchy," he would say, "but we needn't carry that platitude too far." What he really believed in was a matter of speculation. Dull people found him intolerable. Gabriel had always enjoyed his company and even, up to a point, trusted him.

After a glass of champagne in the bar, they went through to the coffee room, where the corner table which Blaise preferred had been kept for them. A senior civil servant from the Treasury looked at Blaise over his spectacles with distaste, a younger man from the Foreign Office with curiosity. Neither of them recognised Gabriel.

"Whatever else may have gone wrong with this club," said Blaise, "and a good deal has, the wine committee, surprisingly, has kept quite a good standard. If you'll accept such a modest offering, I'd like you to try the club claret. But where," he asked when soup was brought, "are the silver soup plates we used to have? Do you suppose they've been hocked? Or has our increasingly bourgeois committee been intimidated by Lord Curzon's precept that a gentleman never has soup at luncheon?"

"Why not?" asked Gabriel.

"Why not indeed? Lady Curzon actually had a soup named after her. Perhaps it was the *pièce de résistance* of her dinner table, and she was afraid that her guests' appetite for soup might be slaked prematurely. But, you know, Curzon also said that a gentleman never dined in Pont Street; which is even odder."

"I'd not heard that," said Gabriel. "But I had a young friend called Jeremy Mitchell-Pearce who would have done. He was amused by such things."

"Yes, I know about him. A bad business, apparently."

"Very bad. That's what I wanted to talk to you about."

"So I assumed."

"Does the name Shaman mean anything to you?"

"Something."

"So I assumed. I will tell you, if I may, the story, and then ask for your comments." He did, omitting only some things about The Fishers of which it seemed better that an official, no matter how unorthodox, should not be officially informed. Unofficially he suspected that Blaise already knew a great deal. That, anyway, was always the prudent assumption.

He finished just before the Stilton was produced. "Some believe in slicing," observed Blaise, "others in scooping. But since the scoopers have already been at work, we really have no choice. Slicing must be right, though, don't you think? On geometrical grounds. A smaller surface to get dry. Now that pansy waiter's gone, what would you like me to say?"

"Anything you can about Shaman."

"We've got a big file but with surprisingly little in it. Not much about him, that is: plenty about what he's done. All spoor, no beast. He and his organisation are for hire, but their principal clients are in Moscow and Prague. Not to put too fine a point on it, they do jobs for the KGB. And in return the KGB shelters them. If they're after you, as you seem to think, you've got a problem."

"It's not our first problem," said Gabriel grimly.

"The point is, old friend, to prevent it's being your last."

"Yes, that is indeed the point, and I'm hoping you may be able to help us."

"How? And for that matter why? Personally of course I'd like to help, but there is a limit to how far I can involve my people in a private, not to say illicit, affair."

"You've just told me that Shaman works for the KGB. Doesn't that make him, or them, a legitimate target?"

"Good heavens, no! Do you remember, at the beginning of the battle of Waterloo, a young officer rushed up to Wellington in a state of great excitement. 'Sir,' he said, 'Bonaparte has come on to the field. Shall we fire at him?' 'Certainly not,' replied Wellington. 'General officers have better things to do than to shoot at each other.' The same applies to intelligence organisations."

"I've never understood that anecdote," replied Gabriel. "If they had killed Bonaparte, the battle would surely have been over before it began. A very worthwhile shot."

Blaise smiled; a smile which had been described as making him look like a crocodile. "That's true. But you can't knock Shaman out, let alone the KGB. Nor can I."

"Of course I can't. But we're a very small thorn in the KGB's side, and Shaman does jobs for pay. If we hit back hard enough, we might be able to make a deal—at least for the moment, here in London anyway. And you wouldn't mind if they withdrew with a bloody nose, would you? Wouldn't that be quite a proper bit of work for your people?"

"Since you ask, no; not if it involves protecting your people. But a touch of impropriety might be feasible. What do you want?"

"Nothing that need embarrass you. Not at this stage. I want you to—"

Blaise checked him with a gesture, hand as slim and elegant as a violinist's. "I think I'm going to need fortification. Let's go and have port in the library."

In green leather chairs, flanked by ancient unread volumes of historical biography, with coffee and port in front of them on a small mahogany table, they talked for a while. The mandarins had gone back to Whitehall, the stockbrokers to the City. They were alone in the big shadowy room.

"I'm doing this," Blaise said finally, "against my better judgement."

"Why?" replied Gabriel. "It's a very slight involvement."

"I don't really give a hang about that. But I ought to be dissuading you from getting into a war you can't win, not conniving at it."

"I'm in the war. I've been in a war for as long as I can remember. I'm old; what does it matter? It's the young ones I must try to save."

"I'd be sorry to lose you."

"Would you? You're not telling me you have a conscience, I hope, or qualms?"

"Of course not," said Blaise. "Silly idea."

Gabriel didn't tell Richard and Diana what he had arranged until, three days later, he received a telephone call from Blaise. Then he asked them into his room. "We're ready to make a move," he said.

"That's a relief," said Richard. "I'm tired of waiting for the opposition to move against us. It's not comfortable."

"I've sent another message to Shaman. But not from me this time. From another source, which I think he'll believe. His KGB friends are being told that we—The Fishers—have an important contact in one of the East European embassies here who is helping us to arrange escapes from behind the Iron Curtain. No names, but they will be told when and where we shall next meet this person. They can hardly ignore such information, coming to them from such a source: and, since Shaman is already their instrument for stopping us, it seems probable that they will use Shaman again for the purpose. So Shaman's men will come to the rendezvous."

"Yes," agreed Richard, "I take your argument. But in the circumstances they could very well suspect a trap."

"Maybe, but they will still have to come. They can't be sure it's a trap, and therefore they cannot ignore the chance of identifying a traitor. My men will be watching for them. We lost them the other day, but this time I am choosing the place. We shall not lose them again."

"You mean you're going to have them followed, or what?" asked Diana.

"Yes. Followed. In the hope that they will lead us to Shaman. Of course, if Shaman himself were to be there, as he was in Highgate—"

"—and at my flat," said Diana.

"Exactly. If he were to come, then so much the better. We would try to take him. But I doubt if he will. It's possible that those who do come will not be content simply to observe the rendezvous; in which case we shall, of course, have to defend ourselves. But, again, I doubt if that will occur."

"Is there really going to be a rendezvous?" asked Richard. "I mean, is there going to be someone they're supposed to think is the traitor?"

"I've been wondering about that. But probably yes, we should play out the scene that far. It will make it easier for us to discern the watchers. There shouldn't be much risk."

Diana said: "Are we allowed to know what this mysterious source is that you expect them to find so credible?"

"I'd rather you didn't ask. It's what you might call semi-official. But they're going to think they've learned about this rendezvous themselves, through their own agents. I've often noticed that people tend to believe what they've discovered with difficulty or by clandestine methods. Because you've tapped a telephone, or even listened at a keyhole, you give more credence to what you've overheard than you would to something you heard normally. It's a fallacy but it happens. I hope it will happen on this occasion."

"And who's going to be at the rendezvous?" asked Richard dryly. "On our side, that is?"

"I hoped you might be."

"I had a feeling that was what you had in mind. Where and when?"

"When? The day after tomorrow. Twelve noon. Better in daylight. Safer and less chance that they'll give us the slip. Where? Somewhere plausible, somewhere not too isolated but not too busy either. Jeremy's house."

"That's a bit macabre," said Diana.

"Does it strike you so? It seemed to me—suitable, poetic vengeance."

"All right," she said firmly. "We'll be there."

Richard looked at Gabriel and shrugged.

Soft rain emphasised the green of the little gardens. A young woman in a blue raincoat was pushing a pram, while a toddler, waterproofed like Christopher Robin, dawdled behind. Innocent, surely. A milkman was loading empties on to a float. Suspicious. In the window of a house on the opposite side of the street Diana thought she saw a lace curtain twitch. This complex of half a dozen small streets made a curiously private world. Visible at the end of the road, barely two hundred yards away, an incessant stream of traffic, red buses, black taxis, messengers' motorcycles weaving in and out, flowed past, but here, in this domestic backwater, the noise and the bustle seemed remote. This was a place where people lived—ordinary quiet lives, most of them. At least, that's what one assumed. But perhaps very few lives would seem quiet and ordinary if one really knew about them, knew about the seething emotions hardly contained, the burning hopes, the nagging fears, the daily hairbreadth escapes from disaster, the infinite variety of dramas being played out, with death as the inevitable end, behind each of those respectable front doors.

Who, after all, could have guessed the stories which began, or the scene which was being set now, behind the red door of Jeremy's house, with the sports car still standing near? Well, maybe that car offered a clue. It was a car for romantics, a car for adventures. Diana, always more given to daydreaming, to elaborate interior monologues, than her friends guessed, let these thoughts blur the hard edge of what they were doing. She mustn't be seen peering around, trying to spot Shaman's men or Gabriel's men—or, of course, they might be women. But not accompanied by a toddler. On the other hand, that very reaction showed what good cover a small child would make.

As Richard mounted the two steps and put his key in the door, she permitted herself a quick glance round. She knew the watchers were there, Gabriel's certainly, Shaman's perhaps, and others must be watching the garden door to the street behind, but nothing remarkable caught her eye. Someone in a parked car perhaps? Those two women with shopping baskets, gossiping at the corner?

The hall smelled a little musty. The damp was encroaching on a home which had lost its occupant. They went into the drawing room.

"Might as well be comfortable," said Richard, and lit what she had taken, on their previous visit, to be smokeless fuel ready in the grate but now realised were ceramic imitations in a free-flowing gas fire. Crossing to the window at the back of the room, he carefully inspected the dripping shrubs in the garden. "I'd better just check through the house," he said. "You wait here."

He was still wearing his overcoat. When he left the room, his right hand was in the pocket. Diana knew it contained the revolver which Gabriel had given him before they set out. She looked at her watch. Quarter to twelve. The house seemed oppressively silent. She couldn't even hear Richard's footsteps on the carpeted stairs. She shivered and moved closer to the fire, which was beginning to give out a cheerful warmth. Piled on a low table in front of it were several copies of *Country Life*, a handsome book called *The Gentlemen's Clubs of London* and another on the Scottish clans. She was just turning, in the latter, to "Mackenzie" when Richard came back.

"Everything seems all right," he said. "No sign that anyone's been here since we were. And no one hiding in the cupboards." He removed his overcoat and threw it across the chair in front of Jeremy's desk, having first taken the revolver from the pocket and laid it on top of *The Gentlemen's Clubs of London*. He peered out of the back window, then walked across the room to the front and gazed out of that window. "We're not overlooked," he said, "not directly. Someone with binoculars in either of the two houses opposite could see slantwise through this window but they wouldn't see where you are. At the back there's a convenient tree blocking the view."

"You don't suppose this room could be bugged?" asked Diana.

"Yes. We did suppose that very thing. One of Gabriel's men came before dawn and swept it. The house has been under observation since then."

"Gabriel doesn't miss a trick, does he?"

"Not many."

An ormolu clock on the chimney piece, after a preliminary whirr, began striking twelve. At the same moment, they heard a car outside, stopping, a door slamming.

Richard, still at the window, stiffened. "Oh my God!" he said.

Diana heard a key being inserted in the front door.

XI

"An Awfully Big Adventure"

"What is it?" asked Diana urgently, but Richard didn't answer. "Who is it?" she said. She heard the front door close and a slow footstep in the hall. Outside, she was vaguely aware, the car drove off. The person in the hall paused, perhaps—from the sound—putting something on the floor. Diana glimpsed a movement past the half-open door, and literally held her breath. Richard had turned from the window.

"Ooh, guesties!" said Jeremy. "Do you know that cartoon? It's by Thurber. I'm sorry; did I startle you? You rather startled me. I didn't know who might be lurking."

He didn't look exactly his old spry self. He was leaning on a stick, and his head was bandaged: but the familiar smile hadn't changed. Richard, having had a few moments longer than Diana to accept the appearance of this *revenant*, was trying to shake his hand and to support him and to greet him all at once. Diana simply found no words. She sat down again abruptly.

Jeremy eased himself into the chair opposite her, stretching his left leg out stiffly. "I'm sorry," he repeated. "I should have warned you. But there were reasons." He glanced at the desk. "I suppose you found that envelope. I'm afraid you'll have to wait a while for Bertha," he said to Diana.

"Who's Bertha?" she said in a small voice.

"My car. The trusty steed. I was glad to see she's still there; no one's pinched her."

"Oh, Jeremy . . ." she began, but was again lost for words.

"Is it too early for a drink? Richard, I'm not very mobile. You know where the booze is kept—unless you two have drunk it all."

"This is wonderful," said Richard, "and there's so much we want to

know. But, first, I must tell you. You've walked into the middle of"—
he hesitated—"a situation."

"Ah. Yes." Jeremy leaned forward and, with his forefinger, delicately
touched the revolver lying on the book in front of him. "So I now see."

Before Richard could explain further, the doorbell rang.

"More guesties," said Jeremy. "Don't mind me. Just carry on with
whatever you were doing."

Richard picked up the revolver and went out into the hall. Jeremy
looked questioningly at Diana, but neither of them spoke. They heard
the front door open and close again. There was a murmur of voices. A
pause.

Then into the room, ahead of Richard, came a surprising figure;
heavily muffled, in a raincoat, gleaming wet, with the collar turned up;
a scarf to cover the lower part of his face; dark glasses; and a squashy
brown hat, tilted forwards.

Jeremy stared, then burst out laughing. "Who are you supposed to
be? Michelin Man?"

Gabriel took off the hat and glasses. "All that matters," he said with
a touch of irritation, "is who I'm not supposed to be. Which is me.
From a distance. But, my dear boy, I am so happy."

They all began talking simultaneously, and broke off in laughter.
"How about those drinks now?" asked Jeremy. "Or doesn't this mysterious situation allow for such frivolity?"

"Oh, yes," said Gabriel. "We must wait a bit anyway."

"You shouldn't have come yourself," said Richard, as he opened a
cupboard well stocked with bottles.

"Who else am I going to send—to maybe get shot at? You weren't
available."

"But Jeremy's right. You're not altogether a plausible figure."

Gabriel shrugged. "If our friends are outside, they'll follow me anyway."

"Or perhaps just photograph you."

"Perhaps. If they identify me afterwards, what of it? They know who
I am. I was foolish to think they might not."

"By 'our friends,' " said Jeremy, "I take you to mean our enemies."

"Just so," said Richard, putting whisky in front of him and sherry in
front of Diana.

"The first thing I should tell you," said Jeremy, "is why I didn't let you know I was still in the land of the living. Jan Van der Bruin put Mrs. Villiers through the wringer. But properly. For hours on end. And he came to the conclusion that it wasn't she who betrayed us. So, if not her, who?"

No one proffered an answer.

"Maybe someone in South Africa. But maybe not. Maybe someone this end. If so, I felt it might be safer just to pop up. A stealthy return. But I didn't expect all this to be happening in the old homestead."

"That is worrying," agreed Gabriel. "But I think we'd better do some catching up all round." He sat down in the chair by the desk. Richard, having completed his ministrations, resumed his post beside the window, watching the street.

"Jeremy, your turn first," said Gabriel. "What really happened to you? We thought you'd been killed."

Diana intervened: "Do you feel up to talking now? Are you really all right?"

"All right's a relative term. But yes, Diana, I'm up to talking—and whatever else may be necessary. Nice of you, though, to ask." He turned to Gabriel. "My story won't take long. Richard, I imagine, will have told you everything up to the time he left."

"I shouldn't have gone," said Richard.

"Don't be an ass. You were needed on the boat. Anyway it wouldn't have helped for you to stay. Luke and I had scarcely got back to the path up the cliff when the opposition started swarming down. My idea had been that we could find cover among the rocks and try to hold them off as long as possible. But we never got that far. Truth to tell, I don't remember exactly what happened. I think I fired a burst before I was hit. And Luke was firing beside me. Then I can remember lying on my face in the sand. I remember the grit against my cheek and in my mouth. I couldn't move but I was in no pain."

He smiled. Not at his friends in the room, though. He's far away, thought Diana.

"Do you know what ran through my mind? That corny old line from *Peter Pan.* "To die will be an awfully big adventure." I wonder what the psychologists would make of that. There was a lot of noise. I was vaguely aware of it, but it all sort of merged into a roaring and a blackness." He paused. "Strange experience. Not frightening.

"When I came to, it was daylight and I was wrapped in a blanket.

There were a lot of black men around—with guns but they weren't threatening me. In fact they weren't paying any attention to me. I had a frightful headache. The rest of me felt numb. I was looking up into an absolutely clear blue sky. There were birds wheeling round. Then this chap came and knelt beside me. Black, of course. In a bush shirt and camouflage trousers. He spoke to me. I didn't think it was a Bantu language but I couldn't understand it. Actually I suppose it was Portuguese. I managed to say 'English' and he tried again. He did speak some English. Not a lot but enough. Pointing to himself, he said 'Doctor.' While he was examining my wounds, I must have passed out again.

"Next time I was feeling better. A woman brought me water and a kind of soup to drink. She didn't say anything; just grinned when I spoke to her. The doctor came back and with him another man, who turned out to be the officer in charge. He spoke rather good English. Well, the long and the short of it was that these chaps were UNITA, some sort of raiding party. They'd been approaching the village when they heard firing. While we were heading for the beach, they must have been coming up from the far side. After we'd had our go, they had theirs. By the time they got down to the beach, I dare say the *Blue Heron* was long out of sight and earshot. Anyway, they found me: and, since I was white and still alive, they were curious enough to carry me up the path and get their doctor to have a look at me."

"Only you?" asked Richard. "Luke? Any of the others?"

"I'm afraid not. I enquired. As for me, it turned out I wasn't really hurt very badly. A bullet through the fleshy part of my thigh and another which just creased me along the forehead. And some bruises. I was very lucky. Except, d'you know, there's a passage in one of Rider Haggard's novels I've been thinking about. Old Alan Quatermain's meditating on all that's happened to him over the years, and he says that he may not have made much money or achieved much but at least he's still alive when a lot of his friends are dead. On the other hand, he says, since he doesn't know whether it's better to be alive or dead, he can't even be sure if that's a good thing. I tell you, coming as near as I did, makes one quite philosophical."

"Be philosophical. Don't think about it," murmured Richard.

Jeremy laughed. "Sorry. After that, though, I really was lucky. Those UNITA chaps might have kept me with them for weeks or months, because they wanted a hostage or for propaganda purposes or just because there was nothing else to do with me. I've read about people who were captured by UNITA being made to march through the bush for hundreds of miles. Not that I was in any shape to march and I don't suppose they wanted to carry me. Anyway, the officer told me they had a man going south next day. I didn't really know what he meant, but I was in their hands; I just relaxed and enjoyed it—more or less. They did carry me for a few hours' march, until we came to a dirt road. We waited, and along came a battered old truck. They shoved me in the back, among a lot of sacks full of heaven knows what. One of them got in front with the driver and away we tooled. I've had more comfortable journeys. But I was still being philosophical. They fed me and watered me. Nobody stopped us, no Cubans, no Angolans. I'm not sure how long it took. I was fairly muzzy. Eventually we met a group of soldiers who weren't Angolan. They were South African, and they were expecting us. Don't ask me why. Our man talked to their man. He was called Hendricks, Captain Hendricks. He introduced himself to me, and said he'd take me with them. Which he did. And that's about it. We got back to South-West, to an army base. I was grilled by an intelligence officer and patched up by the doctor, and then they let me go. I hitched a lift in an army plane, down to Walvis Bay. I called Jan from there."

They had been listening, absorbed. Jeremy said: "Well, don't look so serious. This should be fatted calf time. How about some more dispensing from that bottle, Richard? Then I want to know how come I have the pleasure of this jolly party in my house."

"Oh yes," said Diana. "Any fatted calves you want."

"I'd better explain why we're here," said Gabriel. "We could still be interrupted."

"There's no sign of anything, or anyone, in the street," said Richard, glancing through the window again.

Succinctly Gabriel marshalled the events of the past few days, ending with the point of the present exercise. He looked at the clock, which had stopped because it hadn't been wound; then drew a heavy fob-watch from his waistcoat pocket. "I've been here almost long enough," he said. "Perhaps another five minutes."

"Of course," said Jeremy, "if anyone is watching, they'll have seen me. Pity. I was rather hoping to slip back unobserved."

"You really don't think you'll have been spotted in Johannesburg?" asked Richard. "The opposition aren't tagging Jan?"

"Who knows? But, if so, he hasn't had a scent of them. Incidentally, the American we rescued—Ben Smith—I saw something of him in Johannesburg. He struck me as a pretty good man. We could use him."

"If The Fishers survive," said Gabriel. "This is hardly a time for anyone to join us."

"Come, come. That isn't like you. We've coped with worse problems before. Well, we've coped with problems before. Don't you have much faith in this interesting charade?"

"It's not a question of faith. Until we can get something tangible to work on, we're groping in the mist. A one-way mist. We can't see them but apparently they can see us."

"Now you're back," said Diana to Jeremy, "we're reinforced. I'm sure you'll think of all kinds of moves we can make. I've great faith in you."

Richard felt just a touch, the merest pinprick, of irritation; which he immediately suppressed.

"I'd better go now," said Gabriel, rising. "I want you all to stay here until Sammy calls. He will tell you if his men have spotted anybody and if the coast seems clear outside. Then they will make sure that you leave safely. Jeremy, perhaps you too should come and stay with me for a while."

"Into the Land of Cockaigne? I don't think so. I'd rather stay loose. But you're the one we've got to worry about today. You be careful."

"I shall be all right. Sammy's men are close." He resumed his dark glasses and hat, and turned up the collar of his coat. "Don't come to the door," he said to Richard, who had made a move to follow him. "So, I make my entrance on to the stage again. Do I look mysterious?"

The front door clicked behind him. Richard watched, from beside the window, until Gabriel was out of sight. "Still no one visible," he said. "There's a woman with one of those shopping-baskets on wheels that you push, but she's coming down the street, not the way Gabriel went. Yes, she's passed."

"A shopping-basket," observed Jeremy lightly. "Handy for carrying bombs."

"Don't," said Diana. "There really could be a bomb. I hadn't thought of that."

Jeremy leaned towards her with sudden concern. "You mustn't start imagining disasters. Hark to the voice of experience. In this game you have to do two things at once. You have to be alert to all the possibilities but you mustn't keep dwelling on them. You need them at the back of your mind, not the front. You may think that's impossible but I promise you it isn't."

"I'll try."

Richard looked at them looking at each other. For the next few minutes they all talked desultorily. They should have had much to talk about, but for some reason the conversation was sticky. And the fire, though glowing cheerfully, seemed unable to disperse the chill of a house which had stood empty for a month.

The telephone rang, making Diana jump. Jeremy put out his hand towards it but stopped. "No, you'd better." Richard picked up the receiver, said, "Yes . . . Yes . . . I see," and replaced it.

"That was Sammy," he confirmed. "No one followed Gabriel. He's sure of that. And he's practically sure there's no one watching the house."

"I don't know whether to be relieved or disappointed," said Diana.

"The question is why they didn't take the bait," mused Jeremy. "However. What about lunch? I suppose there's nothing in the fridge but there should be some tins."

"Shall I go and look?" suggested Diana.

"I think I won't stay," said Richard. "I'm going round to my flat. I want to see if there's any mail and I'd like to change into another suit."

"But is it safe?" Diana asked.

"I can't keep away for ever. And I've got this." He picked up the revolver and put it in his overcoat pocket. "We'd better rendezvous at the travel agency and see what Gabriel wants to do now. Six o'clock?"

Outside it was still drizzling. He glanced around, wondering if Sammy's men were indeed keeping an eye on them—and if anyone else was. But he felt now a certain fatalistic recklessness. He thought of Diana and Jeremy preparing lunch in the small kitchen. Perhaps he should have stayed. Why hadn't he? He shook those thoughts out of his head.

His car was parked two streets away, further up the hill. He made a rapid inspection, which had become routine, to satisfy himself there were no traces of interference, no visible signs of a bomb. He knew that the moment of ignition was not, as it seems to be on television, the only moment of danger; bombs can be set to explode when the car goes round a corner or up or down a slope. Perhaps they ought not to be using their own cars at all. Taxis would be safer. He turned into Kensington Church Street and relaxed.

He left the car again just off Belgrave Square, not too near his flat, having already driven past the door for a quick survey of the street. He walked back, glancing into parked cars and down side streets, aware of his own awareness. He let himself into the house and walked up the two flights of carpeted stairs to his flat. He unlocked the door with his left hand; his right hand in his pocket, holding the gun.

On the table in the sitting room were a stack of newspapers and a pile of letters, neatly arrayed by Mrs. Murphy, who was quite used to his absences. Everything seemed all right. He sighed, and started to unbutton his overcoat. Then he stiffened. He had heard something. A movement. Running water. He drew the pistol, thumbing off the safety catch.

Could it be Mrs. Murphy? Possible but not likely. She was supposed to come only for two hours and was generally gone soon after midday. With no one to gossip to and no clearing up after the night before, she would probably have left earlier rather than stayed longer.

He moved quickly and quietly to the far door, which led to his bedroom and, through it, to the bathroom. The door was slightly ajar. There could be no doubt; somebody was in the bathroom.

Richard eased the door fully open. The first thing he noticed was that the bed had been slept in. The bathroom door was open too. Three strides took him past the end of the bed to a point from which he could see into the bathroom. His gun was ready, his finger on the trigger.

He lowered it. "This is a day of surprises," he said.

Irena wore a translucent dressing gown, if that was the word, over oyster-coloured silk pyjamas. She was drying her face with a hand-towel. She smiled at him. "Hello again," she said.

"How did you get in?" he asked.

"That was one of the things they taught me."

"You slept here?"

"Yes. For two nights."

"Didn't you meet my cleaning woman, Mrs. Murphy?"

"She was very nice. I told her you had invited me to stay and given me a key. She didn't seem too surprised."

"And may I ask why? Did you just decide to take up where we left off?"

Irena carefully folded the towel and hung it on the rail. "Must we talk about it in the bathroom?"

"No, no. Be my guest. Apparently you are my guest. I hope I've no other uninvited guests. In the kitchen perhaps?" He backed towards the door. "Or if they aren't here now, are we expecting any of your friends?"

"You needn't worry about that," said Irena. "I came here to get away from them."

Richard checked the kitchen. It was empty. "Why here?" he asked.

"Where else could I go? I had very little money. I thought this was not a place they would look for me. Besides, I wanted to see you, and I knew that you would come back here sooner or later."

"Have you had lunch?" He inspected her costume. "Or indeed breakfast?"

"Only coffee."

"Nor have I. Let's see what there is. Mrs. Murphy generally keeps me provided."

They found pâté and cold chicken and cheese, and, while Irena took food into the living room, Richard opened a bottle of Gewürztraminer.

"I'm afraid it's not chilled," he said, "but unexpected guests have to put up with these little privations."

He looked at her quizzically, and let the silence draw out. She was wearing no make-up, but the effect, combined with her pyjamas, made her, or so he thought, even more attractive; perhaps because it recalled the last time they had been together in this flat. She seemed more confident too, less unhappy than when they had sat, in the gathering darkness, on that bench in Parliament Hill Fields. He knew she was an enemy, that he must be wary of her. It occurred to him that he shouldn't let her near the gun in the pocket of his overcoat, which was now lying across the back of the sofa. She might have a weapon of her own—but not, at the moment, on her. It was going to be very hard to treat her as an enemy.

He chuckled. She responded hesitantly. "They told me," she said, "before I was to meet you the other day, that you would not be hurt unless you tried to detain me. But I heard afterwards that Shaman nearly killed you. I think that's what decided me. Anyway I did decide, that evening; I was going to leave them, the first chance I got."

"For my sake?" Richard asked incredulously.

"No, though I felt I had been a traitor to you and I didn't want to be a traitor to you. It was for my sake and for someone else's. I believe, I hope, that you and Dr. Gabriel can help me."

"Do you now? And why should we?"

"Oh, I'll pay a price. When I was acting as their messenger, I couldn't make a deal. Maybe on my own I can."

"What kind of price?"

"I want you to take me to Dr. Gabriel. I'll explain to you both then."

Richard was serious now. "How can I possibly trust you?"

"You don't have to. I'm in your hands. You make all the arrangements."

Silence fell between them again. Richard thought hard. What Irena was suggesting oddly matched what Gabriel had said the day before. Gabriel's theory had been that, given a suitable bait, Shaman's men would have to take it, thereby unwinding a thread which would lead to Shaman. Now here was a bait being offered which might lead Shaman to Gabriel. But Shaman's men had apparently not taken Gabriel's bait. Ought Richard similarly to back away? But he couldn't, could he? This was not an opportunity he could simply reject or that Gabriel would want him to reject. Nor, truth to tell, did Richard want to. Playing another game with Irena would be dangerous: but it was irresistible.

"Can't you tell me any more now?" he asked. "I need something to go on."

"Perhaps later. I'd better get dressed."

"I'm not letting you out of my sight," he said. "At least not until I've searched that case I saw in the bedroom and your handbag. Sorry."

"Again you don't have to. Let me out of your sight, I mean. You can search whatever you want."

They returned to the bedroom. Irena's handbag was on the dressing table. Richard glanced through it, opened the powder compact, removed the top from the lipstick, but found nothing unusual. Clicking open the smart little maroon suitcase, he ruffled through underwear and tights and handkerchiefs; again nothing unusual. Irena watched him. As he looked up at her, she slipped off the filmy dressing gown and untied the sash of her pyjamas.

"I," said Richard, "am a bloody fool."

He took her in his arms. She made no objection.

Half an hour later they were lying beside each other in bed, his hand resting lightly on her thigh. "I didn't come here for this," she said. "I really didn't. But I'm glad it happened."

"So am I," he said. "I should ring Gabriel."

"Yes." She turned to him, her face—her perfect face—close to his. "Please, Richard, please don't think that this was—well, part of the price. Let me give you something that is."

"No need. Not now."

"I want to. I want to commit myself. And you said you needed something to go on, something to convince Dr. Gabriel. Suppose I tell you that there's someone in your organisation, someone from whom Shaman has learned your plans."

"You wouldn't surprise me."

"You know who it is?"

"Are you going to tell me?"

She told him.

XII

Betrayal

Better not to phone, they thought; so they drove to the travel agency.
"Are you worried about being seen?" Richard asked. "Shaman may be
having it watched."

"He's not," replied Irena. "At least, he wasn't, and he's no reason to
suppose I'd be going there."

The run-down street, as usual, was almost deserted. The shop door
pinged as they entered. Lounging behind the counter, reading a girlie
magazine, was a cheerful young man called Bert, who knew, of course,
that something other than travel business went on in the back premises
but had been brought up not to ask questions; a good habit which
Gabriel reinforced with the occasional five-pound note—and hints of
minor criminality. He grinned at Richard, winked at Irena and waved
them through to the inner door.

Richard knocked. The door was opened by Maria, who looked curiously at Irena but made no comment. Gabriel sat by the fire with a cup
of coffee beside him. He seemed tired, Richard thought; deflated perhaps by the failure of his manoeuvre that morning.

"Allow me to introduce Irena Janocki," Richard said.

"Ah . . ." As though life were surging back into him, Gabriel rose
to his feet, pushing himself up from the arms of the chair. "No wonder
Richard was enchanted by you. What message does the emissary
bring?"

"I'm not an emissary. What I have to say, Dr. Gabriel, is on my own
behalf."

"Indeed? Sit down. Maria, coffee for our guest."

"I should speak to you alone."

"I'm not sure that would be wise. You may say anything in front of Maria. And I'm sure you don't mind Richard."

Richard started to speak but Irena cut in. "Very well. That woman— Maria Konig—has betrayed you." The abruptness of it was shattering.

Gabriel might have protested, but inevitably he looked at Maria. So did Richard. Irena kept her eyes on Gabriel. What might otherwise have been incredible was now impossible to disbelieve. Maria had gone white; she swayed a little; her hand was over her mouth.

"Maria?" said Gabriel. The shock in his voice held pain as well as astonishment.

She turned and ran from the room. Richard moved half-heartedly but she was already out of the door; not the door to the shop but the door to the stairs leading up to the bedrooms. "Shall I get her?" he asked.

"No." Gabriel sank back into his chair. "Miss Janocki, please tell me what you know about Maria." He was appealing to her.

"It's quite simple. Our job was to find out about your organisation and destroy it. We knew certain things. We knew your name. And someone had noticed that Cockney Travel made the arrangements for several people we thought were connected with The Fishers. One of them—we thought the most important one—was Richard. My orders were to"—she hesitated for a moment but then continued firmly—"to seduce him. I was to confirm his part in The Fishers' organisation and learn whatever else I could through him. I may say I learned nothing through him. At the same time one of my colleagues paid similar attention to the woman who worked here at the offices of Cockney Travel, Maria Konig. He had more success."

"Poor child," said Gabriel. He got wearily to his feet again. "I'd better go to her." At the door he paused. "What was the man's name?"

"Kuzov. But she knew him as Georges Marchand. She believes he's French."

Gabriel went slowly upstairs. Richard said: "How much did she tell?"

"Kuzov had to be careful. She would have told nothing if she had felt she was being questioned. But she was less cautious than you. She was in love."

"I had no idea there was a man in her life. She didn't seem the type."

"Oh, Richard, do you imagine that, because she's quiet and shy and not very pretty, she's immune? What sort of women do you suppose read all the magazines and the paperback romances?"

"I wonder if she mentioned him to Gabriel. Probably not; he'd have been suspicious."

"You mean he wouldn't have believed anyone could be genuinely in love with her? As he said, poor child."

They were interrupted by a shout from upstairs, from Gabriel: "Come quick. I need you."

Racing upstairs, Richard pulled the gun from his pocket: but he found Gabriel facing a closed door. "We must break it down," said Gabriel. "She cried out."

Richard hurled himself at the door, which proved quite flimsy. There was a splintering of wood round the upper hinge. He kicked hard beside the lower one, and the door swung inwards. They pushed their way through.

Maria lay on the bed. She was still conscious but there was a great deal of blood. She had cut her wrist with a pair of nail scissors.

Twenty minutes later Richard and Irena waited downstairs. The blood had been staunched and Maria's wrist bandaged. While Gabriel attended to her, Irena found clean sheets. Maria moaned and then tried to speak, but Gabriel wouldn't let her. When she had been put into the bed and made as comfortable as possible, Gabriel had asked to be left alone with her.

"One more casualty," said Richard.

"I'm sorry," said Irena.

"Do you know just how much information she passed on?"

"Not really. Of course she told Kuzov you were going to Africa, or perhaps not even that exactly, but enough for Shaman to guess what was being done there and to arrange for a trap."

"And I suppose she warned him about this morning's bright idea."

Irena shrugged. "I wouldn't know about that. I'd left by then."

"Did you get away quite easily? No minders watching you?"

"Why should there be? I've been working on my own for months. Besides, they knew they had a hold on me."

"But not a strong enough hold, it seems."

Gabriel reappeared but only for a minute; he came to fetch, from an ancient depository of medical equipment in a drawer of the desk, a hypodermic syringe and a dose of some drug with which to ensure that Maria slept. "That will be best for her," he said, "and safest."

"We really need to ask her some questions," said Richard.

"Later. I've been able to talk with her a little. She won't speak of this man or how we could find him. But anything else—to undo the damage she's caused—I think she will. Later, though."

Gabriel was still with Maria when there came another knock at the door. Having glanced through the peephole, Richard opened it. Diana and Jeremy came in, exuberantly as though they'd been to a party; they had evidently enjoyed their afternoon together. But the sight of Irena pulled Diana up sharply. Jeremy, who had never seen Irena before, caught a sense of electricity between the two women and looked at Richard for an explanation.

"I'm glad you're here," said Richard. "Something rather shocking's happened." And he recounted, briefly, the events of the afternoon.

"Now that is a surprise," said Jeremy. "It needs thinking about."

"I'm afraid it's hit Gabriel hard. Maria was the daughter of his closest friend. I believe she's lived with him since she was a child."

"But she kept her lover secret," said Diana. "I've talked to her quite a lot these past few weeks, and she never gave me a hint. I can imagine. She hugged the secret to herself at first, and then began to be afraid."

"She didn't realise what she was doing," said Richard. "It was pillow talk."

"I bet she'd come to realise it," said Jeremy. "One does—when it's too late."

"Kuzov is very good at his job," put in Irena. "He enjoys his work."

"What an awful business," said Diana. "Awful for Maria and for Dr. Gabriel."

There was a tread on the stair, and Gabriel entered. Barely nodding at Jeremy and Diana, he crossed the room and sank heavily into his chair. "She's sleeping," he said. "She'll be all right."

"Is there anything I can do?" asked Diana. "Should I sit with her?"

"Not necessary." And then, to himself: "Betrayal upon betrayal. How our sins return."

"It wasn't a conscious betrayal," said Richard.

"Conscious?" Gabriel said almost angrily. "What is conscious? Max Konig was betrayed."

"I know she was his daughter, but—"

"She wasn't." Gabriel looked up at him, with pain stamped on his face. "Maria isn't Max Konig's daughter. She's mine. I betrayed him."

Richard was at a loss for words. No one spoke. Gabriel continued, still talking more to himself than to the others in the room. "I loved Max's wife. At least I slept with her. She told me she was going to have a child. And at just that time there was a mission. We knew it was dangerous. Max went, and he never came back. Did I send him? Did I persuade him to go? I didn't dissuade him. I didn't go instead. I was King David and he was Uriah the Hittite. Or so I thought. I swear to God I'm not sure."

"Maria's mother?" asked Richard gently. "What became of her?"

"She died. When Maria was born."

"Does Maria know?"

Gabriel shook his head. "No. I brought her up as a daughter, but I told her about Max; what a fine man he was; and that she should be proud of him."

Diana came and sat on the stool at Gabriel's feet, put a hand on his knee. "Maria loves you," she said. "That's why she tried to kill herself. What happened isn't her fault."

"Fault? Who am I to say what is anyone's fault? Except mine. The serpent tempted me and I did eat. But so long ago."

"What we have to do now," said Jeremy, "is deal with the serpent who tempted Maria. Miss Janocki, how can you help us?"

"I can help you. But I don't think we should stay here. This place was safe because of Maria. Shaman wouldn't risk his most valuable source of information, but once he knows that Maria is blown he may come. Remember how quick he was to attack you, Richard, when he learned for sure that you were one of those he wanted."

"That's probably true," said Jeremy. "And I suppose Shadowlawn won't be safe either. Do you know about Shadowlawn, Miss Janocki?"

"Shadowlawn? No, what's that?"

"A house in the country."

Irena shrugged. "I've not heard of it. But that doesn't mean that Shaman may not. I was told only what I needed to know."

Gabriel said: "Shadowlawn is probably safe as long as I don't go there."

"Or me," said Irena. "Shaman will be looking for me very hard."

"We will go somewhere else," said Gabriel. He went to the telephone, dialled with his back to the room so that Irena couldn't see the number and, after a moment, spoke—very quietly. The others could hear only a few words of what he said. Replacing the receiver, he told them: "That is arranged. But it would be better, perhaps, that we should leave after dark. There is no reason why they should expect to hear from Maria before then."

"Ought she to be in hospital?" asked Diana.

"Maybe, but we can't risk that. She'll be looked after."

Richard said: "We must tell Bert to make himself scarce. He can't be left here alone."

Gabriel nodded. "I will do that before he locks up at half-past five. And I must alert the staff at Shadowlawn to be careful. Diana, my dear, you will want to pack your things. I'm sorry that you should have to move again."

"There's no hurry," said Jeremy, glancing at his watch. "It's just five now. Perhaps Miss Janocki would care to tell us what it is she has to offer."

Irena looked at him, summing him up, gauging his hostility; then at Gabriel. "Very well," she said. "What I have to offer is that I will give you all Shaman's organisation in this country. That is, I will give you names and places; enough so that, if you pass the information to the authorities, they can do the job for you. Shaman and his men will be expelled at least."

"That would be very helpful," said Gabriel. "And in return?"

"What I want is not an easy thing, or I shouldn't need you to do it."

Richard said: "Irena, if you're going to bargain with us, you'll have to give us more reason than we have so far to trust you. I presume that all you told me about yourself when we first met was pure fiction. Can we have the truth now, please?"

"I don't blame you. All I can do is tell you the truth and hope that you will believe me. My name really is Irena Janocki, and I'm Polish. Not Canadian. I have a Canadian passport but that was forged. I learned English at the university. Our teacher had lived in America, which is why I have a transatlantic accent. During our last year at the university, I met a young man. When our studies were finished, he joined the state police and he arranged for me to get a job with them as a translator. We lived together for a few months, but he grew bored and left me. There was another girl, of course. It doesn't matter.

"In the spring I had a baby—my son, Stefan. My father was already dead, my mother died soon afterwards. So I was on my own with a child to bring up. The head of my department was kind to me. Yes"— she looked defiantly at Richard and Jeremy—"in return for my being kind to him. I was considered pretty, which my employers found useful. It became part of my job to entertain visiting businessmen from the West, and to learn what I could from them. Occasionally it went further than that. We would be photographed or filmed together, and I suppose they were blackmailed. I didn't know and I didn't ask. Not a very nice job, was it? But I needed the money, and, to be honest, by that time I didn't much care. There was no man in my life; I'd had enough of men. Only Stefan, who was now going to school. I loved him —I do love him—very much. One should never love things very much. It makes one vulnerable.

"Two years ago I was—lent, I suppose you would say—to Shaman for a special job. Not a specially difficult one. The man came very easily. He was rather pleasant. I was sorry for him. But that wasn't the trouble. It was Stefan. He was at an age when children ask questions endlessly. He asked about my work. I lied to him. That's what made me ashamed. So I told the department, and I told Shaman, that I wouldn't go on. I don't know what I expected to happen—that they'd put me back behind a desk, translating magazines? I must have been very naïve. You wouldn't think that someone in my position, with my experience, could be naïve, would you?

"Next day, Stefan didn't come home from school. Just as I was becoming frightened but before I did anything—went to the school or called the police—the telephone rang. Oh, Shaman's timing is always good. He knows exactly when to slip the knife in. I can hear that voice now. He said that my son had gone away for a holiday. The boy wouldn't be harmed, he'd be well cared for, provided I did what I was told. Otherwise I should never see Stefan again.

"I knew Shaman, remember. I knew what he was like, what he was capable of. So I agreed. I would do whatever he told me. That was how it began. Once a month I was allowed to see Stefan, to spend a day with him, like a divorced woman with the right to visit her children occasionally. I would be taken to different places, usually to a house in the country: and he would be brought there too. I wasn't allowed to ask where he was living and he'd been ordered not to talk about it, under threat of punishment. Once he did say something and our next meeting was cancelled. Of course the rooms where we met were always bugged. At least, I had to assume they were and I was afraid of getting him into trouble. The same thing happened if I protested or disobeyed Shaman in any way. Our next meeting would be cancelled. It was quite an effective discipline.

"Then eight months ago a meeting was cancelled for no reason. When I saw Stefan the following month, he was very silent. I wanted to ask him what was wrong. I tried but he said nothing was wrong and I didn't dare press him. Thinking about it afterwards, I felt that he hadn't really been himself for some while, but in those brief meetings, which were tense anyway, it was hard to be sure. A few days later I was sent over here, and I haven't seen him since."

"You say 'sent over here,'" asked Jeremy. "You mean Shaman wasn't with you?"

"I think he came later. One of his men travelled with me. I was fully briefed before we left." She smiled slightly ruefully, at Richard. "They showed me your file. Photographs. The dates and places to be confirmed."

"When you got here, were you working on your own?" asked Jeremy. "How were you to contact Shaman?"

She shook her head. "That sort of thing I shall tell you when we've made a deal, and after you've delivered your part of it."

"And what is it," said Gabriel, "that you want us to deliver?"

"Stefan."

"How can we do that?" asked Richard. "You don't even know where he is."

"I think I do. I told you that he once gave me a hint. I couldn't press him, but I have exercised my charms on people in Shaman's organisation. That's what I'm good at."

"So what did you learn?" asked Gabriel.

"There's a house in what you call 'East Germany'—the German Democratic Republic—in which a number of children are being kept.

All are politically significant in some way. They are hostages for their parents' behaviour. I believe Stefan is one of them."

"Do you know exactly where?"

"At a place called Pachabel. About a hundred kilometres from the border."

"You mean the border with the West?"

"Exactly. It's a lonely house, probably well guarded. The children live there in a kind of school."

"Are you sure about that? Are you sure Stefan's one of them?"

"No, I'm not sure. But it's what I've deduced from scraps of information. I thought you might have ways of checking."

"Perhaps. Suppose the boy isn't there?"

"Then we have no deal. I want Stefan."

"That's a high price you're asking. I doubt whether we could meet it, or that we should try. You expect us to kidnap the boy—if we can find him?"

"I said it wasn't an easy thing. But you solve my problem and I'll solve yours. I have to get Stefan back, for his sake even more than mine: and now that I've run away from Shaman, I'm committed. You're my only chance. Dr. Gabriel, I'm sorry about what happened today to your daughter, but maybe it means that you know how I feel. And at least you haven't lost her for good."

"I hope not."

Jeremy said: "What do you suppose Shaman is doing about you, about the fact that you've gone missing?"

"I told you. He'll be looking for me," Irena said.

"Where? Do you have friends in Britain?"

"Not really, unless you count some of the men I've known—well, professionally."

"Then he may guess, sooner or later, that you've come to us."

"He may. But that won't make much difference. Once he knows that he's lost Maria, you must assume that he could attack any of your people, any of your houses, at any time."

"Those he's aware of," said Gabriel. "Maria won't tell me about this man but I think I can persuade her to tell us what she's told him."

"How old is Stefan?" asked Diana.

"Twelve. I've got a photograph here." Irena delved in her bag. "It's not very recent. I took it myself just before he—went away. He's grown a lot since then."

It was a snapshot in rather badly developed colours. The boy wore a red woollen cap and lumberjacket. There was a background of pine trees and snow.

"Oh, he looks nice," said Diana. Women know that they must praise other women's children.

Gabriel consulted his heavy fob-watch. "I must go and talk to Bert," he said.

They left when dusk was turning into dark. As Gabriel had explained once before, there were very few papers to be removed or destroyed; a few to be burnt, and then just enough to fill a briefcase. Maria was half-awake, half-asleep. Jeremy and Richard supported her, carried her really. Irena and Diana followed. Gabriel led the way.

They went down into the cellar, which was lit by a single unshaded bulb. Gabriel pushed aside a pile of empty crates, cardboard boxes and dusty sacks, to reveal a brick archway. Stooping, they passed through into another cellar. The glimmer of a street-lamp through a high-up grimy window led them to more steps. At the top Gabriel unlocked a door. "Bert should have brought my car round," he said. "Yes, I see it."

Diana realised that they were in the street behind the travel agency. "Will you come with me?" Gabriel said to her. "We'll take Maria. Jeremy and Miss Janocki had better go with Richard in his car."

The Daimler was across the road. They eased Maria into the back, where she immediately sank again into a deep sleep. As Diana slipped into the front seat, she heard Jeremy saying to Richard: "I don't want to leave Bertha. I'll follow." With Irena between them, they strolled off, like three friends, towards the nearest side-turning.

The Daimler glided from those small streets back towards the brighter lights and traffic of the West End. "Where are we going?" Diana asked.

"One of our safe-houses," Gabriel said. "One of our safest, because we've not used it for a long time. Even Richard and Jeremy didn't know about it until I gave them the address tonight. What's more important, I don't think Maria knew about it. We are going to an old friend of mine. Mrs. Westerly. I met her when I first came to England. Her husband was a Battle of Britain pilot. They were married for less than a year before he was killed. Afterwards she took lodgers. Once we could afford it, I persuaded her to take only our lodgers."

"Part of the Land of Cockaigne."

"It was, but she inherited money and didn't need lodgers any more. She had her own life. She said we could always call on her if necessary, but, for one reason or another, we didn't. I've kept in touch, though, Occasionally I visit her for tea."

They passed Baker Street station, and Regent's Park on the right, and then swung left into the darker residential streets of St. John's Wood. The house before which they eventually drew up was a Victorian monstrosity—or a period gem of great character, according to taste. It had a turret and a conservatory and was surrounded by an overgrown garden, dark with bushes.

"Wait here for a moment with Maria, will you?" said Gabriel.

Diana watched him negotiate a twisting brick path and ring the bell. A light appeared in the fanlight above the door, which was opened by a chunky woman with grey hair, wearing trousers. She embraced Gabriel firmly. After a few moments' talk, they came back down the path to Diana, who got out of the car to be introduced.

"I'm Jane Westerly," the woman said, shaking Diana's hand with a grip which hurt. "I think I may have known your father. Long ago. Everything was long ago. I've known this old scoundrel since the Flood. Now let's get this child inside. No, let me. I'm strong as a horse." With Gabriel holding the door, she lifted Maria from the car.

Headlights illumined them. The deep-throated roar of Jeremy's Bertha was followed by the less spectacular arrival of Richard's car. "These your chaps?" asked Mrs. Westerly. "Bring 'em all in. Open house. As you know." She strode ahead of them, holding Maria in her arms.

Maria having been deposited on a sofa, further introductions were effected in the hall, beneath the gaze of a deer's head, flanked by two pairs of crossed swords. For the first time, Diana thought, Irena paled before the fire of a personality more colourful than her own.

"I'll show you to your rooms," said Mrs. Westerly, "then we'll have some grub. Just what I could rustle up. No one here at night but me nowadays. Daily girl in the mornings—useless chit."

The grub turned out to be lavish, a remarkable spread to have been produced, at such short notice, for so many unexpected guests. Vichyssoise was followed by cold chicken and ham, by apple pie and by

Stilton. Three bottles of an excellent Rioja stood, already opened, in the centre of the dining-room table. Mrs. Westerly presided over small-talk as efficiently as she did everything else, filling silences, bringing each of them into the conversation, deliberately averting any direct mention of why they were there. It was her form of discretion.

"Right," she said when they'd finished. "Coffee in the drawing room for the ladies. The men will want to talk. Port on the sideboard. Only late-bottled, I'm afraid. No time to decant the proper stuff."

When Diana and Irena had allowed themselves to be led away, Gabriel fetched the decanter and three glasses.

"What, no nuts?" said Jeremy. "Why have you never brought us here before? We've been missing something."

"I like to keep a few things to myself," said Gabriel. "She's a dear friend."

"And a tower of strength," said Richard.

"She says we want to talk," said Jeremy, "and I suppose she's right. What do we make of Irena's sob-story?"

"I may be hopelessly naïve," said Richard, "but I'm inclined to believe it."

"In other words, she can still twist you round her little finger."

"I'm inclined to disbelieve it," said Gabriel, "in the sense that I know disbelief to be the prudent assumption. Consider. We have no reason to trust Miss Janocki and every reason to distrust her." He held up one finger. "Secondly"—he held up another—"her story is virtually impossible to check. She gave us my poor Maria as a token of her sincerity. But that could be a sprat to catch a mackerel; because, thirdly, this story could hardly be better contrived if the object was to bring us out into enemy territory. The offer is very tempting. On the other hand, consider. The story could be true, and the prospect is indeed so tempting that we can hardly ignore it. Here is a chance, perhaps, to be rid altogether of Shaman in this country. How else could we achieve such a thing?

"So—we cannot lightly reject what Miss Janocki seems to be offering. It's a risk, of course, but continuing to fight Shaman is also a risk, which will inevitably produce more casualties. We might none of us survive such a war. The question, then, is which risk we take. I shall see if it's possible to confirm at all Miss Janocki's story. I shall try, but most probably I shan't learn anything very helpful, certainly nothing conclusive. In which case my answer, on balance, is that, with our eyes open, we have to accept this risk. We have to undertake what she is asking of us."

Richard gazed at the wine in his glass, red as blood.

"Oh Lord!" said Jeremy. "Here we go again."

XIII

A Wicked Stone House

"I'll tell you why I wanted to know," said Gabriel.

"I don't think I want to know why you wanted to know," replied Arthur Blaise. But of course he did, and Gabriel told him. They had met, this time, not in a St. James's Street club but in a small Italian restaurant in Kensington. When Gabriel telephoned Blaise, using a private number which Blaise had given him during a previous affair, and asked if there was anything in the files about a certain house or school at Pachabel in East Germany, Blaise had said he would see and proposed lunch the following day. "But," he added, "I've a feeling, old friend, that I should prefer at the moment not to be observed in your company." Hence this discreet rendezvous, uncharacteristic, it might have been thought, for Blaise whose natural taste inclined to the opulent: but he had once, in the aftermath of war, performed a great service for Giovanni, who, with his fat wife and voluptuous daughter, owned and ran the restaurant, and who, in continuing gratitude, was always ready to provide Blaise with a discreet and secure meeting place.

"We don't know much about it," said Blaise, "but the house exists all right. At least I presume it's the one to which you refer. The locals call it Der Steinhof. In our terms I imagine it's an old farm or manor house. But no one's allowed near it; there's a high fence with guards. What you said seems to be quite right. There are children. Sometimes they're driven out in a private bus. And the rumour is that they're important in some way. In what way isn't clear. The local view seems to be that they are the children of high party officials. A kind of select boarding school, with precautions to keep intruders out rather than the children in. But that may well be wrong. All I can say is that somebody in my service once thought it sufficiently interesting to file a brief report."

"Would it be possible," Gabriel asked, "to find out more? And to get a detailed description of the place?"

"Possible for whom?"

"I told you what we've been offered if this woman is telling the truth. You'd like the information she can provide as much as I would."

"Not quite as much. And not enough to get me involved officially in your clandestine and highly improper business. Yes, if you could drop on my mat a full account of Shaman's activities in this country, I shouldn't spurn it. I would pass it on to the right people and earn good marks. But I have to tell you, as if you didn't know, that your activities are highly unpopular with my more orthodox, not to say stuffy, colleagues. Perhaps more unpopular than Shaman's, because you are apt to rock the boat; which is the worst crime."

"You haven't answered my question."

"I thought I had. Officially my answer is no. I've done too much for you already. Unofficially. . . . But you must have contacts all over Germany?"

"None who could produce this kind of information quickly."

"And what exactly would you do with the information if you had it?"

"I've told you what the woman wants."

"My blood runs cold. Just the sort of thing I mustn't touch. But you might mysteriously get a message within the next few days. Mind you, I say might. And where should it be delivered—now that you've gone to ground?"

"Exactly where I am what you might call holed up is perhaps another thing you'd rather not know. How about my friend Richard's club?"

"Why not?" agreed Blaise.

Richard had moved out of Haggard's Hotel and was staying, with the others, in Mrs. Westerly's house, but he made occasional excursions to his club, which seemed a good post office and comparatively secure. "I doubt if even Shaman's going to throw a bomb through the bay window," he said.

"I wouldn't be so sure," replied Jeremy. "The IRA threw a bomb into Brooks's, if you remember, and machine-gunned the Cavalry Club."

Despite this uncomfortable reminder, Richard felt that he would not be imperilling his fellow-members to any significant degree, and he wanted an opportunity to get out of the house. On the fourth day after Gabriel's meeting with Blaise, the porter handed him a brown foolscap envelope bearing his name. He took it to a far corner of the smoking room.

Inside were half a dozen glossy photographs and two typewritten sheets. There was no address or signature.

The photographs, which were obviously taken from a distance, although some had been enlarged to give the effect of a slightly blurred close-up, showed a rambling two-storey house, L-shaped, enclosing a cobbled or bricked courtyard in the angle, and backed by a hillside, on the top of which stood a fringe of conifers. The enlargement revealed that all the windows on the upper floor were barred. One of the long-distance pictures showed the house, dimly, through the meshes of a wire fence on which hung a notice emblazoned with a skull and a lightning flash.

The typewritten pages were headed simply "Der Steinhof." Then: "The house is situated five kilometres south-west of Pachabel. A turning off the Norburg road leads to it through wooded countryside. The house itself lies in a small valley. It is surrounded, at a distance of about 300 metres, by an electrified fence. A guard in civilian clothes, carrying a shotgun, is in charge of the gate. Two other armed guards, with dogs, patrol the fence.

"The fence can best be approached and the house observed from a ridge on the eastern side. There are no other dwellings in sight, except the lodge, occupied by the guards, beside the gate.

"The house used to have a farm attached, and there are still some barns and sheds in the field behind, but no farming appears to take place now. A gardener cuts the lawn and tends the flower beds in front. He is not from the village, and seems to live in the lodge; he may well, in fact, be another guard.

"According to our observation, the house is at present occupied by eight children and ten adults. (The latter figure is uncertain.) Food shops in Pachabel receive orders, generally by telephone but occasionally in person, from a woman called Frau Lange. (She is described as large with greying hair and spectacles, late middle-aged.) The goods are usually collected by a man driving an old utility truck. Deliveries are occasionally made to the house, in which case the delivery van is always checked when going both in and out of the gate.

"The man who drives the truck also acts as a chauffeur, taking Frau Lange into Pachabel by car, collecting mail and, twice a week, driving the children in a small bus to the Ulbricht Sports Centre on the outskirts of the village. When the children are taken to the sports centre they are always accompanied by two adults as well as the driver.

"Our information, obtained elsewhere (i.e. not from village gossip), is that these are the children of defectors or possibly of people important to the regime who have been allowed to travel abroad. They are permitted no contact with anyone in the village. Individual identities are not known. Ages appear to range from about seven to fourteen. If the children receive letters, they are probably contained in sealed packets, addressed to Frau Lange.

"The house has been used in this way for several years. Care was taken in compiling the above information to avoid drawing attention to the enquiries."

Richard sank back in his leather armchair, visualising an old stone house—a wicked stone house—in a hidden valley, flanked by fir trees. He could almost hear the children's voices, mingling with the noise of talk and laughter from the bar a few feet away. Quite soon, he thought, he might see that house in reality: and, if so, would he ever return to this friendly place? Slipping the envelope into his pocket, he went upstairs to lunch, where, at the communal table, he joined, only a little distractedly, in a conversation about the probable effects of a late damp spring on the breeding of grouse.

Gabriel, Richard, Jeremy, Diana and Irena all sat in the agreeably cluttered drawing room of Mrs. Westerly's house. The top of a piano bore piles of sheet-music. Photographs in silver frames alternated with pieces of Victorian china above the fireplace. A wild variety of books filled the mahogany bookcases; others littered the floor. Afternoon sunshine streamed through the window past faded red curtains.

Mrs. Westerly was upstairs with Maria. The girl had recovered well and, except for a scar on her wrist, should soon, Gabriel said, be no worse—physically—for what had happened: but she was reluctant to leave her room or talk to anyone. Gabriel had spent much time just sitting with her.

But his mind now was on the future, not the past. Lowering the typescript pages which he had just read aloud, he handed the photographs to Jeremy. Diana leaned across to look at them too. Gabriel peered over his spectacles at Irena. "This is an important question," he said. "Think about it carefully. Is it likely, even a little bit likely, that Shaman will realise you may know where Stefan is?"

"I don't believe so," she said.

"Are you sure—because, if you're wrong, they may have moved the boy and be waiting for us?"

"How can I be sure? Shaman is a very clever man. He does guess things. But I repeat—I don't believe he knows or has any reason to guess it. What that paper said was quite right. I simply handed over my letters to Stefan without an address. And his letters to me were delivered by hand; I've no doubt they were censored to keep out any reference to where he was living."

"But you did give us a location."

"I told you, I'm good at finding things out from people without letting them realise what they've said. And I wasn't going to risk anything which might come back on Stefan."

"Hm." Gabriel grunted an acknowledgement which suggested less than total conviction. "Do you suppose anywhere in this house there's an atlas?"

"I saw one," replied Diana. "A *Times Atlas*. Yes, here it is." She picked up the large flat volume and gave it him.

He consulted the index, flicked through the pages and then pored over the relevant map. "I thought so," he said at last. "We have a man not too far away. A man and a route."

"Jeremy and I are off on our travels again, eh?" said Richard lightly.

"Do you speak German?" asked Gabriel.

"We've been over that before. A year at school."

"Exactly. And Jeremy speaks very good German indeed."

"Meaning that I'm elected," said Jeremy. "All on my lonesome. Quite right. Very proper."

Diana and Richard both started to speak, but Irena cut in. "I'll go with him."

"Oh no," said Gabriel. "With all due respect, young woman, I want you where I can see you. But no one is going anywhere immediately. There are things which must be done first. Meanwhile, Jeremy, what you must do is get completely fit."

"Don't leave it too long," said Irena. "Shaman will not sit around doing nothing."

The validity of her warning was confirmed next day, when Sammy telephoned, reporting that the travel agency had been broken into. Nothing had been taken; a cash float of £50, kept in a drawer of the desk in the shop, was untouched. "They're not even bothering to cover their tracks," was Jeremy's comment.

"Why should they?" said Richard. "Shaman wants us to know he's there. He'd like to flush us out. Do we know when this break-in took place?"

"It could have been the night we left," said Gabriel. "I told everyone to keep clear until now. And there's another piece of news. Do you remember Ted Higgins? He has a boat in Harwich," Gabriel explained to Diana. "Or he did. It was burnt last night. Mr. Higgins carried passengers for us occasionally."

"Yes, I knew him," said Jeremy. "The sooner we move the better, if we're to have any organisation left. Actually I've a piece of news too. I telephoned South Africa today. I wanted to tell Jan about developments here, that the leak wasn't his end, but I got Ben Smith, who's been staying with him."

"That's the American you rescued in Angola?"

"Exactly. Well, I said to him, quite casually, "I don't suppose you speak German," and he said he did. He's virtually bilingual. His parents were German immigrants called Schmidt. So I asked him if he'd like to come on a jaunt with me. And he said yes."

Gabriel frowned. "But we know nothing about him."

"I know quite a lot. I spent several days in Jan's house, remember, when I got back to Johannesburg, and he was there. But the important thing is that Shaman doesn't know about him. Anyone who worked with us before may have been blown. Ben Smith didn't and therefore hasn't been. He's catching a plane tonight."

"Well, it's up to you."

"I like him," said Richard. "What I saw of him."

Desirable though it was that they should move quickly, detailed plans had to be laid and arrangements made: and Gabriel wanted to tap his own sources for further information. Acting prematurely in such matters, they all knew, was an invitation to disaster. So Gabriel went his own mysterious way, leaving the little community in Mrs. Westerly's house to wait and live their lives and develop their relationships.

Being a man who noticed things, he was aware that there were cross-currents, perhaps dangerous cross-currents, in those relationships. Mrs. Westerly, a confirmed match-maker, had decided, rightly or wrongly, that Jeremy and Diana were, or should be, interested in each other, and she sought occasions to leave them alone together. Richard was considered, or perhaps considered himself, vaguely responsible for Irena, although whether any affection still existed between them was less clear. Irena now seemed reserved and silent.

Gabriel was too busy to spend time analysing such personal subtleties, except in so far as they might affect the operation he was preparing; and echoes from his own past did warn him of ominous possibilities. But no, he thought; I'm imagining ghosts. Whenever he could, he sat with Maria, trying to unfreeze her with the warmth of his love. And he did make progress. Gradually, with tears, she talked to him; which was useful—he learned what information she had given away—but, much more important, the bond between them, the confidence between them, was at least to some degree restored.

Ben Smith arrived and was ensconced in a small Kensington hotel, which The Fishers had never used and was therefore not liable to be watched by the enemy: but he spent most of his days in St. John's Wood. Gabriel immediately understood why both Richard and Jeremy had been impressed by him. He displayed an air of calmness and competence which was immensely reassuring. He called Mrs. Westerly "Ma'am." "What nice manners that young man has," she said.

Eventually Gabriel was ready to summon them all together—all except Irena, whom he deliberately excluded. Up to a point, they had to trust her: they had to act on the assumption she was telling the truth. But the risk should be minimised. She should be told nothing she didn't need to know. Gabriel found her an enigmatic figure; intriguing, certainly. He addressed her now by her Christian name; which he wouldn't have done, if there had not been something about her which he found appealing. "Irena," he said, "I shall ask you to stay in your room for the next half hour. You understand, I'm sure."

"Of course," she said impassively.

Summer had arrived, and the afternoon was hot. Mrs. Westerly provided two jugs of lemonade, and then retired tactfully. "Irena's in her room," Gabriel had said to her. "Make sure we're not overheard, will you?"

He spread a map of Germany on the floor. "We've discussed various aspects of what must be done," he said, "but now I want to run through the whole plan. You must forgive me if I repeat some things which are familiar.

"I've been in touch—deviously, so I've not been able to ask or learn as much as I would have wished—with our friend in Norburg. He confirms that the situation at the house outside Pachabel, the Steinhof, appears to be as we were told. What I think you don't know, because the need has not arisen for a long while, is that we have a crossing point, over the border, about fifty kilometres from Norburg. I say 'we have a crossing point.' I mean there's a route we have used in the past. I will explain about it later. I asked our friend if it was still available, and he said yes, to the best of his knowledge. On the West German side of the border, there is an inn, a guest-house, mainly for tourists walking in the forest. But not many come. It's a lonely place. I've been there. The proprietor is also a friend.

"I was going to suggest, anyway, that Richard positions himself on the West German side, to be the reception committee. And I think Irena should be there too, not at the crossing point but at the inn, to receive her son. But she can't be left alone. I propose, therefore, to come with her.

"So, three of us in West Germany. There." He indicated a spot on the map. "Now Jeremy and Ben. The Polish cruise ship, *Joseph Machar*, visits England next week. We have friends in the crew. Richard and Jeremy will remember that they've helped us bring stowaways from the East before. This time we shall offer them two passengers going in the opposite direction. You will disembark, twelve days from now, when the ship touches in East Germany. You will be a long way, of course, from Pachabel, but so much the better. The cross-country journey is being arranged. That won't be difficult. The difficult part is when you arrive.

"You have to identify the boy and get him away. If the children are really taken, as we've been told, twice a week to a sports ground, that may be the best opportunity. Otherwise you will need to get into the house. We'll talk about that in a minute, but really you will have to make your own decisions when you see how the land lies. There will be people to help you. They are, I hope, examining the possibilities now."

"It doesn't sound exactly like a piece of cake," said Jeremy.

"I'm afraid not. How do you feel about it, Ben?"

"You got me out of the frying pan," he said. "I guess I owe it to you to jump in the fire."

"You owe us nothing. If—"

"No, no. Just joking. I'm ready to give it a whirl."

Diana said to Gabriel: "I want to go with you and Richard."

"That's not necessary. It's better you stay here."

"I know it's not necessary. But I want to."

Gabriel knew Diana quite well by now, and didn't try to argue.

XIV

The Far Waterfall Like Doom

The inn called "At the Sign of the Black Bear" had a sign outside depicting a black bear, dancing. The timber-and-plaster building looked picturesque enough to be a fake, but wasn't. The forest surrounding it could be the setting for a German fairy tale, tangled and dark, threaded by twisty paths and sun-dappled rides.

Gabriel's party came in two cars, which had been hired, on their behalf, in names not theirs. Four people do not require two cars but seven people do, and they hoped that there would be seven in the party when they left. But, certainly for Gabriel, it was a matter much more of hope than confidence, and his experience gave him the best chance of understanding the real nature of the risk—of what he had sent Jeremy into. He felt, nevertheless, he admitted to himself, just a touch of exhilaration. This was familiar territory from long ago; familiar work from the days when he was young.

"Herr Doktor!" said Hans Grelf, emerging to greet them. His hair and moustache were grey, the lines etched more deeply into the face which had always reminded Gabriel of Mr. Punch.

"Old friend! And Anna—she is well?"

"Thank God. She is inside, wanting very much to see you."

They had been talking in German, but Gabriel switched now to English. He made the introductions. "This is Herr Grelf," he explained, "the landlord of this excellent house."

Grelf chuckled. "Excellent to you maybe. You and I are old-fashioned people. But the tourists, they like things more modern, more shiny. Bathrooms in the bedrooms. Cocktail bars. Things we don't have. But it doesn't matter. Anna and I survive. And survival is much, is it not, Herr Doktor?"

He took Gabriel's battered leather suitcase and Irena's more elegant luggage. Richard brought his own and Diana's. She carried the bits and pieces. The two women, Gabriel had thought, observing them on the journey, made a poignant contrast. Perhaps because of his love affair with England, shaded now with the sweet melancholy of a lost love, he admired Diana, approved of her fair hair, her tweed coat and skirt, her stalwart common sense: and he disapproved of Irena, but, if the truth were told, felt more kinship with her. And, of course, he recognised her beauty.

Anna Grelf had once been quite pretty, plump and blonde. Now she was motherly, although her three children had long flown the nest. Her English, unlike Grelf's, was very limited. She bobbed a curtsy, as she had been taught to do, fifty years ago, when she worked in her father's guest-house. Then she embraced Gabriel.

The room was low-ceilinged, with ancient heavy beams. The polished wooden floor undulated like a calm sea.

"Do you have many people staying?" asked Gabriel.

"Two couples only," said Grelf. "Sometimes people come without reservations who are walking or riding in the forest, but there have not been many this year."

"Good. For us, anyway. You and I, Hans, will have a talk later."

"After dinner? In my room? Like in the old days?"

The bedrooms were simple but scrupulously clean; dark wood, white linen, embroidered bedspreads; wild flowers in little earthenware vases, beside leaded windows open to let in the evening air. The four rooms were all in the same corridor, Richard's and Diana's on one side, Gabriel's and Irena's on the other. The house was actually bigger than it seemed, but the stairs and corridors were labyrinthine, so the effect was of a private wing.

Richard stood by the window, looking out at the trees, which were becoming mysterious in the gathering dusk. He wondered where Jeremy and Ben were this evening. He knew, or at least felt sure, they had disembarked safely. If they hadn't, a message would have reached Gabriel. But now—hiding, fleeing, captured? There had been no word: but no word had been expected. According to the schedule which had been worked out and discussed in unrealistic detail, tomorrow was the first possible—but improbable—day on which the attempt might be made at the house near Pachabel. More likely, even if all the circumstances were favourable, Jeremy and Ben would not be ready to move for several days yet. But, of course, not all the circumstances would be favourable. They never were; which was why excessively detailed planning was unrealistic.

Richard felt guilty because he had rather enjoyed the past week. Preparations for the journey and the journey itself had been leisurely. Gabriel had himself made the arrangements. Their route was circuitous, so that they could be sure they weren't being followed. And nothing untoward had happened. To all appearances they were just four friends on holiday, and it had almost seemed as though that were true. By tacit consent they had spoken very little about the object of their journey but, like chance travelling companions, had talked and laughed and established a kind of intimacy.

He turned away from the window, put on his jacket and went downstairs to dinner.

They had been given a corner table. Gabriel sat with his back to the wall, as he always preferred, so that he could survey the room. He scrutinised the other guests. There was an elderly German couple, who scarcely spoke to one another, and a young Italian couple who talked all the time. The Italians' hands kept touching; honeymooners or lovers. The remaining tables were unoccupied. Anna Grelf bustled in and out of the kitchen, helped by a young girl. Her husband brought the wine.

"This is a jolly nice place," said Diana.

And a quiet one, seemingly. It was hard to believe they had anything more serious to worry about than whether to drink Hock or Moselle. By the time they had finished their dinner, the German couple had retired and the Italians were still totally absorbed in each other. Grelf came, asked if everything was all right and suggested that they take coffee and brandy in the parlour. "With the compliments of the house, naturally," he said. "And perhaps you and I, Herr Doktor, might have our little talk?"

Leaving Richard and the two girls in a room where the severity of black beams and white plaster was relieved by prettily flowered upholstery, Gabriel accompanied Grelf to the office—but it was as much a private sitting room as an office—behind the reception desk. Papers drifted on to the floor from an ancient roll-top desk, but there was a fishing rod in the corner and, on either side of the fireplace, filled now with pine cones, were two comfortable chairs. Grelf produced brandy from a corner cupboard, handed Gabriel a glass and set the bottle on the floor between them.

"Now," he said. "I have done what you asked. My cousin Otto— over there," he gestured in the direction which Gabriel assumed to be the border, "is expecting your friends. If they get to him, he will take them to our old way."

"It's still open? Have the border guards never found it? In all these years?"

"They haven't looked. This isn't a place where anyone tries to cross the border. And we haven't used it for—how long now—fifteen years?"

Gabriel nodded. "But it can be used still?"

"Otto thinks so. We can't be sure because I don't want to risk anyone being seen near it. In the winter, when there is much water, perhaps not. But it should be all right at this time of year."

"Are you in touch with your cousin? Easily?"

"Not easily. And again I do not want to take any risk at this stage. We have arranged a signal. There is a cleft in the hillside across the border which can be seen from this side but not from the other. Each evening, starting tomorrow, we will watch it for an hour. On the night when they mean to cross, Otto will flash a light, so we can be ready to help them."

"I wish I was more confident that they'll ever come. Now tell me about the border guards."

For a while they discussed patrols and dogs and minefields and watchtowers. Grelf drew a sketch-map, which he then, more from old habit than current necessity, burnt, crumbling the ashes among the pine cones. The flame put him in mind of his pipe. He lit it, and looked shrewdly at Gabriel through the curl of blue smoke. "This is something special for you?" he suggested.

"Yes," agreed Gabriel, and explained the situation. "I hope we are not bringing danger to you."

Grelf shrugged. "I told you long ago that Anna and I would always be ready if you called on us."

"I know." And they talked of old times, old perils, old comrades— many, too many, now dead—until the carved clock on the wall struck midnight.

Next day Grelf took Gabriel and Richard for a walk in the woods. Leaving a bridle-path which they had followed from beside the inn, they walked between the trees on a carpet of pine needles. Sunshine slanted in thick beams between the tall trunks. There was very little undergrowth. After some fifteen minutes Grelf held up his hand. "We should be careful now," he said. "It will be better if we are not seen."

He guided them forward to a point where the trees ended. They were on the edge of a steep declivity, at the bottom of which ran a little stream. Without exposing themselves, they peered across to the opposite side of the valley. It was bare, with only a few rocks for cover, and, after flattening out slightly, rose again into a long steep hillside. Across the hillside ran two parallel lines with a sizeable area between them.

Grelf offered Gabriel a pair of binoculars. He put them to his eyes, focussed them and scanned the hillside; then, without a word, passed the binoculars to Richard.

They were powerful glasses. In close-up the line became a fence, ten or twelve feet high, tight-meshed, with rolled barbed-wire at the top. The fence was supported on ferro-concrete posts, to which were attached metal devices of some kind. Periodically there were tall swan-necked lights. Traversing his binoculars, Richard saw that the ground between the two fences had been roughly ploughed. He followed the inner fence leftwards until a watchtower came into his vision, a mushroom of steel girders. On the platform he could see two men. One of them also had a pair of binoculars, and, even as Richard was focussing on him, turned towards Richard. It was an eerie moment. Richard kept quite still and the man turned away again.

"The guard on that watchtower was looking in our direction," Richard said. "Do you think he spotted us?"

"I doubt it," said Grelf. "If he had, he would be looking at us still. And probably photographing us. They are interested in anyone who seems interested in them—or in the fence."

"I've seen it often enough," said Gabriel. "Too often. And in too many places. But I can never get used to it. If anything represents what I've spent my whole life fighting, this surely does."

"They call it the Anti-Fascist Protection Wall," said Grelf. "The wire is razor-sharp. And those things on the posts are SM70 anti-personnel mines. A touch on the wire will trigger them. The story was that they were being removed as part of a deal between our government and the Communists."

"But not yet," said Richard.

"This is a country of fairy tales."

Lowering the glasses, Richard took in the whole scene again. The watchtower was on a ridge, beyond which the double fence sank from view. To his right the valley started to fill in and the fence curved upwards. Another watchtower was just visible far off. The only sign of human occupation beyond the fence was what appeared to be a ruined cottage on the hillside almost opposite where they were standing.

"You see that cottage," said Grelf. "Look above it. You see those rocks. Beside them the ground dips. From there Otto will shine his light. Four times. The guards cannot see it. We can—from here."

"They may not be able to see the light," said Gabriel, "but they might see Otto. Can he get there without being seen?"

"He was born in the village over the mountain. He knows every rock, every tree. He will manage. Now come."

Grelf led them back to the bridle-path. They walked along it for a while, meeting no one, although hoof-marks in the dry dust showed that it was actually used for its proper purpose. Then they diverged again into the trees on the left. The air was hot and stuffy. Richard brushed flies away, and wished that he could brush away the depression, the worm of fear, caused by that evil fence. But the flies came back and so did the darkness of his mood.

Quite suddenly, the trees thinned to reveal a spectacular piece of scenery. They were on the rim of a deep gorge. The hillside with the fence curving upwards now lay directly in front of them, and the reason for the curve had become clear. It marked the edge of a precipitous cliff, not sheer but steep and jagged. At one point water spewed out, bouncing from rock to rock. On the far side of the gorge the hill became, unmistakably, a mountain. Even in summer the impression was Wagnerian rather than pastoral: in winter, Richard thought, with storm clouds and flickers of lightning, it must be awesome.

"Shall I tell him?" asked Grelf.

"Tell him," said Gabriel.

Grelf turned to Richard. "There is an old culvert. Very old. Constructed perhaps in my grandfather's time, perhaps before. Otto and I played in it as children, though we were told not to because it was dangerous. When we were no longer children, nobody else knew about it. The entrance became all covered with brambles. But it runs from beyond the inner fence and comes out there." He pointed towards the gorge.

"You mean in the cliff?"

"Ja. In the cliff. Near that waterfall. There used to be a farm up on the hill, and I think this culvert drained water from the fields. It's broken. It was broken when I was a boy. But a man can still crawl through the pipe, as we used to do."

"But what happens this end?"

"I tell you. It comes out on the cliff. There's a path or maybe just a ledge. But a man can walk along it, at least in summer when there's not too much water. Look, you can see. Just this side of the waterfall. A little above."

Richard peered down. The cliff was green with moss and lichen covering protuberances of rock. With an effort of imagination he could see that there might be a kind of path, widening in one or two places, a route along which an active man with steady nerves might scramble up.

"It is not so hard as it seems," Grelf said. "Where the culvert comes out is behind that bush. It cannot be seen from above. When it rains, there is water, but all mixed with the waterfall."

"Has anyone actually been through lately?" asked Gabriel.

"No. Otto has been a little way but not out this end. We have kept this path to ourselves for the time of need. Now is that time, is it not, Herr Doktor?"

"For us. But I hope we don't ruin it for you. Or will Otto be coming?"

"Oh no. He has his family. But if we are lucky there will be no trouble. They do not watch very closely here, because they think there is no way to cross."

"I'm not surprised," said Richard.

As they walked back to the inn, he tried to visualise Jeremy, Ben and a twelve-year-old boy scrambling like flies up the cliffside. He realised that it wasn't impossible, might not even be very difficult in a physical sense, but it would need cool heads and steady nerves. Rather them than me, he thought, and was ashamed of it.

They found Irena and Diana in the parlour of the inn; Irena glancing through a German fashion magazine, Diana reading an English paperback she'd brought with her. The arrangement was that Irena should not be left alone except in her room, a restriction which she had accepted quite calmly.

Every evening from now on it would be necessary for one of them to go down to the edge of the woods and watch for the signal. Grelf had explained, apologetically, that he couldn't be away at dinner time, leaving Anna to do the work, except in an emergency; so it would have to be Richard and Gabriel taking turns. "And me," insisted Diana.

"All right," agreed Richard. "Come with me this evening and I'll show you the way."

Grelf carefully explained at what point they should turn off the bridle-path. "Keep the sunset behind you and you will not get lost," he said. Nor did they. When they reached the edge of the trees, the hillside in front of them was pink with the reflection of the setting sun, but very soon the shadows engulfed it. The evening was soft and warm, however. Richard and Diana sat on the ground, close together, with their backs against a tree, watching the stars come out above the blackness of the hill. They had taken their bearings before the light went, drawing an imaginary line from a peak to the cleft where the signal should appear.

"*Nox et praeterea nihil,*" said Richard.

"You'll have to translate."

"Night and nothing else."

"You might as well have said that in English."

"It's a quotation. Almost. Anyway—decent obscurity of a learned tongue."

"We didn't expect anything else tonight, did we?"

"No, they could hardly have got here yet."

"Do you really think they'll get here at all?"

"If anyone can do it, Jeremy will."

"Yes."

They sat in silence for a while.

"This is rather like that holiday in the Pyrenees," said Richard. "Remember how we used to sit out after dinner?"

"Yes, it was fun."

" 'And the tedding and the spreading, Of the straw for a bedding. And the fleas that tease in the High Pyrenees . . .' "

"How do you remember so many quotations?"

"It's a gift. Gabriel does it too. 'Never more; Miranda, Never more.

Only the high peaks hoar. No sound: But the boom Of the far waterfall like Doom.' "

"Don't. That's too depressing."

"Sorry. We should have brought a bottle. And sandwiches."

"I know what Jeremy would say to that. 'This is no picnic,' he'd say. And laugh. Richard, put your arm round me. I'm frightened."

"It'll be all right," he said, squeezing her gently to him. "You'll see."

"Oh, I hope so."

Again they sat in silence.

"How are you getting on with Irena?" asked Richard.

"Rather well. We're not exactly soul-mates but we've had a few heart-to-hearts and I actually quite like her. And of course I see why you like her. She is very beautiful."

"Do I like her? Did I ever like her? It's not the same thing, you know. I wonder how Gabriel's coping with her."

"They've a lot in common. They're both foreigners. And that's not altogether a joke."

The dryness of that remark told Richard that she had recovered her spirits. He kept the conversation light, and the remaining half hour of their watch passed quickly as they sat together in the companionable dark.

Meanwhile, Gabriel was with Irena in the parlour of the inn. "I don't think," she said, "that you are so attentive for the pleasure of my company. You still don't trust me."

"Any man would enjoy your company."

"But you don't trust me. You're afraid that, if you leave me alone, I might do something. I wonder what. Send a message? Meet a contact? Run away? I shan't, you know. For the best of reasons. You are serving my interests, and there is nowhere else I would wish to be."

"Life has taught me to distrust people."

"And you think my life has not?"

"I'm sure it has. If I didn't believe you at all, we shouldn't be here. But you must admit, it is a gamble. We are acting on the assumption that—to serve your interests—you have betrayed Shaman and come to us, but, for the same reason, you might have made a deal with Shaman to betray us."

She nodded. "You are logical. Anyway, it doesn't matter. You and your friends are doing what I wanted."

"We'll talk on that basis. So let me ask you something. Suppose we fail. Suppose Jeremy doesn't return or that he returns without your son. What will you do then?"

Watching her closely, he was inclined to trust the shadow on her face. "I don't know," she said. "I'm gambling too. Tell me honestly, what do you think the chances are?"

"There's a good chance. We have some experience in these matters. But life has taught me not only to be distrustful but to be a pessimist. I like to plan for the worst case."

She smiled bleakly. "I'm sure you do. Your race, Dr. Gabriel, and mine have reason enough to fear the worst. I think it sets us a little apart from the others."

Richard and Diana came in, laughing, cheerful in the simplest manner; confirming, Gabriel thought, Irena's observation.

"Nothing," said Richard. "No light. Except the lights illuminating that damned fence. But it's early days yet."

"Early days," agreed Gabriel.

So the days passed and the nights, and a sliver of moon grew towards the full, as each evening one of them, or sometimes two for company, waited at the edge of the wood for a sign which didn't come.

XV

"You'll Say I'm Mad"

Wilhelm Keller was a carpenter and timber merchant, a saturnine man of around fifty, quite prosperous by the standards of Pachabel. He had broad craftsman's hands. He wore an open-necked shirt and coarse grey trousers. He was not talkative but his eyes slid shrewdly between Jeremy and Ben as they debated possible action.

They sat in Keller's office, overlooking the timber yard. He had been sheltering them for over a week now, since they had been delivered, in the night, to his door by the previous man in the chain. Gabriel's arrangements had worked very smoothly. Not that Jeremy was in the least surprised by their efficiency. He had made such journeys before on behalf of The Fishers: but this time he realised there was another network involved. He asked no questions, of course, and was offered no information. He and Ben Smith were simply transported, like inert and clandestine goods, from the port where they were smuggled ashore, across open countryside, through unidentified towns, by car and truck and sometimes on foot, across hundreds of miles of East Germany, to Pachabel. Keller had been expecting them and received them without comment.

Although Pachabel had been referred to in London as a village, it was in fact a small town, large enough for strangers not to be immediately noticed. However, they took as little risk as possible of being seen, making their reconnaissances by night or, when they had to move by day, travelling in the back of Keller's van. With utmost caution they had crawled up to the wire of the Steinhof. Through the slightly open rear doors of the van, strategically parked, they had watched the comings and goings at the Ulbricht Sports Centre, which was less impressive than its name, consisting of a gymnasium, a swimming pool and an unkempt field with goal posts. They studied a large-scale map of the district. The preliminaries were finished: they had learned as much as they could. Now, across the border, not so far as crows might fly but separated from them by a fearful man-made barrier, Gabriel would be waiting. And Irena.

"All right," said Jeremy. "Let me sum up." The Savile Row clothes which he wore in London and which had seemed to Diana a natural extension of his fastidious personality had been exchanged for an ill-fitting mass-produced suit of anonymous grey. His tie was blue wool instead of the regimental or old school tie which he normally favoured. Everything he wore or carried had an East German label. They had not so far been challenged, and he hoped very much they wouldn't be, but, if necessary, their papers showed them to be from Dresden, representing a furniture company. The papers, and a briefing to flesh out the story, had been supplied at the first stage of their journey, by the man to whom they had been delivered off the ship. How well the papers would stand up under scrutiny, and how much of the Dresden background was authentic, Jeremy had no idea but he guessed they would survive at least superficial examination. These were impressive people. But the comforting irresponsibility of the journey was over. The next decisions were his.

"Our preferred option," he said, "was to make contact with Stefan, show him Irena's letter, and somehow, with his co-operation, slip him away. But that looks virtually impossible. We can't get to him. And we can't get a message to him. Even if we found someone to carry a message, it would be no use because we haven't identified him. Similarly, if we managed—heaven knows how—to penetrate the fence without raising an alarm, and to reach the house, we'd be thrashing about with no clear objective. We can't very well wander around asking people where we could find Stefan Janocki. The children may not even be here under their real names. So, option one—not on. Agreed?"

"Agreed," said Ben. Keller said nothing.

"Option two is that we make use of the only time when the children regularly leave the grounds of the house—those trips to the sports centre. We've confirmed that they happen. Every Tuesday and Friday afternoon. But it would be pretty difficult to extract one child without being seen. And even if we could, his disappearance would be noticed very quickly. Within minutes probably. I think we'll have to scrag the guards."

"If we have to, we can," said Ben.

"Agreed. We can. But the alarm still gets raised within two hours at the most. When the children are due back."

"But is there any way we could buy more time?"

"Realistically, I doubt it. What worries me more is that we still haven't picked Stefan out. That damned photo of Irena's just isn't good enough. I had quite a reasonable squint at them last Friday, and, as far as I'm concerned, it could have been any one of the five boys. They're dressed alike. Some are a bit taller, a bit shorter, a bit fatter, a bit thinner, but it would take a mother's loving eye to distinguish. No, that's not quite true. One of them was plainly too young. But that still leaves four."

"Maybe there's another we could rule out. But I admit I wasn't sure. We were quite a way off. Perhaps if we got a closer look?"

"I doubt if we'd be sure even then. I wish I'd asked Irena if the boy has her red hair. You can't really tell from the picture; he was wearing a cap and the colours are out of true."

"And they were wearing caps. So the bottom line is we don't know. Of course, we're assuming he's there at all. Suppose Irena was lying. Suppose she hasn't even got a son."

"I thought I was the sceptic around here. I warned you that was possible when I first roped you in."

"Oh, I'm not complaining," said Ben with a rueful smile. "I've been walking into trouble since I was in knee-pants. I guess it comes natural to me. You're the boss. You just tell me what the plan is."

Jeremy looked at him and liked what he saw—a man who moved and talked easily and slowly, a sensible man, a man to guard your back. I'm not a bad recruiter, thought Jeremy. He said: "All right. If you want me to decide, I will. Tomorrow's Tuesday. The children will be at the sports centre. We'll take all four of them, and pick Stefan out when we've got them away."

"We'll take just those four? What are the others going to do? Sit quietly where we left them? And if we tied them and gagged them, that wouldn't exactly create confidence among the ones we'd got."

"That's a point," agreed Jeremy. "If we're going to use their bus, which is what I had in mind, I suppose we might as well take them all clear of the village."

"Are you good with children?" asked Ben.

"Not particularly. My theory is that, if you treat children and animals like human beings, they respond."

"I hope you're right," said Ben. "Never mind. You're the boss."

Ben turned to Keller, who spoke reasonable, but far from perfect, English. "I'm sorry," he said. "Did you understand that? We're going to try tomorrow."

"I understood enough," replied Keller. "Then, with or without the boy, I drive you to Otto. He will take care of you from then, thank God."

"Yes. You'll be ready?"

"Come," said Keller. He led the way out of the office, down an external wooden stair into the timber yard, which was deserted and shielded from the street by large solid gates. It smelled of freshly cut wood. Indeed, almost half the yard was occupied by piles of lumber. In the other half stood two large trucks, one bearing a roped load of cut planks. Keller walked across to it, slipped his hand between the planks and, with no effort, swung a whole section of the wood outwards as though it were a door, revealing, in effect, a long low cave. "You travel in there," he said.

At two o'clock the following afternoon Jeremy looked at his watch for the third time in half an hour. "Let's go," he said. Keller had driven the truck out of the yard some while before, explaining that he wanted to take a roundabout way to their meeting place. During the previous week he had shown them the roads and the barn where the truck would be concealed and alternative approaches to the sports centre, so that they could move on their own without much danger of getting lost.

It would take less than twenty minutes, Jeremy had estimated, to reach the sports centre on foot. The routine of the Steinhof appeared to be Germanically inflexible; the small green bus arrived at the sports centre on the dot of two forty-five. Again, perhaps because Keller had arranged it so, there was no one in the timber yard. Jeremy and Ben slipped out through a doorway at the rear.

At that hour on a drowsily warm summer afternoon the back streets too were virtually deserted. They walked in a leisurely manner, apparently deep in conversation. None of the few people they met gave them a glance. They turned down an alley, which debouched on to a path running behind a row of cottages. It led on, past the cottages, beyond a spinney to the gravel car park of the sports centre. Access to the car park was from the main road into the village. Neither the car park nor the sports centre itself was visible, Jeremy reckoned, from any house. It had a desolate feel. The grass on the playing field had not been cut lately. The solitary attendant was rarely seen and never, Keller assured them, at this time in the afternoon, when he could invariably be found consuming bread and sausage and beer in the village. Frau Lange had her own key to the changing room. The party from the Steinhof, Keller said, enjoyed an exclusive booking between two-thirty and four. So there should be no one else using the pool or the gymnasium.

Pausing in the shelter of the spinney, Jeremy and Ben surveyed the scene, satisfying themselves that everything seemed normal, that there was indeed no one else in sight.

"Okay?" asked Jeremy.

Ben gave him a mock salute and a grin, and they separated to take up their planned positions. A low straggly hedge around the car park, against which a loose chain dangled from dirty white posts, contributed neither beauty nor security but did provide just enough cover. The bus always came to a halt at exactly the same spot, about twelve feet from the door of the unadorned brick structure in which the changing rooms were housed. Jeremy lay down, at full length, behind the adjacent hedge. Ben took up his position in the small gap between the changing rooms and the gymnasium, the latter being little more than a large wooden shed. The swimming pool shimmered invitingly beyond.

The shade of the hedge felt pleasantly warm. Bees were humming. Jeremy gazed up into a clear blue sky, his mind gradually wandering away—until he jerked himself awake. He consulted his watch again. Ten minutes to go. He wondered if the natural cussedness of things would make this the one day on which the routine was not observed, so that the bus didn't come, or came late, or didn't bring all the children, or did contain other people. . . .

He heard it quite a long way off, coming down the road. Peering through the roots of the hedge, he saw it swing into the entrance of the car park, puffing black smoke from the exhaust. The gravel crunched as it drew up in precisely the usual place, looming above him. The door slid open.

The disembarking procedure too followed a pattern. First the guard emerged, a big man in plain clothes, not visibly armed, though he might well be carrying a pistol. Then came the eight children—five boys and three girls. Finally Frau Lange descended, a sour-looking woman, Jeremy thought, with grey hair and an almost ankle-length grey dress. While the children divided themselves into two groups, boys and girls, she would walk over to the door and unlock it. The driver remained sitting behind the wheel of the bus; later he might join the guard for a smoke and a chat.

Jeremy lay very still. He wondered if anyone looking straight at the hedge could see him. One of the children might suddenly call out. But the procedure unfolded normally. The guard stood, with his back to Jeremy, barely three feet away. Frau Lange opened the door of the changing rooms; he heard the scrape of the key in the lock. The children followed her in disciplined lines, not chattering as might have been expected at their age. He couldn't see them, only their feet, and therefore couldn't try again to identify Stefan. The last of them went through the door, with Frau Lange standing beside it.

He and Ben moved simultaneously. Jeremy hit the guard from behind. Ben, who had worked his way to the corner of the building, needed only a stride to bring him level with the driver's window. The driver had been looking in the other direction, idly watching the children. Ben's powerful hands were about his throat before he knew it.

Frau Lange started to cry out as Jeremy, letting the guard slump to the ground, leaped towards her. He meant to put his hand over her mouth, but, instead of screaming, she fought, kicking and scratching ferociously. Jeremy had no qualms, or only the tiniest vestigial qualm, about hitting her, but doing so effectively wasn't easy. Finally he forced her on to the ground, face downwards, and kneeling on the small of her back, managed to seize her wrists and tie them. She was swearing at him, which enabled him to jam a gag into her mouth. Then he tied her feet. Leaving her writhing on the gravel, he went swiftly to the two unconscious men, first to the guard on the ground, then to the driver in the bus, and, producing short pieces of nylon rope and gags from his pocket, secured them both.

Ben had gone straight into the changing rooms to quieten the children. After a moment in which to recover his breath, Jeremy followed. He could see Ben's back filling the doorway.

Inside was a passage, with duckboards on the floor, and, on either side, a row of showers in front of which plastic curtains could be drawn. The light was dim: the air smelled of steam and damp towels. The girls were grouped on the right, the boys on the left. They held bundles, presumably their swimming costumes and towels, but had not begun to change. A little girl, younger than the rest, was crying. The others simply stood, silently, watching.

Ben was talking to them in his excellent German, his voice calm and friendly, trying to soothe them, saying there was nothing to be frightened of, that no one would hurt them; that, on the contrary, he was their friend, that he had come to help them. But they weren't responding. They seemed less frightened than wary.

Jeremy abandoned any hope that he could immediately identify Stefan. That would take longer than they could afford to spend here. The main thing was to keep control. "Let's get them in the bus," he said in English.

"Come along now," said Ben amiably. "We'll take you all for a little ride in the bus. Then you can go home. Don't worry . . ." For a moment Jeremy thought they would refuse to come, in which case he would have to threaten them, perhaps show a gun. And suppose they still wouldn't move? But they did. One of the older boys led the way, and, still silent except for the crying of the little girl, they walked— marched almost—out of the changing room. With curiosity rather than alarm, they looked at Frau Lange, still struggling, on the ground and at the two inert men.

While Ben shepherded the children on to the bus, Jeremy dragged the two men and then, with some difficulty, Frau Lange into the building. The key she had used was still in the lock. He shut the door and turned the key.

Ben, already in the driver's seat of the bus, switched on the engine. After a quick glance around to make sure that there was no one in sight, no trouble impending, Jeremy climbed aboard, sliding the door shut behind him. The children were sitting, quite obediently. He wondered if they were drugged or psychologically crushed: but no, he thought, rather the opposite. They had learned to survive, to do what they were told and give nothing away. Carefully he examined their faces again. Which was Stefan? None of them seemed to match the photograph exactly but it could easily be any one of three. The fourth, whom he had considered possible originally, seemed at close quarters too unlike.

They were out of the car park now and rolling ponderously, with much grinding of gears, along the road away from the village. There was no traffic. The world seemed asleep. Inside the bus was their own separate world. Well, I'd better try, thought Jeremy and began his speech.

"We've come to help Stefan Janocki," he said. "I've a letter here from his mother." Jeremy produced it. "I wish we could help you all, but the best I can promise is that we won't get you into any trouble. No one will blame any of you for what's happened this afternoon. As my friend told you, there's nothing to worry about or be frightened of. Now I must talk to Stefan. Which of you is Stefan?"

He smiled at them invitingly. No one spoke.

"Please," he said. "I'm telling you the truth. We're here to help. Stefan, this letter really is from your mother. Just look at it. It's in her handwriting. I want you to be quite sure in your own mind that she sent us." There was still no reply. "All right. Pass the letter round." He offered it to the boy who had led the march from the changing room and was now sitting in the front row, nearest to Jeremy. The boy took the letter, read it impassively, and passed it back to the boy immediately behind him. The letter consisted of just half a page in Irena's bold handwriting and the purple ink which she favoured. It said only that the bearer had come from her and that Stefan should trust him. Drafting a letter which would convince her son but convey as little as possible if it fell into the wrong hands had been a difficult exercise, and Jeremy was far from certain that it was adequate.

The heat through the windows made the atmosphere stifling. The bus had turned off the main road now and was heading for the rendezvous point. The scenery was familiar; Keller had twice driven them over the route. They had scarcely more than another mile to go. The letter, after being passed from hand to hand down the bus, had reached the girl in the back row. She too read it solemnly and passed it forward again. The boy in the front returned it to Jeremy.

Trying to keep impatience out of his voice, he said: "Isn't that enough? What else can I do to convince you? Ask me something. Stefan, I've seen your mother. Shall I describe her?"

Still not a word.

Jeremy moved to the empty seat beside the boy in the front, sat down and talked just to him. "You're older than the others and I'm sure you understand how important this is. I must talk to Stefan—for his sake, not mine. Won't you tell me which he is? Or would you like to discuss it among yourselves? There's not much time."

The boy looked Jeremy squarely in the eye. "We have no need for discussion," he said. "We do not betray each other."

It was like a door slamming shut. In the time available Jeremy doubted very much if he could prise it open. The farm where they were to meet Keller lay at the end of this road.

The bus jumped and rattled over deep ruts of sun-baked clay. Jeremy could see the roof of the barn in which Keller should be waiting with the truck and its deceptive load of timber. He left the boy and sat down beside Ben.

"No luck, eh?" said Ben.

"No joy at all. We've only a couple of hours at most before there's an alarm because the bus isn't back at the house. And we need to be well on the road by then."

"Could be much less if that woman worked herself loose. I sure hope you were a boy scout and learned about knots."

The farm gates were just ahead. "The children mustn't see Keller," said Ben, "or the timber truck." Applying the brake, he brought the bus to a halt in the shade of a large oak tree. "Do you want to go ahead and alert Keller?" The plan was to take the bus into a smaller shed behind the great barn, and leave the children there while Stefan was transferred to the hiding place among the timber. But the plan was now in tatters. Jeremy's mind, which always worked coolly and clearly in an emergency, raced through the possibilities.

"Time's a-wasting," said Ben. "What are we going to do?"

"I'll tell you. But you'll say I'm mad."

"Try me."

Jeremy told him. "You're mad," said Ben.

Four hours later the Steinhof was in turmoil. Frau Lange, her normally grey hard features now red and animated with rage, was recounting, for the third time (and the details grew more colourful with repetition), how cruelly she had been attacked and beaten to the ground. A senior uniformed officer of the People's Police took notes. A man in plain clothes spoke on the telephone.

There was the sound of a car outside, a black official car. The man who alighted was not a policeman but the policemen knew who he was. He wore dark glasses. His eyes, had they been visible, might have been pink-rimmed, for his hair was white enough to constitute him an albino.

He evidently knew the way. He went straight to Frau Lange's study, brushing aside the policeman at the door. A hush fell on the room as he entered. Then Frau Lange and the plain-clothes policeman started talking together. He cut them short.

"I have heard what happened. Have they been seen yet?"

"Not yet," said the policeman. "We've established road blocks. My guess is that they will be heading north." At that moment the telephone rang. He picked it up, listened, said: "Yes . . . Yes . . . Good. Thank you." Replacing the receiver, he said: "I was right. The bus has been found. Abandoned, about ten miles north of Pachabel. My men are searching the woods."

The man in dark glasses asked: "Why did you think they would go north?"

"Because the only other main road from Pachabel runs directly south-east towards the border. "But," explained the policeman a touch smugly, "since the border was closed, that road goes nowhere. Just through a few small villages. And if you're imagining that they might try to cross the border, you needn't worry about that. Nobody has ever tried to cross there. It's too difficult. Now, if you want to know where they might attempt a crossing, I have a theory—"

The man in dark glasses interrupted. "Where would you say it is most impossible to cross the border?"

"In these parts? I tell you, no one would try. There are easier places. The most impossible? Around the Schönberg maybe. It's hard even to get near the border. The mountains are very steep."

"You're a fool," said the man in dark glasses. "Give me the telephone."

XVI

Gone Away!

"Who are they?" asked Irena.

"I'm sorry to say they're from Oxford," replied Diana.

The Black Bear, which had been so tranquil throughout the two weeks of their stay, had suddenly ceased to be tranquil: and what had intruded, that Tuesday morning, was farce. The gentle chimes of the clock in the parlour had just struck noon when a crowd of young men burst in. They were clad in beautifully cut tweed coats or hacking jackets and trousers of cavalry twill or dark grey worsted. Their faces were pink, their hair was neatly trimmed. They talked loudly and laughed even more loudly. They were English—or, in the case of the owlish bespectacled one who appeared to be their titular chief (he was addressed occasionally as "Mr. President"), Scots. At least Diana assumed he was Scots, not from his accent, which was impeccably English, but because his name was Mungo.

"Beer, beer, beer," they chorused.

"And wenches," suggested a droopy youth with straw-coloured hair. "At a wayside inn one expects wenches." He put a hunting horn to his lips and blew.

"Shut up, Valentine," the others yelled. "Beer, beer, beer."

Diana recognised some familiar college ties. She half-recognised some faces too, familiar from the gossip columns. And, of course, she knew the type; that was wholly familiar.

Anna Grelf poked her head round the door from the kitchen and withdrew again very quickly. Grelf emerged from his room. *"Bitte, bitte"* he pleaded.

"Ah, landlord," said Mungo.

"The landlord's broken cover," cried Valentine, and sounded another blast on the horn.

"Bitter, bitter, bitter beer," chanted two of the others.

"Herr Oberst," began Mungo.

"That means 'waiter,' " said a plump young man whose checkered waistcoat bulged beneath a white stock. "He's not a waiter. He's the landlord."

"All right, Perry. You're the German speaker. You try."

"Herr Wirt—"

"Gentlemen, I speak English," said Grelf. "Perhaps if you would care to sit at the table outside . . ."

"Beer, beer, beer."

The tide of exuberance eventually receded through the door. Mungo, however, had seen Gabriel's party, sitting in the parlour, riveted by the spectacle. Advancing towards them, he bowed solemnly. "I must apologise for my noisy friends." He pointed to the book lying open on Diana's knee. "I perceive that you are English, compatriots in a strange land. Allow me to introduce myself. I have the honour to be president of our little society. We are called the Henries. You know— Hooray Henries." He grinned, rather disarmingly, Diana thought. "The trouble is, it's too early in the morning. They're not drunk. If they were drunk, they'd be more tractable."

"And what brings you here?" asked Richard.

"We're on tour," said Mungo. "Our summer tour. A riding tour."

"Where are your steeds?" asked Diana.

"Tethered without, madam. Look through the window and you'll see them."

A dozen well-groomed horses were indeed nibbling grass under the trees across the road. The well-groomed young men had seated themselves around a long wooden table. Frau Grelf bustled out, carrying a tray laden with tall golden glasses. Sunshine through branches dappled the grass, a slight breeze making the leaves tremble. It really could have been a scene from an old painting.

"I'd better get back to my friends," he said. "They need a firm hand. Goodbye."

Following his stately departure, Irena said: "I don't understand. Why 'Henries'?"

"Why indeed?" said Diana. "It's a name for people like that. But I don't know why."

"The flower of English youth," said Gabriel acidly.

Through the open window came a clink of glasses, and Mungo's voice: "Gentlemen, the Henries!"

"Hooray!" came the antiphonal response.

The dining room at luncheon was almost empty. The two couples who had been lodging at the inn when Gabriel's party arrived had both left, and, since then, there had been only a trickle of visitors, staying for one or two nights. The Henries consumed a noisy lunch outside. Eventually, with a clatter of hooves and a great deal more shouting, they moved off.

Grelf came in, and, seeing Gabriel, spread his palms in mock despair.

"They're gone?" asked Gabriel.

"Thank the good Lord!"

"I thought they might have wanted rooms for the night," said Richard, "on the 'where I eats I sleeps' principle."

"They are camping out in the woods," said Grelf.

"A long way off, I trust," said Gabriel.

"Were you like that when you were an undergraduate?" Diana asked Richard.

"I was not," he said.

When evening came, it was Richard's turn to keep watch. Diana went with him. The whole procedure had become very much a routine. They sat beneath the tree, looking out across the darkening valley. As the purple of the sky grew deeper, the rising moon became a bright silver penny, illuminating the hillside but blackening the shadows.

"No wonder they call it the Schönberg," said Diana, gazing at the mountain which towered above the valley to the south. "It is very beautiful."

Richard stiffened and gripped her arm. "Diana, look!" he said.

At first she saw nothing. Then she saw it: a pinpoint of light in the blackest part of the hillside opposite them. The light winked on and off.

"Four, I think," said Richard. "Did you count?"

"No. I probably missed the beginning."

"He should do it again. Yes, there."

The light blinked again, four times. It was so small that they might easily have missed it altogether if they hadn't known where to look.

"It really is," whispered Diana.

"Now once more." The light appeared again, on and off, four times.

"They've done it! They're there!" said Richard. "Come on. We must get the others."

They made their way quickly between the trees and then along the bridle-path. There was a bit of time in hand, the arrangement being that the crossing would take place two hours after the signal. The woods were silent, without a breath of wind, which somehow added to the tension; this was the moment of eerie stillness before the storm broke, the fixing of bayonets before the order to go over the top.

Gabriel and Irena were drinking coffee in the parlour of the inn. He stiffened as he saw Richard and Diana come into the room. Grelf, who was carrying a tray of glasses through to the kitchen, also halted. Their news, evidently, was written on their faces.

"The light shineth in darkness," said Richard.

There was no one else in the room, the few other guests having already gone to their rooms or to watch television in the small room set apart for that purpose. "The signal?" asked Grelf.

"Yes," said Richard.

"I shall come with you. Wait, please, for a minute." He vanished into the rear premises, calling "Anna!" Gabriel and Irena had both risen. She gripped Gabriel's arm.

Grelf reappeared, with a coil of thin nylon rope in his left hand and, in his right, a cloth bundle. Unfolding the bundle, he revealed a pair of automatic pistols, which he extended first to Gabriel, then to Richard. "We shouldn't need these," he said, "but it is best to be prepared." He delved in his pocket and produced two clips of ammunition. Gabriel snapped a clip into place: Richard, more clumsily, had to discover how the gun worked.

Grelf led the way from the inn. Looking up at the sky, he said, "There is much light," although whether he considered this a good or a bad thing wasn't clear. He took them again, past the turning to the observation point which had become so familiar, to that other place, a little further on, where they plunged into the trees, following no discernible path, and emerged on the rim of the gorge. The moonlight was, indeed, almost as bright as day.

A narrow crest or ridge of land, between the head of the valley on their left and a vertiginous drop into the gorge on their right, stretched up directly in front of them until it was blocked by the high mesh fence. The two lines of wire and the death strip between them, illumined superfluously by the tall arc-lights, appeared more sinister than ever, an ugly scar across the beauty of the scene.

"The ladies will please wait here," said Grelf. "Within the trees. It is best you should not be seen."

Leaving Diana and Irena in the shadows, Richard and Gabriel followed Grelf. After only a few paces, the ground began sloping sharply down. The walk became a scramble. Sure-footed, Grelf led them along, and down, the right-hand side of the spur. It was steep but not quite as precipitous as it had seemed from above. Soon they were shielded from any observer who might have been looking in their direction from the watchtowers. Richard steadied himself against what was now virtually a cliff-face: but, although the sensation of descending into an abyss was uncomfortable, the climb was not actually difficult. Only a splashing of water broke the silence.

They stepped on to a ledge about six feet wide. Grelf halted, and the others closed up behind him. He pointed forward and down. A succession of protruding rocks, forming a rough stairway, ended in a spray of water, which burst from the cliff and over another, smaller ledge before plunging into the gulf. The straggly shape of a bush, clinging to the thin damp soil, obscured the lower ledge.

"We wait here," said Grelf.

Richard surveyed the position. The edge of the cliff, sharp against the night sky, loomed perhaps twenty feet above them. On the right lay the abyss and beyond it the mountains, rising tier on tier, washed by moonlight. The ledge where they stood was in shadow, but his eyes were now accustomed to the darkness and he could make out, quite easily, the remaining descent towards the bush and the pale spray of water.

"We might as well sit," said Grelf. They did, with relief; Richard felt more secure, seated, resting his back against the cliff.

Gabriel looked at his watch. "We have still a quarter of an hour," he said, "if they are on time."

"Otto will be on time," said Grelf. "He will put them into the culvert exactly two hours after the signal. It should take them then maybe ten, maybe fifteen, minutes. We must hope there is no obstruction."

We must indeed, thought Richard. The minutes passed very slowly. They scarcely spoke, and, when they did, it was in hushed voices; quite unnecessarily, since no one could be within earshot and the noise of the water anyway predominated.

Richard visualised Jeremy and Ben and, with luck, a boy being guided down, through a screen of undergrowth, into a dried-up water course which then vanished into a tunnel or pipe. The culvert must surely be narrow to have remained, for so long, unnoticed. Claustrophobic. And there might be an obstruction. Or Otto might be less clever than Grelf believed. He could have been spotted. The border guards might open fire. But there had been no sound of firing. The silence remained unbroken except for the steady splashing. Unwanted into Richard's mind came that phrase from the poem by Belloc which he had quoted to Diana as they sat beneath the trees: "No sound: But the boom Of the far waterfall like Doom."

The minutes dragged on. Grelf now lay full length, peering down to where the escapers should appear.

Hearing him exclaim, Richard and Gabriel moved quickly over and crouched beside him. A figure had emerged from behind the curtain of water and was squeezing past the bush. It was Ben. "Your friend?" asked Grelf.

"Yes," said Richard.

Grelf whistled. Ben heard him, looked up and waved. Someone else came through the spray. A boy. So this, Richard thought excitedly, was Stefan. Grelf whistled again, and, uncoiling the rope, sent it snaking down to Ben, who caught it and made it fast around his waist. Richard joined Grelf on their end of the rope. It seemed more of a precaution than a necessity; an active man—two active men and a twelve-year-old boy—should be able to negotiate the stairway of rocks without excessive danger.

A third figure was emerging, but it couldn't be Jeremy. Too small. It was another child. A girl. The boy had turned to help her, and she was turning, holding the hand of another, smaller child behind. Then there was another, and another. Richard gaped. Grelf said something in German to Gabriel, whose reply, although Richard didn't understand the

words, needed no translation. Gabriel was expressing equal surprise and
mystification.

Grelf had hauled the rope tight. Richard lent his weight. And the
children, the big ones helping the smaller ones, clawed their way along
it. Jeremy, to Richard's great relief, had finally come into sight, bringing up the rear. As soon as the last child, a boy, had begun working his
way along the rope, Ben waved Jeremy to go ahead as well. Gabriel
extended a hand to the first child, the boy who now might or might not
be Stefan, pulling him on to the upper ledge. The children seemed
remarkably calm, even the little girl who was obviously the youngest of
them. Only when Jeremy had reached the ledge and scrambled up did
Ben start to follow, coiling the rope in his hands as he came.

The ledge was crowded now. The children, herded by the boy who
seemed in some sense their leader, as well as by Jeremy, ranged themselves tightly against the cliff: five boys and three girls. Richard stood
beside Jeremy, smiling, though perplexed. "Hi there!" said Ben, as
Grelf and Gabriel helped him up.

"Is there any trouble?" asked Gabriel. "Are you being followed?"

"Don't think so," said Ben.

Overwhelming relief was Richard's main sensation. "Otto is safe?"
asked Grelf.

"Yup. But he wouldn't come with us."

Jeremy said: "I'm afraid there are rather more of us than you expected."

"There certainly are," said Richard. "Which is Stefan?"

"That's just it. We're not sure. So I thought I'd bring the lot."

Gabriel looked at the children thoughtfully. "They wanted to
come?"

"They came. Shall we proceed? This doesn't seem quite the place for
a chat."

Grelf led the way up towards the edge of the cliff and the stars.
Gabriel helped Ben with the children, talking to them quietly in German. Richard and Jeremy brought up the rear.

"However did you manage to transport them all?" asked Richard.

"In a Trojan horse. It was rather a tight squeeze. I'll tell you our
thrilling adventures later. But there is one thing that worries me. Ben
said we weren't being followed, and I agree; I'm sure we weren't. That
is, there's no one close on our heels. But I fancy we're being hunted.

Just when Otto left us, when he'd shoved us into the mouth of the drain, I heard motor-car engines. And we hadn't seen or heard a car before since we arrived. That's a lonely bit of country."

"You think Otto may have been caught?"

"He'd give them a run for their money."

"Well, there's nothing we can do about it. And anyway you're safely out."

"That's a fairly inglorious summary." Jeremy stood still.

"You can't go back," said Richard.

"No. Of course not."

They came up on to the cliff edge. The rest of the party were already moving towards the trees.

"Irena's here?" asked Jeremy.

"Yes. With Diana."

Indeed they could see the cream linen of Diana's dress. Irena, in plum-coloured slacks and pullover, was barely visible beside her. Then the two women moved out of the shadows into the moonlight, Irena hurrying towards the children. But Diana halted abruptly. Richard thought she was looking at them, at Jeremy perhaps, but then realised she was looking past them. He turned to see what had attracted her attention. There seemed nothing remarkable, no movement; the landscape, the fence, the watchtower lay still in the moonlight. If any alarm had been sounded, he couldn't hear it. But there was something different. The lights along the section of fence nearest to them had been extinguished.

Everything was so clear in the moonlight that the change was barely perceptible and not immediately ominous: but, even as he looked, figures appeared. Two men seemed to come through the far fence as though there were a gap in it, and, at a slow trot, crossed the intervening strip of ploughed land, zigzagging left and right, confidently as though they knew where the mines were laid and could avoid them. When they reached the nearer fence, they cut the wire. Of course, thought Richard, the electricity's off. Now there were more men, perhaps ten or twelve, following. They were all dressed alike but not in uniform. The impression was simply of dark trousers and high dark pullovers. And they were carrying guns.

As he watched, not quite understanding what he saw, Richard was aware that they had seen him. The first man in the main group gestured, pointing, and those close behind him looked in the direction indicated—towards Richard and the others, caught, as most of them still were, in the moonlit open ground between the clifftop and the trees. But the men never halted. They came on, at a steady trot, through the gap in the nearer fence which the advance pair had cut.

"But they never cross the border," protested Grelf in tones of incredulity. "It is most strictly forbidden."

"They're not border guards," said Jeremy.

Gabriel and Ben were already shepherding the children into the cover of the trees. Richard jerked into life. "Let's not wait to find out."

The gap in the fence was hardly more than five hundred yards away. As Richard turned to run, a sharp crack broke the stillness of the evening and a bullet smashed through the leaves of the tree above him. The welcome darkness enfolded him: but he glanced back and saw their pursuers, loping steadily, strung out like a pack of wolves, up the slope from the breached fence.

There was no question of fleeing silently through the wood. Diana had picked up the smallest child, the little girl, and was carrying her: but the whole party panted and stumbled through the undergrowth, leaving a swathe of shattered bracken clear in the dappled moonlight. Grelf was leading the way. Jeremy and Ben fell back on either side of Richard. Both now had pistols in their hands. Richard drew his, knowing, as he did so, how inadequate a weapon it was.

"How far to the village?" asked Jeremy.

"There is no village," said Richard. "Just the inn."

"We can't outrun them. Not with the children."

"They must want us awful bad," said Ben.

"Try and lead them off—up there," said Jeremy, pointing between an avenue of trees. "Delay them." And he sprinted after the children.

There was a moment of utter stillness, the noise of the pursued fading away while the pursuers were not yet close. But, running on that soft carpet of pine needles, Shaman's men, Richard felt (and he had no doubt they were Shaman's men), could be on them without warning.

"You heard him," said Ben. "This-a-way." They ran between the trees for about two hundred yards, until the undergrowth clogged their route behind a fallen tree. They could no longer hear the children.

"Behind that log maybe," said Ben.

They jumped it and flopped on to the ground. Pistols resting on the tree trunk, they looked back along the avenue of trees and waited.

"What do you think Jeremy's doing with the children?" asked Richard.

"Getting them hidden, I imagine," said Ben. "Then he'll come back."

"But we haven't a chance in a gun battle," said Richard, appalled. "There are too many of them, and they've got rifles."

"Do you have a better idea? We'll take a couple of pot shots, then pull back. Perhaps we can lose them."

There was no breath of wind; no sound; then a slight stirring in the undergrowth, which sent Richard's heart into his mouth, but it was only some small woodland creature. Tall shafts of moonlight made the space between the trees look like a theatre set. A set waiting for the players, for the action. Somewhere in the distance an owl hooted.

A man stepped into the open. He was wearing a polo-necked sweater and carried an automatic rifle, his finger stretched beside the trigger. He looked cautiously around. Another man appeared behind him.

"You take the first, I'll take the second," whispered Ben.

Richard's safety catch was already off. No time now for thought or qualms. He aimed, steadying the pistol with both hands. Squeeze, not pull, one was told. He fired, a fraction of a second later than Ben. His target flew backwards like a duck in the shooting gallery at a fair. The other man was down too.

"Come on," cried Ben, who was already on his feet. Crouching low, they plunged between the trees. There was a shout behind them, then a fusillade of shots: but nothing very near. The pursuers were firing blind, just raking the undergrowth. The shooting stopped, and again there was an eerie silence. Ben seized Richard's arm, halting him. They stood quite still, listening: but there was nothing.

Very cautiously they moved forwards, pausing after almost every step. Even the faint rustle of grass or pine needles beneath their feet seemed a fearful treachery, apt to draw a hail of bullets. They didn't dare whisper to each other. Was it better to move or stand still? Should they lie down in the darkest shadows and hope that the hunters would go past? They crept on forwards, more from inertia than decision.

Now between the trees appeared an open space. It was, Richard realised, the main bridle-path. If they could cross it, they might succeed in slipping away. But they weren't supposed to slip away, not if it meant leaving the enemy to search, at leisure, a comparatively small area of woodland in which lay, concealed, the children and Gabriel and the two girls. If a vague thought could be called a plan, Richard decided what they must do. They must cross the bridle-path, fire a shot or two from the other side, and then run, hoping to draw Shaman's men away and then lose them in the larger forest. That would give Jeremy an opportunity to lead his party off in the other direction.

So the thing now was to sprint across the bridle-path. They hadn't spoken but Ben was following just a pace behind. Richard was about to step out from the trees into the full moonlight when he froze. Barely ten feet away to the right stood one of Shaman's men, gun cradled across his arm, watching the path. Richard's pistol came up. He hadn't been seen: he could shoot the man. He looked warily left down the bridle-path. And there stood another man, thirty feet away, gun at the ready. And beyond him another.

In the wood behind he heard a voice, giving orders. He understood, in a sickening instant, how completely they were trapped. The hunters had sealed off a killing ground, and were walking up through the woods, line abreast, to flush the quarry. He imagined them, fancied he could hear them. His mind worked frantically. Could he and Ben lie hidden in the shadows, shoot or knock down the nearest man, break through the line and get away? But the hunters were alert. They would fire at the first movement. And there was no time. No more time to think. No more time to plan. He felt seized by the paralysis which can hold a trapped animal.

He heard Ben's breath, felt the useless weight of the gun in his hand, wondered where Jeremy was, remembered Diana with the child in her arms . . . and heard the sound of the hunters closing in.

But it was a strange sound. A drumming, a throbbing, and not behind him. The sound grew. It was away to the left. Shaman's men had heard it too. It was coming towards them along the bridle-path. And into sight.

Incredibly, absurdly, at full gallop, came the Henries, thundering down the path in the moonlight, dust flying from hooves, Mungo in the lead brandishing a riding crop, Valentine with the hunting horn to his lips and all the others pressing close behind. As they saw Shaman's men they whooped and shouted "Tally-ho!" and Valentine blew the horn.

For a moment the whole extraordinary scene was etched like a black-and-white engraving, action suspended, poised. The cavalry had arrived. But cavalry against machine-guns.

Shaman's men didn't fire. They melted back into the shadow of the wood. Richard let out his breath in a gasp.

Mungo raised his arm, and the cavalcade almost skidded to a halt with much pushing and shoving. "Gone away!" cried someone. Valentine sounded a melancholy blast. Perhaps rashly but too stunned to think about further possibilities of danger, Richard stepped out to greet them.

"Hello, hello, hello," said Mungo. "Spot of bother, what?"

"You might say," replied Richard, and found himself laughing.

"We were camped up there," said Mungo, gesturing vaguely behind him. "And we saw the lights go out, and we saw those chaps, and we heard shouting. Some poor fellow trying to escape from behind the Iron Curtain, we thought. Now's the time, we thought, to do our good deed for the day."

"But you're not from behind the Iron Curtain," said Valentine, puzzled. "We saw you this morning."

"What about the lovely ladies?" asked Mungo. "Are they all right?"

"More to the point," said Valentine, looking around him, "what about the villains? They're still lurking. With guns."

"You've got a gun," said another of the Henries, pointing at Richard.

"But not such a big one," said Valentine.

It was Ben who intervened. "Fellows," he said, "we've still got a problem. Some friends of ours are back there hiding in the woods—"

"I don't think they are," said Valentine.

"What a lot of people in these woods," said the Henry beside him.

"My dear, the noise. And the people," said another.

Looking past them, Richard saw Gabriel, and Jeremy, and the children emerging from the trees, and Irena, and Diana holding the little girl by the hand.

XVII

Children's Party

"I'm very sorry, my dear," said Gabriel.

Irena shrugged. "I never really let myself believe that you could bring him."

"Perhaps when we talk to the other children, we shall learn something. They may tell us where he's gone and then we could try again."

"Perhaps." They sat in silence. Then she said: "No. There won't be another chance. Shaman will make sure of that. He always threatened that, if I disobeyed him, I should never see Stefan again. He'll want that lesson to be learned."

The parlour of the inn was quiet, which was why Gabriel had brought her there. She might deny that she had ever expected their venture to succeed, she might indeed have steeled herself against disappointment, but it must have been a bitter blow when the children came and Stefan was not among them. She had said nothing as they ran through the woods. It was only afterwards, when the danger was over, that Gabriel realised she was standing apart from the children. Jeremy realised it too. "Which is Stefan?" he asked her, already knowing the answer. "None of them," she said.

The Henries, exuberantly, had provided an escort back to the inn, with the smaller children lifted on to their saddles. Richard and Jeremy brought up the rear, pistols in hand, wondering all the time if Shaman's men might reappear from the trees. But nothing more happened. It was almost as though the dark figures which had hunted them were merely shadows or figments of fear, dispersed by the cheerful cavalcade.

"Do you suppose it's the children they want," asked Richard, "or us?"

"Oh, the children," said Jeremy. "The children are important. I don't think they'd have risked coming through the wire for us."

"But they'd have killed us—"

"Killed us or captured us and taken us back across the border. There'd have been no political row because nobody would have known. But all these bright young men were rather too much. They couldn't keep that quiet."

"I hope."

As they approached the inn, Frau Grelf bustled out to meet them. While Diana and the Henries looked after the children, Gabriel, Richard, Jeremy and Ben had a brief discussion. They agreed that, even if there was no further immediate danger, the sooner they got away, the better. And they would have to take the children. Grelf had a car of his own and a shooting brake in which he sometimes collected visitors and their luggage from the railway station in the nearest town, some ten miles away. Using those two vehicles and the hired cars, they could accommodate the whole party.

Gabriel told Grelf what he wanted. "If you take my cars," protested Grelf, "Anna and I will not be able to leave—if it becomes necessary. I am afraid for her."

"I don't think you need be," said Gabriel. "Not now. Certainly not after we're gone. But why don't you come with us? Then you can bring one of the cars back. We can probably persuade the young Englishmen to take care of Anna until you get home."

So it was settled; but Grelf had some arrangements to make on the telephone first. They had planned to leave Germany with one boy; Gabriel carried a passport made out in Stefan's name, with a photograph which looked adequately like him. Now there were eight children to be considered. Grelf's friends in Munich—old friends of The Fishers—would shelter them while Gabriel got in touch with Arthur Blaise. How Blaise would react was a question, but Gabriel, who knew his man, had little doubt that he would want the children; or, if not, that he would at least connive.

The original bargain presumably now fell through. Gabriel could no longer offer Irena's knowledge; it had not been earned. For us this is a set-back, thought Gabriel, for her it's a tragedy. And, while Grelf telephoned and Anna brought food and drink for the Henries and for the children, he sat Irena down in the quiet parlour and insisted that she should drink a glass of brandy.

"They won't hurt your boy," he said. "Shaman still needs him as a hold over you."

She shook her head. "I don't think so. I'm no use to him any more. He'll be more interested in making an example for others."

"What will you do?"

"Go back to England. Of course I will talk to the children. But it won't help. Even if they know where Stefan went, Shaman will move him again now."

"You won't be safe. We must arrange for you to disappear. We're quite good at that."

Irena swallowed what was left of the brandy. "At the moment I don't much care. I want to hit back at those people. I promised that, if you brought Stefan to me, I would give you all I knew about their organisation in Britain. You tried. It wasn't your fault, or Jeremy's, that you didn't succeed. If I tell you anyway, can you hurt them?"

"We can hurt them."

"I shall tell you."

From that moment on everything went as smoothly as though all the difficulties and dangers of the previous weeks had been an illusion. The safe house in Munich proved to be an empty warehouse. At a stained and scratched desk in a dusty office, with last year's calendar on the wall, Gabriel put through a telephone call to Blaise: and emerged smiling. Three hours later a smooth young Englishman arrived to collect them. A few hours more and they were boarding a Royal Air Force plane, to which they had been conveyed, in dark-windowed cars, through a rear gate of the airfield. Before leaving, Gabriel had called Grelf at the Black Bear. There had been no trouble, no sign of the enemy. After a while, Grelf had gone cautiously to the edge of the trees. The broken wire had been repaired. The two men whom Richard and Ben had shot, whether wounded or dead, were gone.

In England Blaise himself met them, a dapper figure on the tarmac. "I must say," was his opening remark to Gabriel, "you don't do things by halves."

"I knew you liked children," said Gabriel.

"I don't like children. But I've a feeling I may like these. Have you got anything more out of them?"

"I haven't tried. They're very silent. Miss Janocki talked to them, and she believes they did know her son but that they don't know where he is now."

"That doesn't really matter any more, does it?"

"Not to you."

"Not to me. You realise the international trouble you might have caused?"

"Isn't that what your colleagues in the Foreign Office are paid to deal with?"

"You realise the trouble you might have caused for me?"

"You like trouble."

"On the contrary, I like a quiet life. And I'm hoping that your Miss Janocki will help us to make life a little quieter. Good-looking woman, isn't she?"

The children had come down the aircraft steps, and Irena, Diana and Ben were with them. Richard and Jeremy stood apart, eyeing Blaise curiously. At the edge of the tarmac five cars awaited them. A man from Blaise's department was talking to a member of the air crew: three more stood by the cars.

"I've arranged a place for the children," said Blaise. "Shall we accommodate her too? We need to start debriefing her."

"Let's ask," said Gabriel. They walked over, and he introduced Blaise, first to Richard and Jeremy, then to the two girls and Ben. Blaise, he knew from past experience, was not concerned about the official anonymity which, in theory, cloaked him. "My enemies," he used to say, "all know who I am. Why shouldn't my friends?"

"I can offer you a safe house," he said to Irena. "As safe as these things ever are."

"I don't want it," she replied emphatically. "I don't want to be kept by any government. I promised information, and I'll give it you. But, if he'll have me, I should prefer to stay with Dr. Gabriel."

"By all means," said Gabriel.

"You're probably wise," said Blaise. "Altogether more comfortable. Better food and drink. My chaps will come to see you later today. You'll be at Shadowlawn?"

"You know the address?" asked Gabriel dryly. "I hadn't really thought: but, yes, we will go there. If, with Irena's help, you can bundle Shaman's men out of the country, it should be safe now."

"Nowhere is safe," said Blaise. "Ever. But we'll see what we can do."

The children, accompanied by the unnamed dark-suited men, were whisked off. Richard and Diana got into the back of one of the remaining cars; Ben sat beside the driver. Jeremy, having helped Irena into the back of the other car, stood, leaning on the door, while Gabriel said goodbye to Blaise.

"I am most grateful," said Gabriel.

"Don't be. I'm not used to it. And you may be right. Perhaps I do like certain kinds of trouble."

They smiled at each other.

The two men whom Blaise had sent duly arrived at Shadowlawn that afternoon. They were polite and sympathetic, seeming not to press at all. Irena found them surprisingly easy to talk to, very different from the kind of interrogators to whom she was accustomed; not really, as Gabriel observed afterwards, because English policemen are different but because these were men whom Arthur Blaise had chosen and trained. Gabriel suspected, but didn't say, that Blaise was also having the house guarded. In the evening he drove up to London and collected Maria, now fully recovered, though still subdued.

The questioning of Irena continued for almost a week, but the crucial facts, the names and places on which Blaise could take immediate action, were all obtained in the first session. No time was wasted. A telephone call to London started the sweep which Blaise had already prepared; supervised by his department, carried out by Special Branch officers from the Yard.

"How odd," remarked Gabriel after dinner at Shadowlawn, "to think that someone else is now fighting our battle for us."

"A nice feeling?" asked Diana.

"Not altogether. I'm always uneasy when I can't see what's going on."

"Well, I think it's fine," said Jeremy. "We've done more than enough running around lately. Relax, boys and girls. Let others take the strain."

"We'll hear what's happened?" asked Richard.

"Blaise will tell us what he thinks we should know," said Gabriel.

Blaise telephoned next day. He called again three days later. The gist of the matter was that a lot of Shaman's men had been picked up, houses and flats had been raided, others were still being watched. There would be no prosecutions: the arrested men were being quietly deported. A couple of diplomats had been told that their presence was no longer acceptable.

"We've not finished yet," said Blaise. "Our files are growing fatter. Meanwhile, we've cleaned a part of the Augean stables."

"There's a name you haven't mentioned," said Gabriel.

"Is there? Yes, I suppose there is. We haven't found Shaman, who-ever he may be. Not hide nor hair nor cloven footprint of him."

"Do you think he's still in this country?"

"I doubt it. We'll go on looking, of course. We'll twist a few arms. But my guess is that he was out before you ever got back."

Gabriel passed the news to the others.

"I'm not surprised," said Irena. "I never thought they would catch him. He does what he likes. He goes where he likes."

"As long as he leaves us alone. . . ." said Richard. "Is it over? Can we all go home?"

"I hope you'll be my guests for a bit longer. We'll see. We'll see."

Irena's interrogation was completed. Gabriel and Blaise lunched to-gether again. Diana said she was needed in the gallery, where her friend Charlotte was thoroughly fed up with coping on her own. After com-muting for a few days, she returned also to her house in the mews. Richard and Jeremy went home too. Irena stayed with Gabriel; Blaise had asked that she should, and where else anyway could she go?

Richard sifted through a pile of letters and junk mail, extracted the cheques, groaned at the bills, despaired of ever catching up with his unanswered correspondence. Deadlines were approaching. He sat down, after postponing the evil hour as long as possible, to his type-writer.

Jeremy announced that he proposed to do nothing at all for a long while. With relief he adorned himself again in silk shirts and Savile Row suits. He took Diana, sitting beside him in his splendid motor car, for Sunday lunch in the country.

It was a beautiful summer and a peaceful one. Although the travel agency had been re-opened, Gabriel spent most of his time at Shadow-lawn, pottering in the garden with his secateurs, walking with Irena beside the river, sitting with Maria in her room. No further attacks were made, anywhere, on The Fishers or their friends. Gabriel kept the organisation quiescent. He wasn't happy about that. There were so many people, so many, whom The Fishers could help: but prudence dictated a pause.

He lunched yet again with Blaise, who told him about the children. Gaining their confidence had been a long and delicate procedure. Bleak experience had taught them to trust no one but themselves, to obey orders but to give nothing. Gradually, however, one or two of them—the youngest—began to soften, and a picture emerged of who they were. Some had been hostages, held, like Irena's son, as a guarantee that their parents would do what was required: others were the children of parents who had defected or who had been taken away by the secret police. No diplomatic protest had been made at their removal from East Germany, no acknowledgement that they ever existed.

"We've checked where we can," said Blaise. "We've traced the father of one of the girls. He was a minor diplomat who defected in Paris. Really he was more than that. He was KGB or anyhow KGB trained. His wife, whom he left behind, has disappeared. We haven't told him yet about his daughter. The other defector whom we've identified is in America. As for the rest, we know about some of them. In at least one case the knowledge is going to be very useful."

"But what will happen to the children?"

"The two who have parents in the West can be restored to their parents—if the parents want them. The rest will be looked after. We shall find them schools or foster homes."

"So they become your hostages? They exchange one prison for another."

"You know better than that. It's not the same thing at all. But what would you want us to do? It would be no kindness to send them back, would it?"

Gabriel sighed. "Poor children."

"On the contrary, lucky children—when you consider the alternative."

"And Stefan. Did any of them remember him?"

"Yes, they did. But he was only at the Stone House for a short while, and was taken away almost a year ago. Apparently that wasn't unusual.

It was a floating population. Children came and went, and the ones who'd gone were never heard from again. No loving postcards."

"What a world!" said Gabriel. "Such wickedness."

"Aren't you used to that by now?"

"Never."

When, later, he told Irena what Blaise had said, she merely nodded. He mentioned it to Richard, with whom he kept in daily contact, and Richard passed it on to Diana. "I suppose there's nothing we can do for them," he said.

Then Diana had a bright idea. "Why don't we give a children's party? I'd like to see that little girl again—Gretel, she was called—and make sure she's all right. Before they're all scattered."

"In your house?"

"No, at Shadowlawn. Plenty of space there."

"Do you think Gabriel would like that?"

"Yes, I do. Anyway I'm sure he'd let us. Heart of gold, your friend Gabriel."

"Your friend as well. He's impressed by you."

"Is he? Good. We'd have Jeremy, of course, and Ben. And Irena's still there, isn't she? And why don't we have the Henries? They'd love to play children's games."

Richard groaned. "What a prospect!"

"Nonsense. It'll be fun. You'll see."

She had made up her mind; which meant that, from then on, she brushed aside all obstacles. Gabriel protested feebly that Blaise might not approve. There would be security problems.

"Let me talk to him," she said. In fact Gabriel talked to him. He had no objection. "Why not?" he said. "As long as I don't have to come."

Jeremy said: "I shall do conjuring tricks. You didn't know I was a conjuror, did you? I'm highly skilled."

Diana wrote to Mungo, whose address she obtained from *Burke's Peerage*. He replied, on heavy crested writing paper, in formal style: "The President thanks Miss Diana Mackenzie for her invitation to a children's party, which he is glad to accept on behalf of the Honourable Company of Henries." And underneath: "Whoopee! What larks!"

She had discussed the party with Irena rather nervously, afraid that she might find the idea painful, even insulting: but Irena, whose mood these days appeared to be one of melancholy determination ("Her Polish blood," according to Jeremy), said that she would like to help. It would be an exaggeration to suggest that the two women were close friends yet but they got on together quite amicably. Sympathy had overcome resentment in Diana's incorrigibly warm heart: and Irena, always enigmatic, had learned long ago to endure.

The day chosen for the party was near the end of September, before the beginning of the Oxford term. Autumn had begun to mellow the leaves, and, although there had been no frost yet, the air was cool, the dew heavy on the grass, and a mist, which filled the valley at dawn, lingered above the river. Gabriel, standing beside the French windows, which were open on to the garden, decided that this was his favourite time of year. The spring was too lively, the summer too fat, for him now; "no country for old men". And the winter would chill him. A September song was right.

But his guests today were young; the Henries, he thought, distinctly younger than the grave-eyed children. They were in the process of having tea in the dining room. Mungo was banging away on an old upright piano; at the moment he was rendering "Swing on a star" with vigour. Jeremy, good as his word, was preparing to do conjuring tricks. The three hostesses, Diana, Irena and Maria, were distributing the tea and cakes provided by Gabriel's cook, who came in daily from the village. The Henries, with Richard as a rather stiff companion, were larking about, and the children, equipped—as indeed were the Henries —with paper hats, whistles, streamers and other items of juvenile entertainment, had begun visibly to relax and, it was reasonable to hope, enjoy themselves.

Gabriel, having greeted them genially and presided over the first games, felt a little tired and had escaped from the noise into the adjacent drawing room. Outside the tranquil valley was bathed in the mild sunshine of late afternoon. The Henries' cars, a weird collection, were parked along the drive, while in a nearby field stood the unmarked green coach which had brought the children. One of the two men who escorted them remained with the vehicle, the other came in with them. A third, the driver of the coach was having his tea in the kitchen. The arrangements were oddly parallel to the way those same children had been guarded and escorted in Germany. But of course what Blaise had said was true. It wasn't the same thing at all. The West and the East were not two sides of the same coin. The moral distinction touched on everything Gabriel's life had been about.

"I've brought you some tea," said Irena, interrupting his meditation. He turned and smiled at her. "Thank you. Is it going well?"

"I think so. I know how those children feel. They still don't trust themselves to let go. Except the littlest ones—Gretel anyway. The young men are good with them."

"They are rather good young men. Very English. Perhaps you and I will never quite understand that type."

"I still don't understand about "Hooray Henries." What does it mean?" Having put the teacup on the table beside him, Irena curled herself on the sofa.

"Jeremy explained it to me," said Gabriel. "He knows a lot of surprising things. The phrase—it should really be "Hurrah Henry"—comes from a story by Damon Runyon. You have read Damon Runyon?" She shook her head. "You ought to. Then it was adopted by English jazz players to mean the sort of young aristocrats who made a great deal of noise in night clubs."

The plausibility of this definition was reinforced by the loud, if not very tuneful, chorus of "Old Macdonald had a cow" which resounded from the dining room. Irena actually laughed. Perhaps, thought Gabriel, an occasion like this is what we all needed; in spite of everything, this is the real world—a place of quiet gardens and noisy young men and children to be amused.

As though she read his thoughts, Irena said: "Is it finished now, do you believe, this private war of yours with Shaman?"

He shrugged: " 'Only the dead have seen the end of war.' But for the moment I expect so. Thanks to you."

Below the lawn and beyond a damp spinney, spectral with wraiths of mist, lay a side road, which meandered from farm to farm until it joined the main London road about two miles away. A black car crested a little stone bridge across the river and glided to a halt beside a gate which led into a meadow beside trees. Shadowlawn was only two or three hundred yards away, but the spinney concealed it from view. The rear door of the car opened. The man in the back seat, tall and thin, touched the arm of the schoolgirl beside him.

"Go," he said gently.

The child had freckles and blonde shoulder-length hair, covered with an unbecoming pudding-basin hat encircled by a blue-and-white school ribbon, and wore a blue serge coat. In the front of the big car a uniformed chauffeur sat impassively behind the wheel. The schoolgirl grinned cheerfully, slid from the car and trotted across to the five-barred wooden gate; without a backward glance, climbed it; and set off in the direction of the house.

The tall thin man in the back of the car watched until the schoolgirl was out of sight, then pulled the door shut. The car slid away.

Jeremy's conjuring tricks really weren't bad, and his patter, as one might have expected, was a pyrotechnic display of wittily precise timing. Mungo made a cheerful straight man, wide-eyed with astonishment when Jeremy named the very card he'd chosen or produced coins from unlikely parts of his anatomy. And the other Henries played up like the audience at an old-fashioned pantomime, jeering ("Bet he can't do it!"), heckling Mungo and crying their choral "Hurrah!" whenever a feat of prestidigitation was accomplished. The children were soon laughing and volunteering to help with the tricks, of which they enjoyed the simplest best. Jeremy had a scarlet bottle inscribed with Arabic characters. When he fed a piece of pyjama cord into it, the bottle hung mysteriously from the cord: when other people tried, it didn't. Mungo stamped and raised his eyes to heaven in rage. The children made them do it again and again.

Diana, leaning against the wall, smiled and let her mind wander. She thought about Jeremy and she thought about Richard. She looked dreamily out of the window.

A girl, perhaps twelve years old, was walking up the lawn towards the house. Probably one of the neighbours' children, thought Diana. Gabriel must have invited her. I suppose, she mused, we could have enlarged the party and had a lot of local children. It might have been more fun for our lot; they've been isolated for too long. A bit of ordinary life is what they need. Blaise might have objected, though, on security grounds. Which was absurd . . .

Surely it was absurd? An alarm bell rang, faintly but insistently, at the back of Diana's mind. The girl in the garden knew just where she was going. She approached the house briskly, glancing neither to right nor left, paying no attention to the laughter which she must have heard from the dining room. Her destination, obviously and quite reasonably, was the open French windows of the drawing room, where Gabriel and Irena were. But this was only a little girl. Diana didn't admit to herself that there was any cause for worry. She simply decided that, as hostess, she should greet the new arrival and make sure the girl was being looked after.

She slipped around, unnoticed, behind the children and the Henries, to the door.

"What are your plans now?" Gabriel asked Irena. "Have you thought about the future at all?"

The evening sun, pouring through the window behind her, illumined the red of her hair, making it glow. "I try not to," she said. "Don't you sometimes feel it would be nice if one didn't have to think at all?"

Gabriel looked at her and thought how lovely she was and how sad. "Some people don't," he said. "Or at least very little. But I come from a thinking race. It may be a misfortune but we're stuck with it. My dear, I should like to help you."

"I don't see how you can."

"Helping people is our business, and we must be practical. You'll need money, perhaps a job—" He broke off. "Hello," he said.

Irena turned to see what had distracted him. A little girl with fair hair and a round hat and a blue coat was standing in the French windows. Her right hand was in her pocket. She was smiling. Out of her pocket she produced a small automatic pistol, and, before Irena could even grasp what was happening, let alone move, pointed it at Gabriel and fired.

Just a second before, Diana had opened the door from the other room. The opening of that door attracted the child's glance for a moment: the pistol wavered as it went off. Diana seized the nearest object, which was a vase on a shelf beside the door, and threw it. Gabriel, who had half-risen from his chair, was punched back by the bullet.

The vase actually struck the girl and then shattered on the floor. Diana sprang after it, knocked the child's gun-hand up as a second shot came. They wrestled. Diana was much the stronger, but the child fought like a wildcat. The pudding-basin hat fell off, and, as Diana finally got a grip that would hold, with one arm round the child's neck, her other grasping the gun-hand, forcing it away, the blonde hair also went askew, then fell off, revealing a head of red curls.

"Stefan!" cried Irena.

XVIII

Gabriel's Horn

"Let me guess," said Jeremy. "No sign of Shaman."

"No sign of Shaman," Gabriel agreed, replacing the telephone rather awkwardly with his left hand. His right shoulder was still heavily bandaged and painful to move, although the bullet fortunately had missed both bone and sinew.

The drawing room was again peaceful and elegant. It was quite hard to believe that in this room, just a week ago, that extraordinary scene had occurred. The French windows were open now, as they had been then: but no small terrible figure stood there. The autumnal garden drowsed in hazy sunshine. Diana and Richard were walking together on the lawn.

Stefan had been taken away, and Irena had gone with him. Had he recognized her when he entered the room? Gabriel thought not. Stefan was a targeted missile and looked only at his objective. Suppose Irena had been in the way: would he have recognized her then? Would he have shot her? Gabriel sighed. He remembered Maria. But this was worse. Stefan had been twisted more deeply, more wickedly, than Maria. When he was held, he had looked for the first time at Irena and had gone limp. He had said nothing, though she tried to talk to him, and after a few minutes had seemed to fall asleep.

"So, what news?" asked Jeremy.

"As you gathered, that was Blaise. They're still not sure what was done to Stefan—hypnotism, drugs, brainwashing of some kind. But he's coming out of it now. He's conversing with his mother quite normally. A bit weepy, but that's natural. He may not remember everything, not for a while anyway."

"Had he been programmed all along just to come here, just to kill you?"

"Oh no. He'd been used for other things. Blaise thinks he killed poor Bardwell."

"Pushed him under the train?"

"Yes. Apparently some of the witnesses said there had been a school-girl near him on the platform, who was never found. No one looked very hard, since it was assumed to be an accident. I imagine that's why they dressed him as a girl. If he was seen, he could vanish afterwards by turning back into a boy."

"He could hardly have been expected to get away from here."

"I don't think he was expected to get away. I just wonder what he had been programmed to do after shooting me. But maybe I prefer not to wonder."

For a moment they were both silent, contemplating possibilities. Then Jeremy said: "Not a nice man, our Mr. Shaman."

"Not nice at all. His main concern was killing me, but he wanted Irena to suffer."

"You're lucky to be alive."

"On the assumption," Gabriel replied slowly, "that being alive is better. We don't really know, do we? It was you who once told us that?"

"So I did. But personally I'm going to continue acting on that assumption. There may be a better world waiting for us, but meanwhile this is quite a jolly one, full of wine, women and song. I'm in no hurry to swap them for nectar, angels and harps."

"*Paradis paint, où sont harpes et luz.* But, speaking of women, I thought, at one time, you and Diana . . ."

"Oh no. Delightful girl, of course. But she's the marrying kind."

They both glanced out to where Richard and Diana were standing, in close conversation, beside the river.

"I just wondered," said Gabriel. "You know—or perhaps you didn't know—I've been grooming Richard to succeed me, to run The Fishers when I've gone? Which might have happened last week."

Jeremy nodded. "That's what I've always supposed. He'll be good. Very sound. Tougher than you might imagine. Tougher than he imagines."

"In many ways it should be you. You're better in the field. But would you be insulted if I said you were one of nature's cavalry officers?"

Jeremy laughed. "I'd be flattered, in spite of the French comment at Waterloo—do you remember?—that Britain had the best cavalry in the world and the worst led. No, you're quite right. I'm not fond of admin and long-distance planning and being careful. The Poles used to say that there were only two suitable occupations for a gentleman. One was a cavalry officer, the other was a poet. And I'm not a poet."

"A very interesting nation, the Poles."

"Aren't they? I might discuss it with Irena one of these days, over a little dinner."

"You like her?"

"She's not the marrying kind. Are you going to have another job for me soon? I take it The Fishers are still in business."

"That business never ends. I've one or two things in mind. I'll let you know."

"You'll sound the tocsin, the call to arms, Gabriel's horn."

"Maybe you are a poet. But there seems to be an idyll we shouldn't interrupt."

He was looking through the French windows to where, beside the river, Richard and Diana were holding hands.

"I'd almost forgotten," said Gabriel, "that people could be happy."

About the Author

Anthony Lejeune was educated at Merchant Taylors' School and Balliol College, Oxford, where he was Newman Exhibitioner in English and Greek. After serving in the Royal Navy and reading for the Bar, he edited the magazine *Time and Tide,* and then became a special writer for the *Daily Express.* He was, for a while, Crime Correspondent of the Sunday *Times* (London) and latterly has written on political subjects for the *Daily Mail* and the *Daily Telegraph,* where he also reviews detective stories. STRANGE AND PRIVATE WAR is his first novel for the Crime Club.